# A BODY AT THE FARMHOUSE

A gripping Welsh crime mystery full of twists

# P.F. FORD

*The West Wales Murder Mysteries Book 4*

JOFFE
BOOKS

Joffe Books, London
www.joffebooks.com

First published in Great Britain in 2023

Cover art by Dee Dee Book Covers

ISBN: 978-1-80405-959-3

*To my amazing wife, Mary — sometimes we need someone else to believe in us before we really believe in ourselves. None of this would have happened without your unfailing belief and support.*

# CHAPTER 1

Detective Constable Catren Morgan pointed at a junction along the road ahead.

'We need to take a left just there.'

As directed, Detective Sergeant Norman slowed the car and turned off the main road. A massive pair of wrought-iron gates opened onto a long driveway that disappeared around a group of distant trees.

A police car was parked inside the gates and a barrier had been erected across the drive. As Norman brought the car to a halt, a uniformed PC asked for their IDs, signed them in and raised the barrier.

'So this is where Tilly Rotherby lives. Jeez, it's massive,' said Norman, setting the car in motion again.

'It used to be even bigger,' said Morgan. 'One of those ginormous old country estates. Then somewhere along the line, the owner developed a keen interest in horse racing. He had to sell off half the land to finance his hobby. Still, he did develop a successful racing stable so I suppose he knew what he was doing.'

'Is he still around?' Norman asked.

'Oh, that was years ago. I may not have it exactly right but I believe the guy in question was Tilly's grandfather, and when he died the estate passed to Tilly's father. But then he died quite young. I think everyone expected Tilly's older brother, Giles, to inherit, but he was left with nothing. When the will was read it specified that Tilly was to inherit everything.'

'But if Tilly was the younger child and the daughter, why leave it to her and not the son? I thought with these sorts of people it was always the son, or at least the oldest child, who got the property,' Norman said.

'I'm not sure but I think the brother was the black sheep, you know? Whatever, his father didn't seem to think he was up to the job.'

'How old was Tilly at the time?'

'Twenty-one, twenty-two, something like that,' Morgan said.

'And the brother?'

'I think he's a few years older.'

Norman shook his head. 'Jeez, I bet he was well pissed off.'

'I can only vaguely remember meeting him, but I doubt he was happy about it.'

'Early twenties seems a bit young to start running an estate,' Norman said.

'I think they had an estate manager.'

'So, young Tilly's worth a few quid, then?'

'I don't know about that. From what I hear, a lot of the people who own these places only look well off. Behind the grand facade they're struggling to make ends meet.'

'I've never been into horse racing,' said Norman. 'It seems to me there must be a heck of a lot of horses that never win a thing.'

'I think the real money is in the stud fees,' said Morgan. 'If you can produce a winning horse, people will pay a fortune to breed from him.'

'And did they produce any here?'

'I'm not sure,' said Morgan. 'I believe they always had two or three stud horses that brought in enough money to keep the stables going, so they must have been winners at some stage. I've no idea if they still have any.'

'How do you know all this?' he asked.

'I knew Tilly when we were kids. She was a few years older than me, so I wouldn't say we were ever friends as such. In fact, I haven't seen her since I was about fourteen. The only reason I know any of this is because I had a pony back then and I used to enter all the local Pony Club shows. It was pointless, really. Tilly's family had the money to buy the best ponies, so she used to win everything.'

'So there's a racing stable right on our doorstep and I never knew,' said Norman.

'As I said, I'm not sure they still have racehorses. Tilly was far more interested in dressage and showjumping, so I wouldn't be surprised if they don't have any now.'

They were driving alongside a red-brick wall, which ended at the gate to a field. Norman stopped the car. They could see a large white marquee to the left of it. A couple of small vans were parked close by.

'That must be where the main event was supposed to be taking place,' said Morgan.

'So, where is the house then?' asked Norman. He pointed to a huge Georgian residence about a mile away across more fields. 'Is that it?'

'Apparently it was, once upon a time,' said Morgan. 'It was sold along with half the estate.'

'So they only kept the land?'

'They kept a farmhouse and a few cottages that were originally built for the staff who worked at the farm and the stables. We're heading for the farmhouse. It's that way.'

She pointed back along the other side of the wall and, as Norman turned the car, an old farmhouse came into view about a hundred yards ahead.

'It's not exactly on a par with the mansion but I guess in its day it wasn't too shabby,' he said.

'It would do for me,' said Morgan.

As they approached the house, the gravel drive widened and they could see three cars and a Land Rover parked to one side, with space for another two or three vehicles. An ambulance waited to the side of the house, its rear doors wide open. A man wrapped in a foil blanket was sitting on the back step of the ambulance, being attended to by a paramedic.

'I think I can fit my car in there,' said Norman, heading for the parking spaces.

As they climbed from the car, a young detective, looking rather pale, emerged from the front door.

'Are you okay, Frosty?' asked Norman. 'Only you look a bit peaky.'

'I'll be all right,' said Detective Constable Winter. He sighed. 'I guess I'll get used to seeing dead bodies one day.'

'I'm afraid there's no quick cure for that,' said Norman. He nodded across to the ambulance. 'Who's the guy?'

'David Griffiths,' said Winter. 'He's the bridegroom. He's in shock.'

'I'm not surprised,' said Morgan. 'It's not exactly how he would have expected to find his bride on their wedding day.'

'That's for sure,' agreed Norman. 'Anyway, Frosty, what have we got?'

Winter pointed towards the back of the house.

'The body is in the barn. DI Southall asked me to make sure Mr Griffiths stays here until she comes back, then I've got to go to the marquee and start taking statements from the catering staff.'

'Did you say the boss is here already?' asked Morgan.

'She arrived a couple of minutes after the pathologist,' said Winter. 'He's examining the body as we speak.'

'Fancy them arriving so close together,' said Morgan. 'I mean, what are the chances?'

Norman ignored the inference. 'How many catering staff are there?'

'Not many,' said Winter. 'Maybe half a dozen. There were supposed to be a few more coming to wait on the tables, but most of them hadn't arrived by the time the body was found.'

4

'Catren can give you a hand when you go up there,' said Norman.

Morgan looked enquiringly at him.

'It'll be a distraction, something to stop you leaping to conclusions,' said Norman.

Morgan smiled.

'Too late for that, I'm afraid,' she said. 'And don't tell me you aren't thinking the same thing.'

'Right now, I've got better things to do than speculate about other people's private lives, especially when those people are both divorced and single,' said Norman. 'And you should, too.'

'What's this?' asked Winter. 'Am I missing something?'

'Take no notice,' said Norman. 'DC Morgan has a vivid imagination.'

Morgan winked at Winter. 'I'll tell you on the way to the marquee.'

'Okay, Frosty, you keep an eye on the groom until the boss gets back. Catren, grab a forensic suit and take a look around the house. I'm going to the barn,' said Norman. 'Which way is it?'

'Down the side of the house and across the garden,' said Winter. 'You'll see a gate in the hedge.'

Norman followed the path indicated by Winter, peering through the windows as he went. The garden was bordered on one side by a dense hedge of yew, which had been encouraged to form an arch over a wooden gate whose hinges creaked when he pushed through. He made his way between two stables, out into a large yard.

A dozen stables ran the length of each side, with a long American barn across the far end. The top halves of some of the stable doors were open, the odd inquisitive horsey face proof that some of them, at least, were occupied. The barn doors were wide open.

Norman stepped gingerly inside and peered around. There was a wide passage down the centre, with either side divided into six stalls for horses.

'It's me,' he called. 'Where are you guys?'

A couple of horses poked their heads out at the sound of his voice. Then the shape of a human emerged from the end stall on the right.

'Down here, Norm,' called the familiar voice of his boss, Detective Inspector Sarah Southall.

Norman made his way to the end of the barn and peered into the stall. The pathologist, Dr Bill Bridger, was kneeling by a body that was stretched out on the floor. A noose was looped around her neck, and a rope hanging from a beam swayed above the body.

Bridger nodded to Norman.

'I'm glad to see it's not just my Sunday that's been ruined,' he said.

'Hi, Bill,' said Norman. 'It's good to see you too.'

'This,' said Southall, 'is, or rather was, Matilda Rotherby, known to her friends as Tilly. She was supposed to be celebrating her marriage at one o'clock this afternoon.'

Norman nodded. 'Is it suicide?'

'At first glance,' said Southall.

'But?' said Norman.

'Bill's not persuaded yet.'

Norman turned to Bridger. 'Is there a reason for your doubts?'

'There's a suspicious-looking cut on her head,' said Bridger.

'Suspicious how?'

'It's quite deep, but there's nowhere near the amount of blood I would have expected from a wound like that. Scalps usually bleed a lot, even from small cuts. It doesn't fit with what appears to have happened.'

'Maybe it's not connected,' said Norman. 'Perhaps she cut her head somewhere else before she came out here.'

'Yes, maybe,' said Bridger doubtfully.

'But you don't think that's what happened,' said Norman.

'I would still expect to see more blood around the wound if that was the case. I'll have a much better idea when I get her back to the lab.'

'Any idea what time she died?'

'Rigor mortis is well established, so I'm guessing she's been dead around ten to fourteen hours, but that is merely a guess at this stage. As I said, I'll know more when she's back at the lab.'

Southall looked at her watch. 'It's ten thirty now, so, until we know better, let's assume she died between eight p.m. and midnight.'

Norman nodded. 'Who found her?' he said. 'Was it the guy down by the house? Winter says he's the bridegroom.'

'A girl called Carys Howells comes in and looks after the horses at weekends. She lives with her mother in one of the cottages at the other side of the estate. She came in at six thirty this morning as usual and found Tilly hanging here.'

'Jeez,' said Norman. 'Is she okay?'

'She's only sixteen years old. From what the first responders say, she was seriously freaked out. She ran home to her mother, who called it in.'

'Poor kid,' said Norman. 'Where is she now?'

'The paramedics couldn't do anything for Tilly when they got here, so they treated Carys for shock instead. She's at home with her mother now. I said we'd call in to speak to them later.'

'Who got the body down?'

Southall pulled a face. 'According to the first responders, the bridegroom says he arrived, couldn't find Tilly at the house and guessed she would be down here with the horses. When he found her he cut her down, thinking he could save her.'

'I suppose that's what anyone might do, but you don't sound so sure.'

'It's all a bit convenient, isn't it?' said Southall. 'If this is a crime scene, he's effectively ruined it.'

'Yeah, but if he's for real, I don't suppose ruining your crime scene would have been the first thing on his mind. And we don't know if it is a crime scene yet. Or, is there something you haven't told me?'

Southall sighed. 'Well, besides the cut on her head, I just feel something's not right.'

'You should never ignore your gut feelings,' said Norman. 'Isn't that what we always say?'

She shrugged. 'I guess it is.'

'To my mind any death is suspicious,' said Norman. 'So, until we know different, we should consider the possibility that there's more to this than meets the eye.'

Two men had arrived to recover the body and stood waiting for Bridger to give them the word.

'I can't do any more here,' said Bridger to Southall. 'Is it okay if my guys take her away?'

'Yes, of course,' said Southall.

The body was quickly and efficiently removed, and Norman noticed a forensic team hovering outside, waiting for permission to get started.

'Did you call these guys in?' Norman asked Southall.

'Yes, I know. If it is a suicide, I'm going to have to explain why I wasted some of my budget on forensics, but I'll worry about that when the time comes.'

'Jeez, all this talk about budgets is driving me crazy. I know there isn't an infinite pool of money, but doesn't anyone realise you can't allocate budgets to solving crimes?'

'Come on, Norm,' said Southall. 'Let's get out of the way and let Forensics do their thing while we talk to her husband-to-be.'

# CHAPTER 2

As Southall and Norman neared the house, Morgan emerged in her forensic suit.

'Find anything?' asked Norman.

'Nothing that says a crime was committed in there,' said Morgan. 'Do you still want me to go and interview the caterers?'

'I think that can wait,' said Norman. 'For now, I'd like you to carry on poking around in the house.'

'It might be nothing, but there is one thing that seems a bit odd to me,' said Morgan. 'I haven't seen Tilly in years, but I know for a fact she's not the sort who would skimp on her wedding day.'

'You saw the size of that marquee,' said Norman. 'I don't think you could call that skimping.'

'Exactly,' said Morgan. 'No expense spared, right? Even when we were kids, her parents had to pay a fortune to have her looking her best.'

'I'm not following,' said Norman.

'What I mean is, where's the hairdresser? The make-up artist? They should have been here by now.'

'Maybe that's an indication of the state of her mind,' said Norman. 'And don't forget there are uniforms down there making sure no one comes through the gates.'

'I thought of that,' said Morgan. 'So I checked with the guys at the gate. They haven't turned anyone like that away. So far, the only people who've been wanting to come in are a couple of teenagers who'd been hired as waiters. It's approaching eleven o'clock now. That's just two hours before the ceremony. No one leaves it that late to get ready on their wedding day.'

'You're right,' said Southall. 'When I got married I had my hair and make-up done at home. They were there by nine that morning, and the wedding wasn't till three. Well done, Catren! See if you can find a mobile phone, a diary, or one of those wedding planner things. That should tell us if she had anyone booked.'

'You think it's relevant, then?' asked Morgan.

'I've no idea what's relevant right now,' said Southall. 'But as Norm said, it might give us an indication of the state of her mind. You know more about Tilly than any of us. If you think it's odd, I think you should check it out.'

Morgan went back into the house, looking pleased with herself.

'Maybe David Griffiths can tell us about the arrangements,' said Norman.

Southall grunted. 'Unless he's one of those guys who leaves everything to the bride to arrange.'

'Yeah, there is that possibility,' said Norman. 'But I prefer to be optimistic.'

If the subtle hint about her pessimism registered with Southall, she chose to ignore it. She marched ahead to the ambulance. David Griffiths got to his feet as they approached.

Southall made the introductions and made sure the paramedics were happy for him to answer their questions.

'How are you feeling, Mr Griffiths?' Southall asked.

'Stunned,' he said.

'That's understandable,' she said.

'Would it be okay if we went into the house?' Griffiths said. 'I'm not sure I feel up to standing out here in the open.'

Southall pointed to a bench nearby.

'I'm afraid we can't let you go into the house just yet. I've officers looking around inside, and as it's a possible crime scene we're going to have to ask you to keep away for a few days. Is there somewhere you can stay?'

'Crime scene? I thought Tilly committed suicide!'

'Sadly, you're probably right, but we need to make sure, so, for now at least, I'm afraid the house is out of bounds.'

'I suppose I can go back to the hotel.'

'Which hotel is that?'

'The Seaview, out on the coast.'

'Oh, yes, I know it,' Southall said. 'I can get someone to arrange for you to stay there for a few days.'

'It's okay, I can manage.'

'If you're sure,' said Southall. 'Is it okay if we ask you some questions now?'

'Of course, although I'm not sure how much help I'm going to be.'

'Was there anything bothering Tilly that you know of?'

'Nothing that would cause her to take her own life. Or if there was, she never mentioned it to me.'

'And she's been okay this week?'

'I've been out of the country on business and only came back yesterday. I stayed in the hotel last night, and came over first thing this morning.'

'Is there any particular reason why you stayed away last night?'

'It was Tilly's idea. She thought it was the right thing to do. It was silly really, we've been together for a couple of years, so it's not as if we've never slept together.'

'Did you live together?'

'On and off. I have my own house down by the coast, and I'm there or out of the country a lot for work, but I come and stay here when I can.'

'Can I ask what you do for a living?' asked Southall.

'I own an offshore wind business. We build and install wind turbines out at sea, around the UK and Europe. That's why I'm away a lot.'

She smiled. 'You must be in high demand at the moment.'

'We make a living.'

'I'm sure you do,' said Southall.

'Isn't being apart on the night before a wedding one of those old superstitions?' suggested Norman. 'Don't some people think it's bad luck for the bride to see the groom on the night before the ceremony?'

'Actually, this wasn't a wedding ceremony,' said Griffiths. 'The fact is, we were secretly married two weeks ago in a registry office. This was more of a reception to celebrate the wedding.'

'Is there any reason you got married in secret?' Southall asked.

'Tilly didn't want to upset any of her friends by choosing bridesmaids or a maid of honour, then you've got all these people who think they should be sitting at the top table. And I'm not a big fan of church weddings anyway, so, in the end, we decided it would be better to please ourselves and disappoint everyone else.

'We booked the local registry office, kidnapped a couple of witnesses from the wedding before ours, and went to the pub for a quiet lunch afterwards. Today is, or rather was, intended to be a peace offering for all the friends and relatives who weren't at the real wedding.'

'So, Tilly wasn't the type to offend anyone?' asked Norman.

'She was the sweetest person, with a heart of gold,' said Griffiths. 'Yes, she was a fierce competitor on a horse, but outside of that she'd do anything for anyone. She even hooked up with a local charity so she could give free riding lessons to disadvantaged teenagers.'

'That really is having a heart of gold,' said Norman.

'I know this is going to be hard,' said Southall. 'But can you take us through what happened when you got here this morning?'

Griffiths licked his lips and stared at some distant point, as if it would help him remember.

'I left the hotel at around six fifteen and arrived here at about six thirty. As I said, it seems crazy to be staying in a hotel that close, but that's what Tilly wanted. Anyway, when I got here, I went around to the back door and found it wide open. I went upstairs but there was no sign of Tilly, so I guessed she would be down with the horses.'

'It didn't bother you, finding the back door wide open that early?' asked Norman.

'Tilly is an early riser, and she was always leaving doors open. Anyone would think she had been raised in a barn.'

'Right. I see,' said Norman. 'Sorry, I didn't mean to interrupt. Please carry on.'

'I went down to the stables and called out, but there was no one around. That surprised me, as there's a girl who usually comes in and does the horses at the weekend.'

'And you thought she would be there?'

'She's usually here not long after six, but there didn't seem to be any sign of her. Then I found Tilly in Henry's stable. I got Henry out of the way, cut the rope and lowered her down.'

'How did you manage to reach high enough to cut her down?' asked Norman.

'There was a feed bucket lying just outside. I grabbed it and turned it upside down so I could stand on it. I know CPR and I tried to save her, but I think she must have been dead a while. Next thing I knew, there were police officers and paramedics everywhere . . .'

He bowed his head and began to cry softly.

'I'm so sorry,' said Southall. 'It must have been a terrible shock.'

'Roughly how long was it from when you arrived at the house and getting to the stables?' asked Norman.

'I don't know,' said Griffiths. 'Probably no more than five minutes. I would like to go now, if you don't mind. I'm really not feeling too good.'

'Just a couple more questions,' said Southall. 'You said you found Tilly in Henry's stable. Who's Henry?'

'Henry's her favourite horse,' said Griffiths. 'She's had him for years.'

'Where is he now?'

'I put him in the stall opposite.'

'And he was definitely in with Tilly when you found her?'

'Yes.'

'And the gate to the stall was closed?'

'Oh, yeah, he couldn't have got away if he'd wanted. The poor old thing was a bit spooked, but then so was I when I saw her hanging there like that. Now, please, can I go?'

'Of course,' said Southall, 'but we will need to speak to you again.'

'I'll do anything I can to help, but right now I need—'

'Of course.' The DI's voice was firm. 'We'll speak again tomorrow.'

Griffiths got to his feet.

'One more question,' said Norman. 'Do you know if Tilly had booked anyone to do her hair and make-up?'

'Without a doubt. She wouldn't turn up at an occasion like this without getting glammed up first. There are two girls she uses for that sort of thing. I can't tell you their names, but it was always the same two. Why do you ask?'

'Because we figured that would be the case, but they haven't arrived.'

'Is that important?'

'Probably not,' said Norman. 'We were just curious.'

Looking bemused, Griffiths rose to his feet and headed for his car.

'Shall we have a look around the house?' Norman asked Southall.

'Catren's outside. Let's go and see what she's found.'

Morgan, who had been joined by Winter, was waiting by the car.

'Any sign of a mobile phone?' asked Southall.

'No, but I've only looked downstairs so far.'

'Okay. I'd like you two to go down to the marquee and speak to the caterers now. We'll have a look around upstairs and then go and speak with Carys Howells.'

Morgan held aloft an evidence pouch. 'I have found this diary, though.' She handed the diary to Southall, who eyed it with interest.

'Have you had a look inside?'

'I did have a quick flip through.'

'Does it have an address for the beautician and hairdresser?' asked Southall.

'There's a home mobile number for Donna Price, the hairdresser. I tried ringing but it goes straight to voicemail. Do you want me to keep trying?'

'If it's a business number, it's possible you won't get an answer on a Sunday,' said Southall. 'But you could leave a message asking her to call you back. We need to know why they missed their booking, and where they were on Saturday evening.'

'Okay,' said Morgan.

'When you've finished speaking to the caterers, get off home and rest. I want you wide awake in the morning.'

'Come on, Frosty,' said Morgan. 'I can leave that message on the way to the marquee.'

# CHAPTER 3

Southall and Norman donned forensic suits, latex gloves and bootees, and made their way through the front door of the farmhouse into a lavishly decorated hallway.

'From the outside it looks like the sort of quaint, draughty old place that's going to be full of ghosts,' said Norman. 'But it's a bit different when you get inside, isn't it?'

'Yes,' agreed Southall. 'Tilly must have had expensive taste.'

They had a quick scout around downstairs to get the lie of the land, then made their way upstairs.

'Jeez, I hate to think how much this oak staircase cost,' said Norman. 'The quote I had for new stairs in my cottage made my eyes water, and it's nothing like as grand as this.'

'Don't you think it's rather too grand for a farmhouse?' said Southall.

'Perhaps she was trying to recreate the big house,' suggested Norman.

At the top of the stairs, they found a long landing with five doors leading off. They made their way along, opening the doors to the left and looking inside. The three rooms appeared to be guest bedrooms, each pristine and undisturbed.

'Nice, if a bit clinical,' observed Southall. She opened a door at the far end, to the right. 'I'm guessing that's the guest bathroom. It's got that hotel feel to it. You know, impersonal.' She pushed open the next door. Standing in the middle of a thick white carpeted floor, a massive double bed took up most of the space. 'This must be Tilly's room.'

Norman followed her inside. 'What, no wardrobes or dressing table? Are you sure?'

Southall pointed to a door in the corner. 'I'm betting that leads to an en-suite bathroom and a dressing room.' She stopped and took in the room. 'It doesn't look as though there's anything to see in here. Definitely no sign of a struggle.'

'The bed hasn't been slept in,' said Norman. 'If we can find out what time she normally goes to bed, it might help us narrow down the time of death.'

Southall walked around the bed and opened the door in the corner. 'As I thought. Dressing room, and en-suite bathroom.'

'How the other half live,' said Norman wonderingly. 'I'll never live in anything this grand.'

'You sound impressed.'

'No way,' said Norman. 'It's nice enough, but it's a waste of space. Clean and simple, that's how I like it.'

'Let's have a look in this dressing room,' said Southall. 'You take the wardrobe; I'll take the drawers.'

'I wish I knew what I was looking for.'

'Me too. I expect we're wasting our time, but there's no harm in looking.'

Norman worked his way through the first wardrobe. 'Tilly must have had a different coat for every day of the week, but she was tidy. There's nothing in any of the pockets, not even an old tissue.'

'Ew,' said Southall.

'Yeah, I suppose I should be grateful for that,' he said. He moved on to the next wardrobe and opened the doors. 'Jeez, look at all these skirts and dresses. And the shoes! Who needs so many shoes?'

'She was just a girl who likes shoes, Norm.' Southall looked over his shoulder. 'There are lots of us around.'

'You'd have to be a centipede to need this many shoes.'

'You need to get used to the idea, Norm. I think Faye's a shoe girl. I bet she's got dozens of pairs.'

Ignoring Southall's comment, Norman felt his way through the clothes hanging in the wardrobe and then knelt down and examined the shoes. 'Half of these look as if they've never been worn.'

'Maybe she's a collector not a wearer,' said Southall. 'I bet she's got a load of matching handbags too.' She opened a cupboard. 'Here we go.' She began searching through them.

Norman finished with the shoes and opened the next wardrobe to reveal a couple of jackets, three pairs of trousers and a pair of jeans. 'Aha! Men's clothes.'

'Griffiths said he stays here sometimes,' said Southall.

Norman lifted the jackets from the rail and rummaged in the pockets, but found nothing. He looked at the size of the jacket and read it out to Southall. 'I guess that's about Griffiths's size.'

'I think so, more or less,' said Southall. 'What about the length of the trousers?'

Norman took a pair of trousers and held them against himself. 'Three or four inches too long for me. But then I'm not exactly a giant.'

Southall turned to look. 'They'd be about right for him.'

'Okay, so we'll assume this is his wardrobe.' Norman took out a solitary pair of shoes. 'Shoe size eleven, in case you were wondering.' He returned the shoes to the wardrobe.

Southall had been working her way through the handbags.

'This seems a bit odd to me,' she said.

'What's that?'

'I've only got three handbags at home, but I guarantee you'd find something inside every one of them, even if it's just a few old receipts, or a packet of tissues. I only tend to remove the important things like my purse, phone and keys. Everything else stays where it is. Yet every one of Tilly's handbags is completely empty.'

'Is that so odd?' said Norman. 'Maybe she was just obsessive about stuff like that. Don't forget, I found nothing in any of her pockets.'

'Yes, possibly, or maybe there was a reason for her obsessiveness. Perhaps she wanted to make sure there was nothing to be found.'

'You mean you think she had a secret of some sort?'

'It's possible, isn't it? Suicide or not, it could be the reason for her death.'

Norman closed the door on the wardrobe he'd been searching and stepped across to the last one. 'Well, unless there's a clue to the secret hidden in this fourth wardrobe, I have no idea what it might be.' He reached for the door handle. 'Crap. It's locked. Now, why would this one be locked when the others aren't?'

'Maybe the answer to our secret is in there,' said Southall.

'Have you found any keys? I don't want to bust the door open if I don't have to.'

'Hang on, I've still got a couple more drawers to search.' She pulled a drawer open. 'Now this looks the sort of place a woman might hide something.'

Curiosity piqued, Norman craned his neck to see. 'Why there?'

'How many men do you know who would go searching through a drawer full of sanitary products?'

'Ah, right. I see what you mean.'

'I've often wondered why you guys are so squeamish about these things.'

'I dunno. I guess it's one of those taboo subjects,' said Norman. 'It shouldn't be, but it is. For guys my age, maybe it's because when we were kids, our mums and sisters made a big secret out of it — you know, whispers and hushed voices. But you're right, I wouldn't dream of looking through things like that if it wasn't a criminal investigation.'

It didn't take Southall long to find a small purse. She unzipped it and produced a handful of small keys.

'Here we go.' She threw them to Norman. 'I bet it's one of these.'

Norman worked his way through the keys until he found the right one. He unlocked the wardrobe doors and pulled them open. 'Crap. More men's clothes.'

'You sound disappointed,' said Southall. 'What were you expecting to find? A body?'

'At least that would have been a secret worth dying for, rather than a bunch more clothes,' said Norman.

'Now ask yourself why those particular men's clothes are in a locked wardrobe,' suggested Southall.

Norman took one of the jackets from the wardrobe and held it up. He did the same with a pair of trousers. 'Not Griffiths's size. Different style, too. There's even a tweed jacket that looks like something a country squire would wear. I can't see Griffiths in that, can you?'

'No. It's not quite the image he projects,' Southall said.

'Maybe this is the secret that made her so obsessive about emptying her handbags and pockets,' Norman said, and Southall nodded. 'It adds up, doesn't it? Then again, would she really keep another man's clothes in the same dressing room Griffiths uses? I mean, if she was worried about him searching her handbags and pockets, wouldn't she keep what's in this wardrobe somewhere else?'

Southall shrugged. 'Yes, you would think so.'

'Maybe Tilly came up with a convincing enough reason for keeping this wardrobe locked,' said Norman.

Southall grunted. 'It would have to be a damned good one.'

'Perhaps the clothes belong to another member of the family,' suggested Norman. 'Catren said Tilly has an older brother.'

'Yeah, Giles Rotherby. I suppose that might work,' said Southall. 'Griffiths is hardly going to be jealous of her brother, is he?' She looked at her watch while Norman felt around in the jacket pockets. 'Time's getting on. Let's finish up here and then see if we can get a few minutes with Carys Howells before we head back to the office.'

Norman stopped. 'Hang on a minute, Sarah. I've found something in here.' He slipped a hand into one of the pockets and held up his trophy for Southall to see. 'Well, look at that,' he said with a broad smile. 'Whoever this guy is, he left his mobile in his pocket.'

Southall looked at the phone. 'That's not exactly the latest smart phone, is it?'

'No way,' said Norman. 'It's one of those with huge keys, like for an old person.'

'But Giles Rotherby is in his early forties,' said Southall. 'Why would he need a phone like that?'

'I dunno. Maybe he's got bad eyesight.' He was trying to switch it on, but nothing happened. 'It looks as if the battery is flat. I suppose it would be if it'd been left here for more than a couple of days. Should we take it as evidence? I mean, it's probably irrelevant if it's her brother's and it's locked away in the wardrobe.'

Southall considered for a moment. 'I think we should take it, but maybe not make it a priority at this stage.'

'Your wish is my command.' Norman slipped the mobile phone into an evidence pouch.

'Right, let's go and speak with Carys Howells.'

# CHAPTER 4

Norman drove them along a rough track to the six cottages, which formerly housed the staff employed on the estate farm. They formed a small, neat terrace, their red-brick walls and rusty brown tiles giving them a warm and welcoming appearance. They were positioned closer to the huge country mansion than the farmhouse.

'It's a lovely spot to live in,' said Southall as they approached the cottages.

'I don't think I'd want to live out here if this track was the only means of access,' said Norman.

'Isn't that the price you pay for rural living? You're not one of those people who wants to cover the country in concrete and tarmac, are you?'

'Of course I'm not,' said Norman. 'But it wouldn't hurt to level the track and put some gravel down, would it? I'm not asking for a motorway. I just want to get there without having my car shaken to pieces.'

'Once a city boy, always a city boy. Is that it?'

'Definitely not. I wouldn't go back to London in a million years. I'm just saying it doesn't need to be this bad.'

Cottage number one had a small wooden front porch that had seen better days. A small boot rack provided a home for two pairs of knee-length wellington boots, and a shorter pair of mucker boots, all upside down.

The door was answered by a tall, slim, dark-haired woman. Large, round spectacles seemed to magnify her brown eyes and give her a slightly owlish appearance. She looked a little worn down by life, though Norman guessed she was probably in her mid-thirties. He showed her his warrant card and made the introductions.

'Are you Mrs Ffion Howells?'

'It's Ms.'

'Oh, right. Well, Ms Howells, is it possible for us to come in and speak to Carys?'

'I'm afraid not. The paramedics gave her a sedative and she's completely out of it right now.'

'Of course. It must have been a terrible shock for her,' said Southall. 'What about you? Would you be able to answer a few questions?'

'About Tilly? Yes, I suppose so, if it will help.'

She led them into a tiny, shabby sitting room.

'We know Carys looked after the horses for Tilly, but did you know her?' asked Southall.

'We were friends years ago, but we drifted apart. You know how it is.'

'Any particular reason for that?' asked Norman.

Ffion sighed impatiently. 'How about Tilly owns an estate, and I rent a tiny cottage? You could say we don't exactly move in the same circles.'

'But you did move in the same circles once?'

'We used to compete at the same horse shows, that's how we first met. We used to travel all over, and to make life easier we shared the transport. Our fathers used to take it in turns to drive. But that all stopped when I got pregnant with Carys.'

'And you didn't go back to riding?'

'It costs a lot of money to keep show horses and compete. My parents paid for most of it until I became a single mother. Then that all stopped.'

23

'That must have been hard,' Norman said.

'Being disowned by my parents and finding myself alone with a baby on my eighteenth birthday was a bit of a blow,' she said bitterly.

'Yes, it must have been difficult,' said Southall.

Ffion grimaced. 'It certainly wasn't plain sailing, but I was lucky. My employers were fantastic. They gave me lots of time off and even found me somewhere to live. Looking back on it now, I can honestly say that it was when I found out how strong I was. And, of course, I've got my lovely Carys, so it wasn't all bad news.'

'How long have you lived out here?' Southall asked.

'Just over two years.'

Southall smiled. 'It must be a great place for Carys if she loves horses.'

'Oh, she doesn't love horses. She never had the slightest interest in them until about a year ago.'

'She's not a budding showjumper, then?' Southall said.

'Good heavens, no. We couldn't afford it anyway. She wanted a weekend job, and Tilly was seeing David Griffiths and fancied a lie-in every weekend. As far as Carys is concerned, it's just a way of earning herself a few pounds.'

'It's handy, though, with you living so close to the stables,' Southall persisted.

'It's just a pity the owner didn't keep her promise to spend a bit of money and do the place up. Hopefully, the new landlord will bring these houses up to date.'

'I thought these cottages were part of Tilly's estate,' said Norman.

'They were until a couple of months ago when the people who own the big house bought them.'

'D'you know why Tilly sold them?' he asked.

'No idea,' said Ffion. 'Maybe she got fed up with her tenants complaining about how run down they are.'

'Can I ask how you came to live here?' asked Southall.

'Much as I love Carys, children are expensive to keep,' said Ffion. 'I needed to cut costs, and that included finding somewhere cheaper to live. I saw this place advertised and thought it would be nice to be out in the country. I didn't even realise it was one of Tilly's cottages until I came out here to see it.'

'It didn't rekindle your friendship then,' Southall said.

'As I said, we move in different circles. She barely recognised me.'

'So, you didn't get on?' Southall asked.

'We didn't have anything to do with each other. I paid the rent and asked for the improvements she had promised. She took my money and ignored my requests.'

Southall frowned. 'But doesn't that make it awkward for Carys?'

'Carys may only be sixteen, but she's her own person, and she makes her own decisions.'

'She's a bit wild?' Southall asked.

'That's not what I meant,' said Ffion indignantly. 'I believe in letting her make up her own mind about what she wants in life, but she knows she can always come to me if she wants a second opinion.'

'Can I ask where you were this morning between six and six thirty?' asked Norman.

'I was here, in my bed. Carys is quite capable of getting up without my help.'

'On your own?' he asked.

'Yes. On my own. Or at least I was until Carys came screaming in through the back door.'

'What time was that?'

'About six thirty. Your call centre will be able to tell you what time I called them. Carys came back about five minutes before that. It took me a good five minutes to calm her down and find out exactly what she'd seen.'

'And you didn't go down to the stables yourself?' Southall asked.

'I was more concerned with trying to calm my daughter. As far as I'm concerned, Carys comes before anything else.'

'And she's okay now?' Southall said.

25

'The doctor said she's as well as can be expected, though she'll probably be having nightmares for years to come, poor kid.'

'We're still going to need to speak to her,' said Southall. 'We'll be back at the farmhouse in a few days. Will it be okay to come over and speak to her then?'

'I suppose so, but if you upset her—'

'Ffion, I promise we'll do our very best not to upset her, but you must understand that she was the person who found the body. She might know something vital to our investigation.'

'All right, but I want to be there too.'

'Of course,' said Southall. 'We'll come here. As she's only sixteen, we wouldn't dream of questioning her without you being there.'

* * *

'Where to?' asked Norman when they were back in the car.

'Let's go and see if Forensics have finished with the barn. I'd like to take another look around if we can.'

Southall's phone pinged to announce a text message. She looked at the message then turned to Norman.

'Are you doing anything tonight?'

'Are you asking me on a date? I thought you and Bill Bridger were an item.'

'No, I am not asking you on a date. Dr Bridger is doing the autopsy this evening.'

Norman scowled. 'Actually, I have a prior engagement and, to be honest, I'd rather be anywhere else but there.'

Southall ignored his protest. 'He wants to know what time we'll be there.'

'Sarah, I'm serious. I really do have something else on. You know I wouldn't normally ask, but just this once I'd like to miss out on the slicing and dicing.'

Southall stared at Norman, but he wasn't to be moved. 'Are you sure? Can you really not make it?'

'You're not going to insist, are you?' he pleaded.

She sighed. 'I suppose I could let you off just this once.'

She tapped a reply to Bridger, then slipped her phone into her pocket.

'Does everyone think that?' she asked.

'Think what?'

'You know. About me and Bill Bridger.'

'Did you really think no one knew?' He smiled. 'You arrived at my house arm in arm with him, remember?'

'You mean for your housewarming?'

'Yeah. You have to admit it was bit of a giveaway. And then this morning I hear you and him arrived within two minutes of each other,' he said.

'That doesn't prove anything.'

'No, but it's enough to feed the rumour mill,' he said.

'Catren Morgan is a gossip.'

'She likes to think there's a bit of spice mixed in here and there.'

'And if there isn't any, she'll invent it,' Southall said. 'Whatever happened to privacy?'

He looked at her. 'Are you saying there's nothing going on between you two?'

Southall was silent.

'So, you're not denying it then?'

Southall folded her arms. 'I don't need to be judged by you, or her.'

'No one is judging you, Sarah, especially not Catren. I think you'll find she's happy for you.'

'I don't need her to be happy for me.'

'Aw, come on, lighten up. There's no need to get shitty about it. It's no big deal.'

There was a minute or two of uncomfortable silence, until Southall said, 'Talking of your housewarming, how did it go with Faye?'

'What do you mean, how did it go with Faye?'

'Well, you know . . .'

He looked straight ahead. 'No, sorry. I have no idea what you mean.'

'Yes, you do. When we went home there were just the two of you left.'

'That's because you all went off and left her,' he said.

'But she wanted to stay.'

'Yeah, that's right, I believe she did.'

'So, what happened?'

'I'm sorry?'

'She had no car to get home.'

'Yes. And?'

'Oh, come on, Norm, you know exactly what I mean. Faye almost begged us to leave her there with you.'

'Oh, I see. So, it's okay for you to pry into my private life, but it's wrong for anyone to speculate about you and Bill Bridger.'

'Well, no, that's not what I'm saying . . .' Southall trailed off.

'I think you'll find it's exactly what you're saying,' said Norman. 'But the thing is, you're not asking me because you think it's shocking that Faye and I might have spent the night together, are you? Of course not. You're asking because you'd like to think something good happened, and that me and Faye are happier as a result. Am I right?'

'Well, yes, I suppose you are.'

'And that's exactly what Catren's hoping for you. Now, is it really such a bad thing that she wants you to be happy?' He turned to face her.

'Is that really what she wants?'

'Sarah, it's what we all want. And as for Catren, I know for a fact she thinks the world of you. She's the sort of person who wants everyone to be happy. If she can have a little fun with it at the same time, well, that's just how she rolls. You know how much she likes to tease.'

'And you're sure she's not telling the whole world?'

Norman pulled up outside the farmhouse. 'Trust me. If I thought there was any danger of her embarrassing you, I'd put a stop to it.'

They climbed out of the car and set off for the stables.

'What's this prior engagement you have tonight, then? Anyone I know? It wouldn't be Faye by any chance, would it?'

Norman smiled. 'Nice try.'

'I could always call her and ask.'

'Yeah, you could,' said Norman. 'But, to quote a good friend of mine, "whatever happened to privacy?"'

Southall couldn't prevent a wry smile of her own. 'Touché.'

They arrived at the stables just as the forensic team were packing their equipment away.

'Anything we should know?' asked Southall.

One of the team pulled his mask off his face. 'We've got hundreds of fingerprints, which is probably way too many to help us narrow it down in any meaningful way. And we haven't found any evidence of a fight, but there are some marks on the floor of the barn that could be rubber from the heels of her boots.'

'You mean like drag marks?' she said.

'Yes, possibly, but they're not consistent, like two neat lines, so we'll need to compare the samples with her boots to be sure. Anything else of interest has been marked.'

'What about the house?'

'We're just going over there now.'

'I've got an autopsy to attend later,' said Southall.

'No problem. If we find anything important, I'll send you a report overnight.'

'Perfect. Thank you,' said Southall.

# CHAPTER 5

They heard the snorts of horses, and a couple of heads appeared over the stable doors.

'Did anyone think about who is going to look after the horses?' asked Southall.

'Catren said she'd contact Animal Welfare to get us over the next couple of days,' Norman said. 'After that, I suppose it's up to David Griffiths to sort something out.'

'We mustn't forget about them,' said Southall. 'They've done nothing wrong, so there's no reason for them to go hungry.'

They stood at the entrance to the barn.

'I assume these are the drag marks,' said Southall, pointing to faint traces marked with forensic tags.

'I see what he means about them being "possible" drag marks,' said Norman. 'They're not exactly crystal clear, are they? We'd probably have missed them if they hadn't been tagged.'

They made their way to the stable where Tilly Rotherby's body had been found.

'What are we looking for?' asked Norman.

'I don't know, Norm. Anything that doesn't look right, I suppose.'

Norman pointed to the rope hanging from a beam above them. 'Okay, so let's start with that rope. It must have been cut about eight feet above the floor. There wasn't much more than a foot of rope attached to the noose, so that means it must have been hanging at least six feet from the floor. Tilly didn't look like a six-footer to me, and there's nothing to stand on apart from that bucket, which doesn't look tall enough, so how the hell did she manage to get her head through it?'

'David Griffiths said there was a horse in the stable when he found the body. Maybe she sat on him when she put the noose around her head, and then got him to walk away,' Southall said.

He looked at her. 'Are you saying you've now decided it definitely was suicide?'

'Not at all,' she said, 'just how she could have done it.'

'So, you reckon she threw a rope over that beam, made a noose at one end, tied the rope off on the other side of the stable, got on the horse's back and then manoeuvred the horse under the noose?' Norman pointed to the various parts of the rope as he spoke, striding across to where the rope was tied to a metal eye screwed into the wall.

'Yes, something like that,' said Southall.

'I suppose she could have done it that way,' said Norman gloomily. 'But in that case, I need to know why she would want to kill herself. I mean, this is one hell of a way to go. Why not just take a few sleeping pills?'

'Perhaps there's a meaning behind it and we just haven't worked it out yet. Maybe it's some sort of message, or perhaps there's something about David Griffiths that we don't know.'

Norman sighed. 'Yeah, maybe. But how bad would he have to be to make her want to do something like this?'

'Come on,' said Southall. 'Let's have a look around the rest of these stables.'

In the stall opposite, an old grey snorted and pushed his head over the door.

'This must be Henry,' said Southall, stroking his nose. 'If only he could speak. He could tell us what happened.'

'And maybe he could tell us why,' said Norman.

They wandered around the barn for twenty minutes but found nothing of particular interest. A door at the far end led them into a room full of saddles, bridles, and various other pieces of horsey paraphernalia. What seemed like hundreds of rosettes were pinned to a cork board on one wall and on another, a shelf was crammed with trophies.

'This must be the tack room,' said Southall, switching on the light.

'Are you one of those horsey people?' asked Norman. 'Only, if you are, you've kept it pretty quiet.'

'Like many little girls I went through a pony phase. I even went to riding lessons. I never had one of my own, though. My parents couldn't afford it.'

'It can't be the cheapest of pastimes,' said Norman.

'It's not just the money, it's a full-time commitment. Looking back now, I'm glad they couldn't afford it because I don't think I would have kept it up for long and they would have wasted all that money. The smell of this place brings back memories, though. Leather and saddle soap, I think it is.'

'And don't forget the horse droppings,' said Norman. 'That's the smell I'm going to remember from this place.'

'There's nothing wrong with horseshit. You should collect some for your garden. It's great fertiliser for roses.'

'Is that right? Well, it just so happens my roses are doing just fine as they are. I think.'

'Don't you know?'

'I haven't got round to doing the garden yet. I was thinking of getting someone in to sort it all out for me. To be honest, I have no idea where to start.'

She glanced at him. 'I understand Faye's a bit of a gardener.'

'Really? Well, fancy that,' said Norman noncommittally.

They spent the five minutes following this exchange poking around in silence.

'I don't think there's anything for us in here, Norm, do you?' Southall said, finally.

'It would help if we knew what we were looking for, but I think you're right. I can't see anything here that jumps out at me.' He pointed to a top hat sitting amid the trophies on one of the shelves. 'I didn't expect to see one of those in here,' he said.

'I think you'll find women used to wear them as dressage riding hats.'

'I'm not the best person to ask about riding apparel,' he said. 'There wasn't a lot of call for that sort of stuff where I grew up. Catren's my go-to person when it comes to farms and animals and stuff. I'll try to remember to ask her, but I can't promise it will be at the top of my to-do list.'

Southall smiled. 'Come on, let's go.'

She led the way out of the tack room and back towards the car.

'What did you think of Ffion Howells?' asked Norman.

'As a person, or as a murder suspect?'

'We don't know this is a murder. I meant as a person.'

'There's clearly some animosity towards Tilly, but her main focus is her daughter. She'd be way down my list of murder suspects,' Southall said.

'Yeah, I think I'd go along with that,' said Norman. 'Of course, if this is a murder, everyone's a suspect, aren't they, but some people are more suspicious than others, right?'

When they reached the car, Southall looked at her watch. 'You'd better get off home when we get back,' she said. 'We can start again in the morning. We'll have the preliminary autopsy report by then.'

# CHAPTER 6

Southall was pleased to find that everyone was on time the following morning. Even Detective Constable Judy Lane was present, despite being on leave.

'What's the matter, Judy, can't you keep away?' she asked. 'You're not supposed to be here until tomorrow.'

'I called Catren last night, just for an update. She told me what was going on and, well, I didn't have anything to do today so I thought I'd come in and help. I hope you don't mind,' Lane said.

'Of course I don't mind. Just make sure you take some time off in lieu when you get the chance.' Southall turned to Norman. 'Is there an email from Forensics, Norm?'

'I'm just reading through it now. They say they've taken lots of fingerprint samples for analysis but you already know that. Apart from that it doesn't look as if they found anything to get excited about.'

'Right, then, let's make a start,' said Southall, looking around the room. 'As you all know, we're here to investigate the death of thirty-six-year-old Matilda Rotherby, known to everyone as Tilly.'

She used a small magnet to fix a photograph of Tilly to the noticeboard.

'Dr Bridger did an autopsy last night, and his preliminary result shows that Tilly died of asphyxiation.'

'I guess that can happen when you tie a noose around your neck, and jump off a horse's back,' said Norman. 'Does he give the time of death?'

'Now he's got her in the lab, he's narrowed it down a bit. He now thinks she died between ten and twelve on Saturday night,' said Southall. 'And, while I take your point about jumping off a horse's back, in this case it's not quite as simple as that. Dr Bridger is certain she didn't hang herself.'

'So, what are we saying here?' asked Norman. 'Was she dead before the noose was put around her neck?'

'Yes.'

'How does he know?' asked Winter.

'If someone had put the noose around her neck while she was conscious, there would almost certainly be scratches or marks of some sort on her neck, or possibly fibres under her nails, where she tried to pull the rope away, but there are none.'

'I don't understand,' said Winter. 'If there are no marks, doesn't that prove she didn't struggle? I know I'm new to all this, but to me that suggests suicide.'

'Normally I would tend to agree with you on that,' said Southall. 'But pooling of the blood suggests she was lying on her back after death and wasn't strung up until later. Also, when the rope was removed from her neck it was clear the marks that were left underneath had not just been made by the rope, but that she had also been strangled with something else. Dr Bridger thinks it was probably a leather strap. He's confident that whatever happened on Saturday evening, Tilly Rotherby did not commit suicide.'

'There was no shortage of leather straps in that tack room,' said Norman.

'Yes, a horse's rein would fit the bill quite nicely,' said Southall.

'So, if there were no scratches, does that mean she didn't resist when the strap was put around her neck?' asked Morgan.

'Didn't Dr Bridger find a wound on her head?' asked Norman. 'She wouldn't have resisted if someone had knocked her out.'

'Whatever hit her was sharp enough to slice through the scalp, and there was none of the bruising you would associate with a classic blunt-force trauma type of wound. Also, because there was very little blood, Dr Bridger thinks the head wound was inflicted post-mortem.'

'So, if it wasn't a blow to the head that knocked her out, do we know how she came to be unconscious?' asked Norman.

'We're not sure yet but, hopefully, Toxicology will be able to answer that,' she said.

'You think she was drugged?' he asked.

'Dr Bridger has his suspicions and says it can't be ruled out at this stage.'

'So, someone drugged her, strangled her with a rein, and then put a noose around her neck and tried to make it look like suicide,' said Morgan.

'The drugging has to be confirmed but that's more or less how it looks,' Southall said.

'Is there anything else of interest we should know about?' asked Norman.

'A couple of things,' said Southall. 'First, it appears Tilly had sex not long before she died.'

'Does that mean she was raped?' asked Morgan.

'I'm assured there's no evidence to suggest she wasn't a willing participant.'

'Any idea how soon before she died?' asked Morgan.

'That's not so easy to pinpoint,' said Southall. 'Probably within an hour or two.'

'But you can't say for sure?' Morgan said.

'I'm afraid not. Do you have a theory, Catren?'

'What about kinky sex gone wrong? Don't some people think being strangled at the same time takes the experience to another level? Perhaps that's where the rein comes in, only someone took it a bit too far, and then panicked and staged a suicide.'

'That's a bit elaborate for someone in a panic,' said Southall. 'Staging the scene suggests it was planned.'

'But, if Catren's right, and we've got the time of death right, we can rule out David Griffiths as her killer,' said Norman.

'That's assuming he's not lying about where he was,' said Southall. 'We need to check that out.'

'But if he's telling the truth, we're looking for a lover, who could well be her killer,' said Norman.

'There's one more thing,' said Southall. 'Tilly was three months pregnant.'

'Maybe that's why she agreed to get married,' said Morgan.

Southall raised an eyebrow.

'Maybe she was having doubts but finding out she was pregnant made up her mind for her. She wouldn't be the first one, would she?' Morgan said.

'Surely that would depend on who the father was,' said Norman.

'Okay, so perhaps she knew Griffiths was the father,' said Morgan.

'Or perhaps Griffiths found out he wasn't the father and that's why Tilly's dead,' suggested Norman.

'There are several possibilities,' said Southall. 'Hopefully, if the DNA gathered is viable, it will help us to identify who she had sex with before she died.'

'And maybe it will also tell us who the father is,' said Norman.

'Does this mean it's a double murder as it's mother and baby?' asked Winter.

'That is one of those grey areas that's become a legal minefield,' said Norman. 'According to the law, a three-month-old foetus isn't a child, and even if it was classed as a child, the prosecution would also have to prove there was intent to kill that child. If the intent was only towards the mother, the law doesn't recognise any offence against the unborn child. It's a nightmare and almost impossible to prove.'

'That doesn't seem right,' said Winter.

'I'm afraid there are a lot of things in law that don't seem right,' said Norman. 'But like it or not, it is what it is, and we can only work within the law.'

'Let's not get sidetracked by discussions about the legal system or we'll be here for weeks,' said Southall. 'Let's just focus on this case and find out who killed Tilly.'

'Do you want me to run the office?' asked Lane.

'I can't think of anyone better,' said Norman.

'Okay, but, as I missed yesterday, can you take me through what we know so far, and then I'll get a proper whiteboard up and running.'

'That's a good idea,' said Southall. 'Then we're all up to speed.'

'Right,' said Norman. 'Briefly, from the beginning: Carys Howells found Tilly Rotherby hanging in a stable just before six thirty a.m. She ran home to her mother who then called 999.

'David Griffiths says he arrived at around six thirty, looked for Tilly in the house but couldn't find her, so he assumed she was with the horses. He claims it took him about five minutes to get from there to the stables.

'When he got to the stables, he found Tilly hanging from the ceiling. There was a horse in the stall when he found the body, so he moved it to the stall opposite and then cut Tilly down to see if he could save her.

'First responders arrived fifteen minutes later and found him trying to give CPR, but it was too late. Tilly was already dead, and, as we now know, had been dead since around ten p.m. the night before.'

'Didn't he realise she was dead?' asked Winter.

'Obviously not,' said Norman. 'Or, maybe he knew very well that she was dead but wanted to mess up the crime scene.'

'You mean he could be the murderer?' asked Winter.

'Sure, he could be, but perhaps he's telling the truth and he was just desperate to save her. How many members of the public do you think would recognise a dead body? I reckon half of them wouldn't have a clue. And most wouldn't know how to do CPR either.'

'Okay, but if he was so keen to save her, why did he move the horse first?' asked Morgan.

'He says he had no choice. The horse was freaking out and he needed it out of the way,' Norman said.

'So, why not just open the gate and let it out?' asked Morgan. 'Why waste time putting it in another stall? And another thing, why didn't he remove the noose from around her neck? I think it would be the first thing someone would do.'

'Both good points,' said Southall. 'We'll ask him when we speak to him.'

'There is some other stuff we know from her diary,' said Southall. 'Tilly had arranged for someone to come in to do her hair and make-up, yet no one arrived. It's possible she may have cancelled them but that seems a bit odd for some-one who supposedly liked to look her best.'

She looked at Catren Morgan.

'Their names are Donna Price and Glynis Jenkins,' said Morgan. 'Donna called me back last night.'

'We need to speak to them,' said Southall.

'I've arranged to go and see them this morning,' said Morgan.

Southall nodded. 'Good. Take Frosty with you.'

'Do we have any suspects yet?' asked Lane.

'David Griffiths says he cut Tilly's body down to try and save her,' said Southall. 'But he could just as easily have done it to mess with the crime scene. In the absence of anyone else with a motive at this stage, he's my prime suspect.'

'So, you want to know all there is to know about him, right?' asked Morgan.

'When you get back from speaking to Donna Price, I'd like you to check him out, please, Catren. Background, finances, the lot,' said Southall.

Morgan nodded.

Norman turned to Southall. 'Have we covered everything?'

'Tilly had no landline but we know she did have a mobile phone,' said Southall. 'So far, we haven't found it, but we do know the number so we should be able to get a call history.

And, yes, we have tried calling the number, but the phone appears to be switched off.'

'I'll put in a request for that call history, and see if they can identify the location where it was last used,' said Lane.

'And, as I mentioned, we do have Tilly's diary,' added Southall. 'Judy, I'd like you to have a look through it this morning.'

Lane nodded. It was just the sort of thing she loved doing.

'Catren, talk us through what we know about the Rotherby family.'

'I used to know Tilly when I was a kid, but I haven't seen her in years. I can tell you her father died ages ago, and I'm sure her mother had moved on to greener pastures even before that. There's also Tilly's older brother, Giles Rotherby, who probably wasn't happy about being overlooked in the will in favour of his younger sister, but I have no idea where he is, or what he does.'

'Frosty, there's a job for you when you get back,' said Southall. 'I want you to find out all you can about Giles Rotherby.'

'Yes, boss, no problem,' said Winter.

'Right. You all know what you have to do. Norm will be with me. We're going back out to the stables, and then we'll speak to Carys Howells and David Griffiths. We'll see you back here later.'

## CHAPTER 7

The door swung open to reveal a feisty-looking woman in her forties, with long dark hair. A smaller, younger woman, her hair a startling shade of blonde, peered out at them from behind her.

'I'm DS Morgan and this is DC Winter,' said Morgan, showing her warrant card. 'We spoke yesterday. You're Donna Price and Glynis Jenkins, right?'

'You've come to the right place,' said the dark-haired woman. 'I'm Donna, and this, behind me, is Glynis.' She looked Morgan up and down. 'If you're looking for a make-over, I'm sure we'd have some fun working on a gorgeous young thing like you, but I'm afraid your friend will have to wait outside. We don't *do* men, if you know what I mean.' She smiled at Morgan suggestively.

Morgan smiled. 'Sounds like an intriguing proposition, but I really haven't got the time right now. Perhaps we can arrange it for another day.'

Donna grinned and winked at her. 'Any time, love. You just let us know.'

Winter gave a discreet cough.

'As I said yesterday, I'm hoping you can answer a few questions we have,' said Morgan.

'Why? What have we done?'

'Nothing, as far as I know,' said Morgan. 'But you might be able to help us with a case we're working on.'

'Well, you'd better come in, and we'll see what we can do,' said Donna.

She swung the door open and stood aside.

'This way,' said Glynis, leading them through the hallway and into a chintzy lounge. 'Take a seat,' she said, pointing to two armchairs. She settled herself next to Donna on a cosy settee.

Morgan was starting to enjoy herself, but she could see Winter was rather uncomfortable so she decided she'd better make it business-like.

'I understand you had a booking to do hair and make-up for Tilly Rotherby yesterday,' she said.

'That's right,' said Donna. 'She cancelled on Saturday morning.'

'Isn't that leaving it a bit late?'

'Tilly is like that. She can blow hot and cold over nothing at all. She'll be as nice as pie one minute, and the next she's showing you the door. You often feel like you are walking on eggshells around Tilly.'

'But she was a regular client?'

'How many clients do you think we've got out here? It's not like being in town where people walk in off the street. We can't afford to turn anyone away, especially someone who's such a good tipper.'

'She was generous, then?'

'She appreciates the fact that we are prepared to go the extra mile to keep her happy.'

She gave Morgan that knowing smile again. This time Morgan ignored it.

'Did she give a reason for cancelling?'

'All she said was that she had changed her mind and was calling the wedding off.'

'She was calling the whole wedding off?'

'That's what she said.'

'How did she seem when you saw her?'

'Oh, we didn't see her. It was all done by email.'

'You didn't speak to her?'

'I tried calling to ask why she was leaving it so late to cancel, but she never answered the call.'

'Did you call the house phone?'

'Her mobile,' Donna said. 'I think the landline was only there for the broadband. If she did use it, she never gave us the number.'

'So, you have no idea why she was calling the wedding off?'

'I assumed she'd fallen out with him again — that boyfriend of hers. David Griffiths, or whatever his name is.'

'You don't like him?'

'I don't really know him, but I've heard stories about him, and I've been told he's not what he seems.'

'What does that mean?'

'Apparently he's a liar, a bullshitter and a cheat.'

'I know they had a stormy relationship,' added Glynis. 'She's told me as much on more than one occasion. She's never actually said so, but I got the impression he might even have knocked her around on occasion.'

'You must have been angry with it being called off so late,' said Morgan.

Donna smiled. 'Normally I would have blown a fuse getting a cancellation at such short notice, but Tilly paid anyway, for messing us around, so we haven't actually lost any money. In fact, a day off with pay isn't something that happens often when you're self-employed, so it turned out to be a bit of a bonus.'

'And she has actually paid, even though you didn't see her?' Morgan asked.

'She always pays by bank transfer, and that's what she did this time.'

'You don't seem particularly surprised that she called the wedding off at such short notice,' said Morgan.

'She's been talking about getting married for a year or more, but I was never convinced she really wanted to go through with it.'

'Why do you think that was?' Morgan asked.

'I dunno. Perhaps, underneath it all, she knew he was full of shit.'

'Then why would she have stayed with him so long?'

'If I had a pound for every woman who's stuck with a man for all the wrong reasons, I could retire tomorrow. You know what it's like. You must come across them all the time in your line of work,' Donna said.

True enough, thought Morgan. 'Can you tell me where you were late on Saturday afternoon, and the night of the wedding?'

'We were here,' said Donna. 'Can I ask why you're asking all these questions? Has something happened?'

'I'm afraid Tilly was found dead yesterday morning.'

'Oh, my God,' gasped Glynis, and burst into tears.

Donna put her arms around her. 'She was very fond of Tilly,' she explained. 'She'll be okay in a minute.'

'You don't look surprised at the news, Donna,' said Morgan.

'I'm sorry, of course I am, but I've been around long enough that not much surprises me anymore,' she said. 'What was it, suicide?'

'What makes you say that?' asked Morgan.

'Well, you didn't say she'd been murdered or had an accident, did you? There isn't much left after that, is there?'

'I'm afraid I can't give you any details,' said Morgan. 'And I don't think we have any more questions for now.'

'If we can help in any way, just let us know,' said Donna, as she showed them out. 'Tilly could be difficult at times, but underneath it all I liked her.'

She opened the door and stepped aside to let them out.

'There is one thing,' said Morgan, pausing in the doorway. 'Do you have Tilly's phone number?'

Donna frowned.

'It's just routine,' said Morgan. 'Some people have more than one number.'

'Just a minute.' Donna disappeared for a moment then returned, offering Morgan a business card. 'This is our number in case you need to get in touch, like when you want to book that makeover. I've written Tilly's number on the back.'

Morgan took the card. 'Thanks,' she said. 'You've been very helpful.'

\* \* \*

As she climbed into the car next to Winter, Morgan showed him the card.

'You didn't mean that, did you?' asked Winter, as he pulled away.

'You mean about booking a makeover? Why not? Every girl likes to be pampered now and then.'

'I think she was offering to give you a bit more than a makeover.'

'You think so?'

Winter grinned. 'Don't tell me you didn't realise what she meant. I mean, come on, you even said it yourself.'

'Said what?'

'You said it was an intriguing proposition.'

'Don't you think it would be intriguing?'

As Winter began to blush, Morgan saw an opportunity for a bit of fun.

'The way I look at it, life is full of opportunities to experience new things,' she said. 'How can you know whether you like something or not if you've never tried it?'

'But that Donna. I mean, she's a . . . a *she*.'

'I can see why the boss was keen to get you on the team,' said Morgan. 'I expect you noticed that Glynis is also a woman.'

'Well, yeah, of course I did.'

'And your point is?'

'Well, Donna's old enough to be your mother.'

'I don't think she's quite that old,' said Morgan, 'and I don't think that's actually what you're getting at. Anyway, age means experience, and in my opinion there's nothing wrong with a bit of experience.'

Winter was blushing furiously now. 'I just didn't know you were that way inclined.'

Morgan was laughing out loud now. '"That way inclined",' she repeated. 'What's that supposed to mean? It's a good job I'm not the sort to take offence.'

Winter looked as if he wished he could disappear.

'As it happens, I'm not inclined one way or the other,' said Morgan. 'You could say I'm undecided. Not that it's any of your business.'

'You're right, it's not my business, and I'm sorry if I spoke out of turn,' said Winter. 'Can we change the subject?'

'You started it.'

'Yes, I did, and now I'm sorry.'

'Just so you know, your narrow-minded attitude doesn't offend me,' said Morgan.

'I'm not narrow-minded. I really don't care what you do or who you do it with.' Winter was beginning to sound angry.

'Good. Because I'm not going to change who I am to suit you. I'm afraid you'll just have to learn to put up with me as I am.'

# CHAPTER 8

Southall called the Seaview Hotel before they left Llangwelli station.

'Right,' she said to Norman. 'David Griffiths is happy to answer a few more questions. He says he'll wait for us to get there.'

'Magnanimous of him,' said Norman.

'I've also spoken to the hotel manager and asked her for copies of any CCTV footage they have from eight pm on Saturday until eight the following morning. She's going to have them ready for us to collect.'

'It's all systems go then,' said Norman. 'Where shall we begin? The estate, or the hotel?'

'Let's try the estate first,' said Southall.

\* \* \*

'Where do you want to start?' asked Norman, parking the car next to the farmhouse.

'Let's have another look at that barn. Now we know a bit more about the cause of death, perhaps we can figure out what happened.'

'I'm sure these stables weren't full yesterday,' said Southall as they walked through the yard towards the barn.

'I think Catren asked Animal Welfare to move them out of the barn and into the stables so they wouldn't have to keep walking through our crime scene,' said Norman.

Southall nodded. 'Good thinking, Catren.'

'Yeah, she's pretty switched on,' said Norman. 'I can't think why anyone who worked with her before us would suggest she was useless.'

'She's not useless, Norm, she's outspoken. A lot of senior officers want their female officers to be meek and mild, and not question their orders. Catren doesn't fit that mould, so I suspect someone couldn't handle it and that's why they moved her out to Llangwelli station. Perhaps they hoped she'd become so demoralised out here that she'd leave.'

'Well, that hasn't worked, has it? In fact, I think she's about ready for promotion.'

Southall nodded. 'Yes, I think you're right.'

'Have you spoken to her about it?'

'I've dropped a few hints. D'you think she'll be able to pass the exam?'

'There are a few areas where she lacks specific knowledge, but I'm pretty sure she'd be prepared to do whatever it takes to fill in those blanks.'

'Then perhaps it's time I had the conversation with her. It would be a shame to lose her but we're here to help people develop, not to hold them back.'

'You're not going to recommend they get rid of me to make way for her, are you?' Norman said.

Southall stopped in her tracks, mouth agape.

'Don't be ridiculous, Norm,' she said, finally. 'That's not even up for discussion.'

'Really?'

'Really. And I can assure you Superintendent Bain wouldn't entertain the idea.'

'You've spoken to him about me then?' he asked.

'As you know, we speak regularly about everyone on the team. I think I've mentioned before that he values you very highly.'

'Yeah, but are you sure he means it?' Norman still sounded anxious.

'Come off it, Norm. He didn't seek you out and beg you to join the team because he thought you were useless, did he?'

'Well, no. I suppose when you put it like that . . .'

'Is there any particular reason why you're feeling so insecure this morning?'

'I'm sorry, Sarah. It's just . . . even I need a little reassurance now and then, you know?'

She grinned. 'And there I was thinking you were superhuman.'

'Huh! My only superpower is an uncanny ability to get the wrong end of the stick.'

'Well, switch it off for a while, will you? The last thing we want to do now is waste our time chasing shadows.'

By now they had reached the barn.

'Right,' said Southall, sliding the door open. 'Now we've massaged your ego, do you think we could get on with our work?'

'Er, yeah, right. Of course.'

Southall led them to the end stall and stopped. 'Let's just take a minute to look before we go in, shall we?'

In the middle of the stall, the cut rope still dangled from the beam above.

'Remember yesterday I was asking how she could have got her head through the noose?' said Norman. 'Well, now we know she was dead before that happened, I've got two new questions. We're assuming our murderer was trying to make it look like Tilly committed suicide, right? So, question one, how the hell did they manage to get her up there? I mean, even though she wasn't a big woman, it would have taken a lot of strength to raise her up that high.'

'That's a fact,' said Southall.

'Question two. How did Griffiths really manage to cut her body down? I mean that loose end is dangling eight feet in the air. Would standing on the upturned bucket be enough? I'm not sure he's tall enough to reach that high.'

'I'll leave it to Griffiths to explain that feat when we speak to him later,' said Southall. 'But I might have an idea of how Tilly was raised up there in the first place.'

'You have? Okay, let's hear it,' said Norman.

'David Griffiths said there was a horse in here when he arrived.'

'Yeah, but we've only got his word for that.'

'I don't think he's lying,' said Southall. 'Don't forget Carys found Tilly first. She would know if there was a horse in here.'

'Does Griffiths know Carys was here before him? He says he thought she would be but he didn't see her.'

Southall beamed. 'My, my, you are on the ball this morning. Whatever you were doing last night, I think you should keep on doing it.'

'Yeah, I plan to,' said Norman. He cleared his throat. 'Anyway, you were just about to explain your theory.'

'Okay. For now, let's assume there was a horse in here. What if our villain used the horse to lift her up?'

'Seriously?' said Norman.

'Why not?' she said. 'You could throw the rope over the beam, with the noose reaching the ground, drag Tilly inside and slip the noose around her neck. You put a saddle on the horse, tie the rope to the saddle and make the horse walk forward. The horse pulls the rope and raises Tilly's body, then you slip the end of the rope through that ring on the wall and tie it off.'

Norman nodded thoughtfully. 'And you don't think Tilly was too heavy for a horse to pull?'

'Come on. Any horse would be powerful enough.'

'In that case, Sarah, I think you might be on to something.'

'It's probably a bit more complicated than that, but if you had time to get everything ready beforehand . . .'

'It works for me,' said Norman. 'And if it had to be planned, that's clearly premeditation.'

'It's something to think about,' said Southall. 'We'd have to test it and, of course, proving it's possible doesn't necessarily prove that's what happened.'

'Even so, it makes sense. I think you might well have cracked it,' said Norman.

Southall put a hand on his arm and raised a finger to her lips. They both listened.

'What is it?' he whispered.

'Can you hear a phone ringing? It's very faint, but I'm sure that's what it is.'

Norman frowned. 'I can't hear anything.'

Southall pointed to the far end of the barn. 'It's coming from that stall on the right.'

They hurried to the stall she had indicated and stopped outside.

'I still can't hear anything,' said Norman.

'It's stopped now,' said Southall. 'Bugger! I'm sure it was a mobile phone.'

'Let's have a look around,' said Norman. 'We might still find it.'

They spent a good five minutes searching the stall but found nothing. Norman even heaved up the food manger and peered underneath, but there was nothing there.

'Damn,' said Southall. 'I must have imagined it.'

Norman chuckled. 'Maybe it was someone calling a random number about a car accident — you know the ones, it wasn't your fault — so they might try again. They always call me a second time when I don't answer.'

'I wish,' said Southall. 'Come on, Norm, let's go. Maybe we can get Forensics back here later.'

Norman followed Southall out of the stall. Just as he turned to close the gate, they both heard a familiar 'ping' from the corner where the food manger stood.

'You definitely didn't imagine that,' said Norman. 'I heard it too. Someone just sent a text to that phone, and the sound came from over there.'

51

'But we already looked there,' said Southall.

'Then we obviously didn't look closely enough.'

Norman hurried back to the manger and bent down to listen.

'What are you doing?' asked Southall.

'If it's like my phone, it'll ping again in a minute or two,' he said. 'It drives me mad, but it'd be handy in this situation.'

Sure enough, the sound was repeated.

'It's definitely behind this food thing,' said Norman.

He lifted the empty manger from the wall and turned it over. 'Aha!' He set down the upturned manger and fished in his pocket for a pair of latex gloves. 'Got the little sod,' he said, prising away a mobile phone that had been taped to the back of the manger.

Southall held out an evidence pouch, and he dropped it inside.

'D'you think that's Tilly's phone?' Norman asked.

'I'll try it,' said Southall, pulling her own phone from her pocket. 'But why would she hide it there? And how come we didn't hear it when we were trying her number yesterday?'

She found Tilly's number, called and waited, but the phone before them remained silent.

'No self-respecting killer is going to hide their mobile phone within yards of the crime scene,' she said. 'So, whose phone is it? And why is it hidden like that?'

'Whoever owns it must have access to this barn,' said Norman.

'The thing is, anyone could slip in here unseen,' said Southall. 'There's no obvious security, is there? They don't even have a guard dog.'

'Yeah, I've been thinking about that. Catren told me they used to have stud horses here. Now, I don't know much about these things, but aren't they supposed to be valuable?'

'I think so. Some of them are worth millions.'

'So, being valuable, they would need to be insured, right? And wouldn't an insurance company insist they had decent security measures in place? I mean, if you made a claim and you didn't have any security they'd laugh in your face, wouldn't they?'

'Let's take a look at these horses and see if we can identify the studs,' said Southall.

'Not being rude, but I doubt I could tell a racehorse from a donkey,' said Norman. 'D'you think you can?'

'I think I know a stud horse from a riding-stable pony, and we can always find an expert if we need one.'

They went back to the main yard and slowly made their way from stable to stable.

'Apart from Tilly's horse, Henry, and maybe two others who have a bit of quality about them, these are all ponies,' said Southall. 'They're the sort you find in riding stables all over the country.'

'I take it that means they're not stud horses, then?'

'Henry is the only male here, and he doesn't have all the necessary equipment to be a stud,' explained Southall. 'The others are all mares.'

'So, Catren was wrong when she said she thought it was the stud fees that provided the money to keep the place going,' said Norman. 'But we've both seen the inside of that house. Tilly must have had an income from somewhere.'

'Come on, Norm,' said Southall. 'Let's go and speak with Carys Howells, and then I think we need to ask David Griffiths some serious questions about Tilly Rotherby and her business affairs.'

## CHAPTER 9

Ffion Howells wasn't pleased to find the two detectives on her doorstep again.

'Do you have to do this now?' she demanded. 'Carys is only sixteen, and I've kept her off school because she's still in shock. Can't it wait?'

'Ms Howells, your daughter happens to have discovered a murder victim,' said Southall. 'So, I'm sorry but, no, it can't wait.'

Ffion's eyes widened. 'Murder victim? I thought Tilly had committed suicide! That's what Carys said.'

'Well, I don't know where Carys got that from, but it's not the case.'

'Are you sure? She'd hanged herself, hadn't she? That's how Carys found her. It must have been suicide.'

'You sound very sure about it,' said Norman.

'People committing suicide hang themselves, don't they?'

'Do they?' said Norman. 'I think you'll find sleeping pills are a much more common method.'

'Did you go across to the stables after Carys came home?' asked Southall.

'As I told you yesterday, Carys came home in a terrible state. It took me five minutes to calm her down and find out why she was so upset. When she managed to explain, I called 999 to report it.'

'And you didn't go over there to see if you could do anything to help?'

'I'm not about to waste my time on people who don't want to live. I thought it was more important to stay here and look after my hysterical daughter, who, by the way, has her whole life ahead of her.'

'We still need to speak to her,' said Southall. 'Is she here?'

'She's upstairs.'

'Could you ask her to come down, please?'

'She's still in bed.'

'Maybe she is,' said Norman. 'But, as my boss has said, this is a murder investigation. The sooner she comes down here, the sooner we can ask our questions, and the sooner we can get out of your hair.'

Ffion pulled the door open to let them in, muttering darkly about heavy-handed policing and human rights. If she was spoiling for a fight, she was wasting her time. Southall and Norman had heard it all before.

'I'll go and wake her, but I think it's all wrong—'

'It's all right, Mum.' Carys was standing at the bottom of the stairs. 'They've got their job to do. If I can help, I think it's only right that I should.'

Tall and slim like her mother, Carys even had the same dark hair, but wore hers tied back in a ponytail. Despite being deathly pale, she was still strikingly pretty.

'Hello, Carys, how are you?' asked Southall.

'How do you think she is?' snapped Ffion.

'Mum, it's okay,' said Carys soothingly. 'I'm fine. I can handle this.'

'Is there somewhere we can sit down?' asked Southall.

Carys, who seemed to have taken control of the situation from her mother, led them through to the small scruffy lounge, where they sat down, Southall and Norman on one side of the room, Carys and Ffion sitting together, facing them. They had decided beforehand that Southall would ask the questions, while Norman took notes.

'I understand this isn't going to be easy for you,' said Southall. 'But we need you to tell us exactly what happened yesterday morning.'

Carys took a deep breath. 'Right. Well, I usually get up at five forty-five, but yesterday I must have dozed off again, so I was a bit later than usual. I suppose I must have got to the barn at about six twenty.'

'Are you absolutely sure about the time?'

'Because I was in a rush, I forgot to put my watch on, so I'm guessing, but I know it was just after six fifteen when I left here.'

'Okay, so you reached the barn at six twenty. Then what happened?'

'I always grab a bucket of food for Henry on the way to the barn. He's my favourite, so I always see to him first. When I opened the barn door, I could hear him freaking out, so I ran down to see if he was okay. That's when I saw her, just sort of hanging there.'

She reached towards Ffion who pulled her close.

'It was horrible,' said Carys. 'I can't stop seeing her, every time I close my eyes.'

'What happened after you saw Tilly?' asked Southall.

'Nothing at first. I just stood and stared. Then I screamed, and I ran straight back here to Mum.'

'She was in a terrible state when she arrived,' said Ffion. 'I don't want you putting her through that again, d'you hear?'

'Believe me, we do understand, Ms Howells, but we have to ask these questions.'

'It's okay, Mum, honest,' said Carys. 'I want to help if I can.'

'Just a few more questions for now,' said Southall. 'Are you quite sure Henry was in the stall?'

'Oh, yeah. Poor old thing. I probably should have let him out, but I didn't think. I just panicked and ran.'

'That's understandable,' said Southall. 'I think I would have done the same at your age. What happened to the bucket of feed?'

'Sorry?'

'You said you were carrying a bucket of feed. What happened to it?'

Carys looked puzzled. 'D'you know, I can't remember. I suppose I must have dropped it. I'm really not sure.'

'Okay,' said Southall. 'Did you see anyone else around?'

'No,' said Carys. 'But I don't usually. The whole point of me seeing to the horses at the weekends was so Tilly could have a lie-in.'

'How did you get on with Tilly? Was she a good boss to work for?'

'I hardly ever saw her. She used to leave my money in the tack room, and she'd leave a note with it if she wanted to tell me anything.'

'Your mum told us you weren't interested in horses before you began working at the stables.'

'I'm not mad about them. I can take them or leave them, you know? To me it was just a convenient job.'

'But don't you have to know what to do?' asked Southall. 'I wouldn't know where to start unless someone showed me.'

'Oh, yeah, Jimmy showed me the ropes for the first couple of weekends.'

'Jimmy? Who's Jimmy?'

'He does the horses in the mornings from Monday to Friday, and we split the evenings between us.'

'He's a stable lad?'

'I suppose that's what you'd call him, or at least it was until last Friday.'

Norman and Southall exchanged a glance.

'What happened on Friday?'

'It was his last day. He told me he was only doing the horses part time while he found a proper job.'

'And did he find one?'

'As I said, he left on Friday, so I suppose he must have.'

'Did he tell you what his new job is?'

'No. I haven't seen him to speak to. I only knew he'd gone because Tilly left me a note asking if I knew anyone who could take his place.'

'Does Jimmy have a surname?' asked Norman, pencil poised over his notebook.

'I think it's Denman.'

'I don't suppose you know where he lives?'

'Sorry, no. It can't be far, though, because he comes in on a mountain bike.'

'I think that's enough questions for now,' said Ffion, her face like thunder.

'We'll need you to come to Llangwelli police station and make a proper statement, Carys. Can you do that?'

'Yes, of course. Do I have to come today?'

'No, but I'd like you to come soon, while your memory is still fresh.'

'Should I ask for you?'

'If I'm not there, ask for a nice young detective called Judy Lane. She'll look after you.'

'What's going to happen to the horses?' asked Carys.

'Our animal-welfare people are looking after them for now,' said Southall. 'But I don't know what'll happen in the long term.'

'I'd like to help. I could feed them before I go to school, and when I come home.'

'I don't think that's a good idea, Carys,' said Ffion.

'I'll be all right as long as I don't have to go back into that barn, Mum, honest. I won't have time to muck them out, but I can go over and feed them.'

'You won't have to go into the barn,' said Southall. 'Our Animal Welfare people have moved them into the main yard.'

For a moment, Ffion looked ready to disagree, but she heaved a petulant sigh and waved her hand dismissively. 'I really don't think you should, but I'm too tired to argue.'

'I imagine our people would really appreciate your help,' said Southall.

'Yes, great, thank you so much,' said Ffion between gritted teeth. She was already on her feet and heading for the front door. 'Now, I really think it's time you left.'

The two detectives followed her to the door. As she was about to close it behind them, Southall turned back.

'Did Tilly tell you she was pregnant?'

For the briefest moment, Ffion's eyes widened in what looked like shock. Then the angry expression took over again and she spat out, 'What makes you think she would tell me? I already said she had no time for me and that we didn't speak.'

'I wondered if she might have mentioned it to Carys, and she had told you.'

'She had no more time for Carys than she had for me, so it's hardly likely, is it?'

'No, I suppose not,' said Southall.

'Now, if you don't mind.' Ffion started to close the door.

Southall and Norman were still saying their goodbyes when the door closed in their faces.

* * *

'I was watching Ffion's face,' said Norman as he started the engine. 'Jeez, that woman did not like Tilly one bit.'

'Yes, the bad vibes were coming off her in waves whenever Tilly was mentioned.'

'I thought she was going to explode when you asked if she knew that Tilly was pregnant,' he said.

'Yes, that was an interesting reaction, wasn't it?'

'Maybe it goes back to when Ffion got pregnant all those years ago,' said Norman.

As Norman popped the car into reverse, Southall looked back at the house.

'D'you think a house like this would have an underground telephone line?' she asked.

'Out here in the sticks? No way. It would be much too expensive to lay an underground cable all the way out here for half a dozen houses. Anyway, why are you asking? Didn't you notice the telegraph poles along this so-called access road?'

Southall looked embarrassed. 'Of course I noticed. I was just testing you.'

'Yeah, right,' said Norman with a wry smile. 'But you were going to make a point. What was it?'

'There doesn't appear to be a telephone cable going to that house and with no landline, Ffion would have used a mobile phone to place the 999 call.'

'Does that matter?' he asked, beginning to drive away.

'Probably not.'

'You're not happy about those two, are you?'

'For a kid who's just come upon a corpse, Carys is very calm and collected, whereas her mother seems to be having trouble dealing with what's happened. And was it me, or does Carys seem to have remarkably good recall considering what's happened?' Southall said.

'Yeah, she was quite precise about most of it, wasn't she? Ffion didn't convince me either. I get the protective mother thing, but there's something about her demeanour that's not quite right,' Norman said.

'It was a bit strange, wasn't it, almost as if Carys was the one in charge.'

He nodded. 'She was definitely more in control of her emotions than her mother.'

'Well, as you've already pointed out, Ffion really didn't like Tilly.' She looked thoughtful. 'It all seems to have gone bad after she got pregnant with Carys.'

'Yeah, but if her daughter means so much to her, would she really involve her in a murder?'

'I don't know, Norm, but I think we need to have a good look into her background. We need to find this Jimmy Denman too. I want to know where he fits into it all.'

'We are only a small team, you know.'

'I know, Norm, but that's never stopped us before.'

'How do you want to play it with Griffiths?'

'What have you got in mind?'

'I thought I might try and wind him up a bit and see if he's got a short fuse, if that's okay with you,' he said.

'Yes, that's fine, I can work with that.'

# CHAPTER 10

The aptly named Seaview Hotel sat perched atop a cliff, look-ing out to a horizon that on a clear day like today, seemed a million miles away.

Southall headed straight for Reception.

'I'm DI Southall and this is DS Norman,' she said, show-ing her warrant card. 'You have some CCTV footage for us, I believe.'

'One moment,' said the receptionist, and picked up the phone. 'The manager wants to speak with you.' She mur-mured something into the receiver, then looked up at them. 'She's on her way. She'll just be a moment.'

Almost immediately, a smartly dressed forty-something woman made her way towards them.

'DI Southall? Can I just check your ID, please? I'm sorry, but what with the data-protection rules and what have you . . .'

With a smile, Southall handed over her warrant card. 'We'd be disappointed if you didn't check.'

'This all seems to be in order,' said the manager. 'But I'm still not sure . . .'

'As I said when I called, this is a murder enquiry,' said Southall. 'I can get a search warrant if you prefer, but then you'll have a car park full of police cars, and police officers everywhere. I don't think you want that, do you?'

The manager sighed resignedly, reached into her pocket and produced a small memory stick. 'It's all on here,' she said. 'Room plan, guest list, and footage from every camera we have for the full twelve hours.'

'Thank you, that's very helpful,' said Southall.

'I'm all too happy to help if it means we can avoid a major disturbance.'

'Can you tell us where we can find David Griffiths?'

'I believe he's having a coffee in the garden.'

'D'you know him? Is he a regular visitor?'

'No. He's never been here before this weekend, but we don't get many visitors who ask if they can re-book their room because their house has become a crime scene. It rather sticks in your mind.'

They found Griffiths sitting in a neat, tidy garden at the side of the hotel, gazing out to sea.

'Morning, David,' said Southall. 'How are you today?'

'To be honest, I'm still trying to get my head around what's happened.'

'I can understand that. Is everything okay with the hotel?'

'Yes, it's fine. My room has even got a private patio.'

'Good,' said Southall. 'We'll let you have the farmhouse back as soon as we can, but I'm sure you can appreciate the need to be thorough.'

He shrugged. 'I don't really have much choice, do I?'

Southall offered him a smile. 'I'm afraid not. Are you up to answering a few more questions?'

'As I said yesterday, anything I can do to help. Only, I think I told you all I can remember about what happened.'

'There are a couple more points about yesterday, and then some more general questions,' said Southall, producing a folded sheet of paper from her pocket. 'They'll probably seem a bit random because I haven't had time to put them in order.'

Norman was rather surprised at this, but as Southall unfolded what he could see was a blank sheet of paper, it dawned on him what she was doing.

'That's okay,' Griffiths said. 'I understand. My own thoughts are all over the place at the moment.'

'Right,' said Southall, glancing at the paper in her hand. 'We forgot to ask you what time you arrived at the hotel on Saturday.'

'I'm not sure. I guess it would have been around eight fifteen. Does it matter?'

'Probably not,' said Southall. 'We just like to have these little details for our timelines.'

She looked at the sheet of paper again and seemed to hesitate, allowing Norman to step in.

'When you found Tilly hanging in the stable, you said you cut her down,' he said.

'Yes, that's right.'

'Do you always carry a knife with you?'

'There's always a sharp knife in the tack room. They use it for cutting the string on the hay bales.'

'So, you went to the tack room, got the knife, and then came back and cut her down. Was this before you put the horse in the stall, or after?' Norman asked.

'What are you suggesting?'

'I'm not suggesting anything. I'm just trying to establish the order of events.'

'I went to get the knife first, and it was only when I got back that I realised the horse was going to be in the way.'

'You could have just opened the gate and let him out.'

'Yes, I suppose I could, but I wasn't thinking straight. Tilly had a rule that the horses were never to be allowed to wander around on their own, and I guess I've had it drummed into me so often I didn't think about it.'

'How did you manage to reach up that high when you cut the rope?' asked Norman.

'I'm sorry?'

'The rope was severed about eight feet above the ground. I'm guessing you're a little under six feet tall. I'm just curious how long your arms must be.'

Griffiths sighed. 'I already told you. There was a feed bucket on the floor outside the stall. I grabbed that, turned it upside down and stood on it.'

'And you held on to Tilly as you cut her down?' Norman said.

'Of course I did. I wasn't going to let her drop, was I? I'm not sure what you're trying to suggest, Sergeant.'

'I'm just trying to work out how long Tilly must have been left hanging there while you were getting all this stuff together.'

Griffiths's jaw tightened. 'I don't like your tone, or what your questions seem to be implying, Sergeant.'

Norman stared levelly at Griffiths. 'I'm sorry if you don't like my questions, Mr Griffiths, but we're trying to find out who killed your wife. Sometimes that involves asking questions people object to.'

Griffiths sat back. 'Well, I understand that, but surely you can imagine how I was feeling. I was terrified.'

'Yeah, I guess most people would be scared in that situation,' said Norman. 'But most of them would have been running around like headless chickens, not staying cool and thinking straight, like you seem to have done.'

He stared impassively at Griffiths, who swallowed once or twice but said nothing. Finally, Southall broke the tense silence.

'When we were in the tack room, we were surprised to see three shelves stacked with trophies.'

'They're Tilly's. She won a lot in her heyday.'

'Oh, right. I didn't realise she was that good,' said Southall.

'Apparently, at one time there was even talk of her going to the Olympics.'

'Really? Wow, she must have been good,' said Norman. 'Anyway, in the centre of the lower shelf, there's a top hat.'

'That's right. It's Tilly's,' said Griffiths.

'I'm sorry. Did you say it belonged to her? Why did she have a top hat?'

'Years ago, riders often wore a top hat when they were competing in dressage events. It's banned now on safety grounds. Tilly told me she was less successful after the ban. She believed the top hat brought her good luck, so she felt it deserved pride of place among her trophies.'

'That would explain it, then,' said Norman.

'Is it important?'

'I shouldn't think it's important, or even relevant. I was just curious, since I don't know much about horses and dressage.'

'On a more serious note, we haven't managed to find Tilly's mobile phone,' said Southall. 'Do you know if she kept it anywhere special?'

Griffiths shook his head. 'No. She usually had it on her, or at least close by.'

'Have you got her number? I just want to make sure we've got it right.'

'Yes, sure.' Griffiths picked his phone up from the table, found the number and passed it over to Southall. She showed Norman so he could make a note of it, then handed the phone back to Griffiths.

'What can you tell us about Tilly's business arrangements?' asked Southall.

'We tended to keep our businesses separate from our private lives,' Griffiths said.

'You had just married,' said Norman. 'Presumably you were planning on living together at least some of the time. Surely you must have spoken about your finances, like who'd be paying the bills and all that.'

'Not really. We just sort of muddled along, you know?'

'No, I'm not sure I do know,' said Norman. 'I can't believe you didn't know anything at all about her finances.'

'Well, I knew some, of course.'

'Some? Like what?'

'I know she had stud horses, and she made money from the stud fees. And she owned half a dozen cottages. The rent from those brought some money in.'

'And that made her enough to keep the estate going?'

'Well, yes, I suppose so.'

'You suppose so,' said Norman. 'You've got your own business, Mr Griffiths, and you're successful, right?'

'I like to think I do okay.'

'So, it would be fair to say you've got a business brain?'

'I think so.'

'Half a dozen tatty rental cottages in Wales are going to bring in how much? I reckon four to five grand a month if you're lucky. Are you telling me you seriously think that's enough to run an estate on?'

'I see. No, on its own that's not enough. It's the stud fees that bring in the real money.'

'Where are these famous stud horses that bring in all this money?' asked Southall.

'In the stables, of course.'

Southall shook her head. 'No, they're not. There's only one horse in those stables that could ever have been a stallion, and that's poor old Henry. And I suspect he was gelded long before he ever got the chance to prove himself.'

Griffiths stared at Southall in disbelief. 'No, you've got that all wrong. There are three of them.'

'So, where are they?' asked Norman.

'I don't know. Perhaps Tilly moved them for some reason.'

'I hope you're right,' said Southall. 'Oh, and by the way, the cottages won't be bringing in any more income. Tilly sold them to the owner of the mansion.'

'That's not right. They're part of the estate. Why would Tilly sell them?'

'We were rather hoping you might be able to tell us that,' said Norman.

Griffiths looked blank.

'You see the problem we have here, David,' Southall said. 'We know Tilly sold the cottages months ago, and it appears she may well have sold the stud horses too, and yet she still seems to have been living very comfortably. So, where was the money coming from? You?'

'Tilly never, ever, asked me for money. As I said, we never really spoke about that side of things.'

'So, you want us to believe that you know nothing about her business dealings, and she knew nothing about yours?'

'That's just how we were. We didn't pry into each other's business lives. We didn't feel we needed to know.'

'Did you pry into each other's private lives?' Southall asked.

'We had no secrets, if that's what you mean.'

'Oh, really?' said Southall. 'You knew Tilly was pregnant, then?'

Griffiths spluttered into his coffee. After a few minutes, he said, 'Yes, of course I knew. We were keeping it quiet because she'd had a couple of miscarriages.'

'Were you the father?' asked Norman.

'What sort of question is that?' snarled Griffiths.

'Actually, it's a very relevant question,' said Southall. 'You see, Tilly had sex not long before she died, and you told us you had been away all week and hadn't seen her.'

'Had she been raped?'

'We don't believe so. There's no evidence to suggest she was anything but a willing participant, and that suggests the possibility of a lover,' Southall said.

'I don't believe this,' said Griffiths. 'Of course the baby was mine.'

'We could prove that if you would allow us to take a DNA sample,' said Norman.

'I don't have to prove anything. I know the baby was mine. I also know I'm not under caution, which means I don't have to answer any more of your questions. So, I suggest you clear off and leave me alone.'

'It's true, you're not under caution at the moment,' said Southall. 'But we seem to be finding more questions than answers where you and Tilly are concerned. I have a feeling we will be speaking again before too long, Mr Griffiths.'

\* \* \*

Norman started the car and headed out of the car park. 'D'you want to go back to the house now?'

'Let's head back to the ranch,' said Southall. 'We need to get the mobile phone to the tech guys, and we need to start going through this CCTV footage. I'd also like to see where we are with the background check on David Griffiths.'

'You don't like him, do you?' asked Norman.

She shook her head. 'Men like that make my skin crawl. I wouldn't trust him as far as I could throw him.'

'What was all that business with the blank sheet of paper?' asked Norman. 'And did I see you batting your eyes at him?'

'Look, I probably wasn't very good at it, but I was playing soft cop to your hard cop,' said Southall. 'I just wanted to see how he would react if I seemed a bit scatty.'

He smiled. 'Well, I have to say your simpering woman act wasn't very convincing.'

'Well, I think I've told you before that most people reckon I'm a hard-nosed bitch.'

'Being a tough, independent woman doesn't make you a hard-nosed bitch, Sarah.'

'Some people think it does.'

'Well, maybe those people don't know the real Sarah Southall.'

Southall stared out of the car window and absorbed the compliment, mightily grateful to Norman for his support.

'Good act or not, did you see the way he was looking at me?' she said. 'I'm pretty sure he thinks I'm clueless and that I'd be a pushover.'

'Yeah, I did clock that,' said Norman. 'He's a predator all right, but aside from the fact you think he's a creep, what did you make of him otherwise? He did look genuinely shocked when you told him the stud horses were gone and the cottages had been sold.'

'Yes, but was he shocked to think Tilly had sold them, or shocked to think he wasn't going to inherit them?'

'That's the million-dollar question, isn't it?' said Norman. 'But if his business is doing as well as he says, I can't see why he'd be bothered about how much Tilly was making from those cottages. It would be like loose change, wouldn't it?'

'I smell a rather large rat where Mr Griffiths is concerned,' said Southall. 'I can't wait to see what the search into his background uncovers.'

'And I'm sure he lied about knowing Tilly was pregnant,' said Norman. 'He almost choked on his coffee when you told him.'

'Yes, it wasn't difficult to see it was an act, but I couldn't decide why. Was it because he genuinely didn't know, or because he didn't think we'd find out?'

'D'you know, I hadn't thought of it like that,' said Norman. 'I was thinking he was all about the money, but if he already knew she was pregnant, and he's not the father, that's a pretty good motive for murder. Money or jealousy, take your pick.'

'Or maybe there's something else we don't know about yet,' said Southall. 'Whatever, he's definitely in the frame.'

# CHAPTER 11

Southall, followed by Norman, went into the main office. She was surprised to see Morgan and Winter working at their desks.

'I didn't think you'd be back yet,' Southall said to Morgan.

'We only got in about ten minutes ago.'

'How did you get on with Donna and Glynis?'

'They say they weren't there yesterday because Tilly cancelled on Saturday morning. Apparently she paid them in full because it was such short notice.'

'That bit makes sense,' said Norman. 'According to David Griffiths, Tilly hated to offend anyone. He said she had a heart of gold.'

'That's not what Donna and Glynis say. According to them, Tilly was a good customer but difficult, and would often fly off the handle for no reason.'

'What else did they have to say?' asked Southall.

'They said they were half expecting Tilly to cancel the wedding. Apparently, she had mentioned calling the whole thing off before.'

'That's odd,' said Southall. 'According to David Griffiths, they were already married. He says they tied the knot two weeks ago in a registry office. This thing yesterday was just a party for all those who didn't attend the actual wedding.'

'Donna and Glynis say David Griffiths isn't what he seems,' said Morgan. 'Maybe they're right and he's feeding us a load of bullshit.'

'Did they say why they think that?' asked Southall.

'They've heard rumours that he's a liar, and a cheat.'

'That could be just spiteful gossip. People love to spread rumours about others,' said Norman. 'It doesn't mean they're true.'

'There is one more thing the girls mentioned about Tilly,' she added. 'It may not be relevant, but apparently she was happy for them to "go the extra mile" with her.'

Norman frowned.

'They're gay, Norm,' explained Morgan. 'For a consideration, they were willing to—'

'Oh, gotcha. You mean Tilly didn't really have a preference.'

'It seems not,' said Morgan. 'As I said, it's probably irrelevant, but you never know.'

'I suppose some guys might take umbrage and consider it a threat to their masculinity,' said Norman. 'But is it a sufficient motive for murder?'

'Nothing would surprise me with some men,' said Morgan. 'How did it go with you two?'

'Well, we've upset Ffion Howells and pissed off David Griffiths big time,' said Norman. 'So I think you could say we've done a good day's work.'

'According to Carys Howells, there's a part-time stable lad called Jimmy Denman who looks after the horses during the week. We need to find the guy and speak to him.' Southall produced the evidence pouch containing the mobile phone. 'And we found this mobile phone hidden in one of the stalls inside the barn. Luckily, someone sent a text to it while we were standing there. We can't get into it, of course, but that's what we have a tech department for.'

'And we've got this,' said Norman, holding the memory stick aloft. 'It's CCTV footage from the Seaview Hotel where

David Griffiths was staying on Saturday night. With a bit of luck, it will show us if he was telling the truth about what time he got to the farmhouse.'

'D'you think he's lying?' asked Morgan.

'Let's say I don't trust a word that leaves his mouth,' said Southall.

She turned to Lane. 'What about you, Judy? Anything of interest in Tilly's diary?'

'Unfortunately, she wasn't one for pouring out her heart and soul. It seems to consist mostly of times and initials, as if she was recording when and whom she met, but unless you know who the initials belong to, it's difficult to make any sense of it.'

'Does she mention locations?' asked Southall.

'Not that I've noticed. I just assumed most of these meetings took place on the estate. The initials that crop up most often are BR, AT, FN, JY, and DD, and there's one person she refers to as Dy. On the last Friday of every month D and G are booked in, and I'm assuming that refers to Donna Price and Glynis Jenkins.'

'Was that Sunday meeting crossed out?' asked Southall. 'Only we know Tilly cancelled the appointment.'

'No, it's still in the diary and hasn't been altered.'

'That's interesting,' said Southall. 'Were any meetings arranged for Saturday?'

Lane flipped open the diary.

'Yes, there's Dy, but there's no time, which is unusual.'

'And she hasn't made any comments about any of the meetings?'

'Some of the DDs have been crossed through. I wondered if that meant it was a no show, but that's just a guess.'

'I don't suppose there are any contact details, phone numbers, or anything like that?' asked Norman.

'I'm afraid not,' said Lane.

Norman nodded. 'That would have been too easy, wouldn't it?'

'I'll take a look at her finances when I get time,' said Lane. 'Maybe I can find something there that will help us identify some of these people.'

'Right. I think you all know what you've got to do this afternoon, so I'll let you get on,' said Southall. 'But don't forget to eat. I don't want anyone missing lunch.'

'I'm glad you're here, Frosty,' said Morgan. 'Because it's your turn to make the teas.'

'But I make lousy tea.'

'Then you obviously need more practice. Go on, off you go. I make my share, and Judy always makes hers, so it's your turn.'

'But that means I'm going to have to make five!'

'Yeah, well, you could always make tea when there are just the three of us, but you keep finding excuses for putting it off,' said Morgan. 'This is what happens when you try to dodge your turn.'

'It's called karma,' added Lane with a sweet smile.

Winter made his way reluctantly to the small kitchen. Southall retreated to her office, picked up her phone and dialled the number for the control centre.

'Hi,' she said. 'This is DI Southall at Llangwelli station. There was a 999 call placed at around six thirty yesterday morning, regarding a woman found hanged in a stable. Yes, that's right. I'd like to know the exact time of the call, and I'd like a recording of the whole conversation, please.'

Norman slipped off his jacket, rolled up his sleeves, settled at his desk and plugged the memory stick into his computer. Four folders popped up on the screen before him, three of which were labelled as CCTV footage.

'Jeez, three cameras with twelve hours of footage each. Holy crap, it'll take two or three days to get through that lot,' he muttered. It wasn't true, of course, because he would fast-forward most of the film. Sometimes he just liked to have a little gripe to himself.

He nodded to Winter as he set a mug of tea beside him, opened a notebook and put a pencil next to it.

'Okay,' he muttered, clicking on the first file. 'Let's start with the guest list and room plan.'

Griffiths had stayed in Room Two, which didn't take long to find on the plan.

'Of course. He said he had a room with a private patio.' Norman watched and made notes, muttering a running commentary to himself. 'Now, let's take a look at these videos. We'll start with this one from Reception.'

He set the file scrolling at double speed and almost immediately had to slow it down as a man appeared carrying a small holdall. It was David Griffiths. Norman made a note of the time stamp on the video.

'Twenty eighteen. I guess that's close enough to what he told us.' He watched as a man and woman arrived while Griffiths was signing the register. After an exchange of smiles and greetings, Griffiths moved off across the reception area towards his room. On the screen, the couple were checking in, but Norman had seen what he wanted.

He spent the rest of the afternoon working his way through the footage. He slowed it down every time someone came into Reception. He saw the couple from earlier make their way through to the bar, less than half an hour after their arrival. So far, David Griffiths hadn't reappeared.

Southall emerged from her office while the others were getting ready to go home.

'Okay, it's nearly five. Has anyone found anything they want to share?'

'Griffiths was right about what time he arrived at the hotel,' said Norman. 'And if he left again, he didn't go through Reception. But I've still got the other cameras to go.'

'They can wait until tomorrow,' said Southall. 'Anyone else?'

'From what I've found so far, I'd say the best approach might be to take everything David Griffiths says with a pinch of salt,' said Morgan.

'Why's that then?' asked Southall. 'Anything concrete?'

'I haven't got as far as I would have wanted, because I got sidetracked by his business,' said Morgan. 'You'll soon see why. I started with his Facebook account. According to his profile, he's a forty-two-year-old entrepreneur who lives in Aberystwyth. He also says he's the chief executive of a company called OffTurbUK, which was formed three years ago. The company deals in wind turbines and is also based in Aberystwyth. It's listed at Companies House but they don't seem to have submitted any financial results to date.

'I think the name is a shortened form of Offshore Turbines, but although he mentions it in his personal profile, there's no Facebook page for the business. I thought that was a bit odd, so I took a look at LinkedIn. He's listed on there too, but the information is sparse to say the least. There's only one contact number listed, which I tried, but the line was dead. However, there was a website, so I had a look at that.

'Sure enough, an Offturbuk.com website does exist, and at first glance it looks like the shop window to a thriving business, but when you check out one or two rival websites, it's not hard to see the OffTurb website has been cobbled together using pages from various other sites, with only the company name altered. They've used the exact same photographs, in the exact same places.'

'The website is fake?' asked Southall.

'We'd need to go up to Aberystwyth and take a look, but I believe the whole business is a sham,' said Morgan. 'I've checked Google maps, and the address they list does exist. The thing is, I would expect a business like that to need a lot of room — those turbines are huge — but what I'm seeing is a Portakabin on the edge of a business park, not a big factory unit or warehouse on an industrial estate.'

'Is there a bank account?' Southall asked.

'Sorry, I haven't got that far yet. I'll get on to it in the morning.'

'So, from what you know so far, you reckon your make-up and hairdresser ladies were right to think he's not what he seems, do you?'

'It looks that way,' said Morgan. 'I'm afraid that's all I can tell you for now. As I said, I got a bit sidetracked.'

'Don't worry, you've done well,' said Southall. 'We already had our doubts about David Griffiths. Now you've confirmed that he's definitely someone of interest.'

'What about you, Frosty?' asked Norman. 'Any luck with the brother?'

'His full name is Giles Augustus Rotherby,' said Winter. 'He was born in May 1982, so he's now forty —five years older than Tilly. He was educated at Eton, and in 2003 went on to Swansea University where he studied Business Law.'

'Did you say Swansea?' asked Norman. 'It costs a fortune to send a boy to Eton. Wouldn't he have been expected to go on to Oxford or Cambridge?'

'Sending your son to a posh school doesn't necessarily mean you're going to end up with a genius,' said Winter. 'As my grandfather would say, you can take a horse to water but you can't make it drink.'

'You mean Giles is thick,' said Morgan.

'I mean he seems to have an aversion to hard work,' said Winter. 'He lasted less than a term at Swansea.'

'Any idea why he dropped out?' asked Norman.

Winter shook his head. 'No. D'you want me to find out?'

'Maybe, but it's not a priority at the moment,' said Norman.

'After he dropped out,' Winter continued, 'Giles seems to have run off to London where he lived in a small flat leased by his father and had a succession of bartending jobs in various London clubs. But he never seemed to hold any of these jobs down for more than a few months. He finally came back home when his father died.'

'Presumably thinking he was going to inherit the estate,' said Norman.

'But Tilly inherited instead,' said Southall. 'So, I think it's safe to assume his father thought he wasn't responsible enough to run the estate, but I wonder, was that the only reason?'

'Maybe they just never got on,' said Norman. 'It happens, right?'

'Yes, but if it was that bad, would his father have let him live in his London flat?' Winter said.

'Good point,' said Norman. 'What happened to the flat? Is he still living there?'

'As far as I can make out, the lease was terminated when the father died,' said Winter.

'Terminated by whom?'

'I haven't been able to find that out.'

'So, where's he living now?' Norman said.

'I haven't been able to find that out either. He seems to have spent the first ten years after his father's death living on the family estate with Tilly, but after that he went off the radar. I'm assuming he's either living rough, or maybe sofa-surfing and sponging off his rich friends.'

'So, currently of no fixed abode,' said Southall. 'I can't imagine he would have been very happy losing his inheritance, and his home in London. If that didn't foster resentment, I don't know what would.'

'It would be a powerful motive for murder,' said Norman.

'Yeah, but why wait until now?' asked Winter. 'He instigated procedures to challenge the will immediately after it was read, but he didn't take it all the way.'

'Do we know why he stopped?' asked Southall.

'My first guess was that he didn't have the money to pay for it,' said Winter. 'But then he ended up living on the estate for ten years, so maybe he struck some sort of deal with Tilly. The thing is, if he was that resentful about the will, then surely, in the ten years he was living there, he would have had plenty of opportunities to bump her off.'

'Yeah, but he would have been the obvious suspect,' said Norman. 'Much better to disappear for a while and then strike.'

'From what I've found out so far, I don't see him as the type of person who would think that far ahead,' said Winter.

'Maybe he left because they fell out and Tilly had him evicted,' said Morgan. 'If he wasn't resentful enough to kill her before, he would have been after that.'

'Frosty, you won't be able to do this until tomorrow, but can you get hold of the solicitor he used and find out why he dropped the legal challenge?' asked Southall.

'Consider it done,' said Winter.

'Okay, I think you've all done very well,' said Southall. 'So if you want to get off home, I'm not going to stop you.'

'I'm going to stay,' said Lane. 'I want to get the board set up, draft a to-do list and start getting everything booked and catalogued.'

'I'm miles behind,' said Morgan. 'It'll be easier to do the financials tomorrow, but I need to catch up with this background stuff, so I'll stay.'

'I'm in no rush to get anywhere, so I'll stay too,' said Winter.

Southall looked at Norman.

'I've already made a start on that CCTV footage,' he said.

'None of us are robots, guys,' said Southall. 'We all need rest and sleep.'

'Yeah, we know we don't have to stay,' said Morgan. 'But we're a team, right? So, if one stays, we all stay.'

Southall looked at the clock. 'Only until seven p.m. At seven, every member of the team goes home.'

'I've just found more proof that Griffiths is full of bullshit,' said Morgan. 'The house by the coast he says he owns is actually a holiday chalet. I'm going to trace the owner in the morning.'

'Nice work, Catren,' said Southall. 'Perhaps the owner will be able to tell us more about him.'

'It's not looking good for Griffiths, is it?' said Norman. 'That hole he's digging just seems to get deeper and deeper.'

'Right, guys,' said Southall. 'Don't forget I don't want to see any of you here after seven. We'll start again at eight in the morning.'

## CHAPTER 12

By the time Norman had driven home, made himself dinner — in the form of a bacon sandwich washed down with a cup of strong coffee — it was eight p.m. He settled himself in his favourite armchair, set his notebook and pencil on the table by his side, opened his laptop and plugged in the memory stick he'd slipped into his pocket before leaving work.

'Okay,' he said to himself, clicking on a folder. 'Let's get on with this.' He opened the folder containing the CCTV footage. 'Now, where was I?' He flipped his notebook open and read his notes. 'I suppose I really ought to watch the car-park footage first, and then I can finish with Reception.'

Alternately speeding up and slowing the film, he watched the first few hours of car-park footage. A few cars came and went but he found nothing unexpected, and by midnight all activity had ceased. He scrolled quickly through the next few hours until by four in the morning, boredom had set in and he stopped the video. He made a note of where he'd got to and closed the file. He could come back to this one later.

He did the same with the footage from Reception, watching a handful of non-residents entering and making their way to the restaurant, but there was no further sign of Griffiths after he'd checked in.

Between eleven o'clock and midnight, all the non-residents were making their way out to their cars. At eleven thirty, the couple who had checked in after Griffiths provided the single moment of interest when they staggered across the reception area, heading for their room. At first Norman thought they were both drunk, but then he realised the woman was actually sober and merely staggering under the weight of her apparently comatose husband.

'Jeez, I wouldn't have wanted his head on Sunday morning,' muttered Norman.

He fast-forwarded through to four a.m. and then stopped. He set the laptop to one side, climbed stiffly from his chair, and made his way to the kitchen. He grabbed a beer from the fridge and, humming quietly, made his way back to his chair and once more set the laptop on his knees.

He opened the third camera folder. At first, he thought he was looking at the garden to the side of the hotel, where they had spoken to David Griffiths, but soon realised this camera was set up high on one of the hotel walls and showed a view of the back of the hotel, where some of the ground-floor rooms had doors leading out onto private patios. They all had six-foot-high fences between them, which provided privacy. A wide path ran along the back of the gardens towards the side garden.

'Aha!' muttered Norman. 'The rooms with patios. So, if Griffiths was in the second one along, this is how he could have got to the car park without going through Reception.'

He started the video at four times normal speed, reached for his beer and settled back, quite sure that, any minute now, he would see Griffiths leave his room and head off along the path.

The time stamp read one a.m. when a movement caught Norman's attention. He rewound a couple of minutes and set the video playing at normal speed. As he watched, a door swung open onto the patio of Room Two, and in the gloom a man made his way out to the path.

Convinced that this was Griffiths, Norman held his breath as the man appeared to undo the bolt securing the gate.

Then, to his surprise, instead of opening the gate, he went back through the patio to his room. As he passed through the door to his room, a wall light came to life and flooded the patio in light.

Disappointed, Norman muttered a curse and took a swig of his beer. He continued to watch David Griffiths's patio, until he spotted movement on the patio behind the next room along. As the door swung open, a pale, ghostly figure emerged and turned to close the door. Norman couldn't make out who it was in the darkness, but there was enough light to show them walking across the patio, undoing the bolt on the back gate and stepping out onto the path.

The figure briefly disappeared behind the fence, then the back gate to Griffiths's patio opened and the figure reappeared. Illuminated by the wall light, the figure turned out to be a woman, wearing a flimsy white negligee that gave her the look of a ghostly apparition. Fascinated, Norman watched as she glided across the patio and in through the door into Griffiths's room, pulling it closed behind her.

Norman rewound the video until he found a frame with a good view of the woman's face, then he zoomed in.

'Well, hello again,' he muttered. 'Down in Reception you were acting like you'd never met before. I wonder, does your husband know what you're up to?'

He paused the video, went back to the guest list and wrote down the names of the people booked into Room Three. Then he returned to the video and watched some more, noting the time when the woman made her way back, carefully bolting the gate before crossing the patio, opening the door and disappearing from view.

# CHAPTER 13

'Are you okay, Norm? You look like you've been up all night,' Southall said, when Norman arrived for work the next morning.

He held up the memory stick. 'You know when you start watching one of those TV series intending to just watch the first episode, but you get so involved you can't stop? Well, this CCTV footage is a bit like that. Sure, there are hours when literally nothing happens, but, trust me, the good bits more than make up for the boredom.'

'If it's that good, you'd better share it with the rest of us.'

'I edited all the relevant footage together like a highlights reel. Give me a couple of minutes to get set and then I'll talk you through it while you watch.'

Soon, he called for their attention.

'Okay, I'll play it on the bigger monitor so you can all see . . . So, here we see David Griffiths parking in the hotel car park. It's within a couple of minutes of the time he said he'd arrived, so there's no issue there. I've let this footage roll on so you can see this second car, which arrives a couple of minutes after Griffiths.'

On screen, the second car pulled up. A woman climbed out of the passenger seat and stomped off towards Reception, leaving the male driver to gather a suitcase from the boot and hurry after her.

'Okay, now this is footage from Reception. We see Griffiths sign in and collect the key to room number two, which is on the ground floor. Watch what happens as the man and woman from the car park arrive.'

They watched the next few seconds in silence.

Southall frowned. 'Was that bit relevant?'

'What did you see?' asked Norman.

'Apparent strangers saying hello,' said Southall.

'Right,' said Norman. 'Apparent strangers. Remember that.'

He pressed play.

'Just before nine p.m., the couple come back through Reception and head for the restaurant and bar. A handful of non-residents come to the restaurant, stay for two or three hours and leave. All as normal. I checked the plan and there's no other way in and out of the bar and restaurant besides through Reception. At no point during the rest of the evening does Griffiths reappear. The only bit of interest is this.'

He played the footage of the couple staggering back across Reception towards their room.

'At first, I thought they were both plastered, but it's just him. At one point — here — he actually falls to the floor and she has to help him up. Going by her body language I'd say she wasn't exactly happy about the state he was in, but I don't think it was a new experience for her either.'

They watched as the woman struggled to help the man get up off the floor. He must have been really heavy.

'I'd have left him there,' said Morgan.

'I know what you mean,' said Norman. 'But she knows he'll sleep like a log, and you'll soon see she had good reason for wanting him out cold.'

He paused the film, which now had an image of the outside of the hotel.

'Okay. Now, each of the ground-floor rooms has a private patio separated from its neighbours by a six-foot fence.

French doors open onto this patio and there's also a gate allowing access to a path, which runs along the back of the hotel and out to the car park.

'The path along the back must be a security nightmare, which is probably why they have the CCTV there. When I started watching, I thought I was going to see Griffiths sneaking out to the car park, but something totally unexpected happens.'

He set the video running again.

'Okay, it's one a.m. Griffiths comes out of his back door. Just as I expected, he crosses the patio and unbolts the gate, but instead of heading for the car park, he goes back inside. I thought maybe he'd forgotten something, but watch what happens in the next room along.'

They stared at the screen, seeing the ghostly figure appear from the next room and make her way across her own patio, unlock the gate, walk around to Griffiths's room and go in.

'Now that's an unexpected complication,' said Southall.

'Ain't it just?' said Norman.

'Do we know who the woman is?'

'Oh, yeah,' said Norman. 'Remember the apparent strangers Griffiths spoke to in Reception just after he checked in? Well, according to the hotel register, this particular stranger is called Rhona Pritchard.'

Norman zoomed in on her face.

'The drunk she was struggling with earlier is her husband, Thomas.'

'What do we know about them?'

'I have an address from the hotel register but I haven't checked it out yet,' said Norman. 'But now you can see why she wanted to get her drunk husband back to their room and snuggled up in bed. I bet he was sleeping like the dead while all this was going on.'

'Don't you think she looks a bit old for him?' asked Winter. 'I don't want to be unkind, but Griffiths is forty-two, and she looks nearer sixty. Are you sure she's not his mother?'

'Why would his mother be sneaking into his room, half undressed, at that time of night?' asked Norman. 'And I really wish you hadn't put that idea into my head, Frosty.'

'Does she stay all night?' asked Morgan.

'She returns to her own room just after two a.m.,' said Norman. 'I can only think of one reason why she'd be creeping into another man's room at that time of night, and I don't think it was because he needed help with a crossword.'

'I'm still finding it difficult to picture them together,' said Winter.

'Maybe he likes her because she's like his mum, even though she's not, if you see what I mean,' suggested Morgan.

'Can we just forget about her being his mother and take it at face value for now, and assume they're lovers,' said Norman.

'Are you thinking what I'm thinking?' asked Southall.

'D'you mean that this was prearranged?' asked Norman. 'Yeah, I reckon it must have been. There's no way they could have met and planned something like that after they arrived.'

Southall nodded. 'Is there anything else?'

'Yeah, one more thing.' He started the video again. 'At five thirty, Griffiths opens the door onto his patio, walks to the car park, gets into his car and drives away.'

'He told us he left the hotel at six fifteen,' said Southall. 'Do you think he had a phone call about Tilly?'

'Well, if he did, he didn't seem to be too bothered about it. You can see for yourself, he's in no hurry, wherever he's going.'

'Yeah,' said Morgan. 'But what if he arranged her death? In that case he knows there's no need to rush. Tearing around like an idiot would only draw attention to himself.'

'So, what do we think?' asked Southall. 'Now we know Griffiths left the hotel forty-five minutes before he told us he did, we need to find out why. Did he go somewhere before he went to the estate, or did he get to the farmhouse much earlier than he said?'

'If he did get a phone call, it can't have been about Tilly,' said Winter. 'She wasn't found until after that.'

86

'That's what we've been told,' agreed Southall. 'But perhaps it's just what someone wants us to believe. What if she was found earlier but someone doesn't want us to know?'

'You think a sixteen-year-old would lie to the police about something like that?' asked Winter.

'Even a cute teenager can tell lies to the police if they have a strong enough motive,' said Norman. 'But it doesn't have to mean Carys lied. Maybe someone else found the body before her, called Griffiths but didn't report it to the police. This is a murder, right? So, we know for sure that at least one person knew Tilly was hanging there before Carys found her.'

'Or perhaps I'm right about Griffiths paying someone to bump Tilly off,' said Morgan. 'Maybe that person called him to say they wanted a bit more money. It could be they left some incriminating evidence where we would find it and he had to get over there and remove it before anyone else saw it.'

Southall looked at Norman. 'What do you think, Norm?'

'I'm not saying he has nothing to do with Tilly's death, and I'm not saying Catren's wrong about him employing a third person to murder her, but it seems to me he's just too calm for that scenario. I reckon he had arranged to be somewhere that morning before he went to the farmhouse.'

'You mean he had an appointment with someone,' mused Southall.

'I don't know where, and I don't know why,' said Norman.

'Paying the killer?' suggested Morgan.

'Do you want us to bring him in?' Norman asked Southall.

'Hang fire on that for now,' she said. 'If he's as smug as he appears to be, he'll think he's too clever to get caught. When we're sure he's involved we can arrest him. In the meantime, let's carry on with the background checks. Judy, please notify the necessary authorities so he can be picked up if he tries to leave the country.'

Lane nodded and reached for her phone, while the others headed back to their desks.

* * *

Twenty minutes later, Morgan called out to Norman. 'What was the name of that woman in the video?'

'Rhona Pritchard.'

'Wow! It certainly is a small world,' said Morgan. 'Guess who owns the chalet Griffiths calls home?'

'Ha! Now it's all starting to add up,' said Norman. 'What's her address?'

As Morgan read it aloud from her screen, Norman checked the address listed in the hotel register.

'One and the same,' said Norman. 'So, we were right about them knowing each other before Saturday night. I wonder how often she calls in to check on her tenant.'

'She could well be a frequent flyer,' said Morgan. 'According to this street map, her house is only a couple of minutes from the chalet.'

'D'you still think you need to run up to Aberystwyth to check out his business?' asked Norman.

'Definitely,' said Morgan. 'And, if you like, while we're up there, we could check out the chalet and call in on Rhona Pritchard.'

'Let me have a word with the boss.'

Norman went to Southall's office and stood in the doorway, leaning against the frame.

'Someone needs to go up to Aberystwyth,' he said. 'We need to see if Catren's right about this bogus business. It turns out the woman in the video owns the chalet Griffiths says he lives in. I thought we could kill two birds with one stone.'

'Okay, that makes sense,' said Southall. 'Are you going now?'

'I was thinking Catren and Frosty should go.'

Southall raised her eyebrows.

'Catren did the groundwork, finding the business and tracking down the owner of the chalet. So, it's her job,' said Norman. 'And, anyway, if we're going to recommend her for sergeant, she needs to demonstrate she can take the lead when necessary. And Frosty's spending all his time stuck in front of a screen when he'd be much better out on the street gaining experience.'

Southall nodded slowly. 'If you're happy for them to handle it.'

'They'll be fine.'

'Okay. Let's just have a quick catch-up and they can get going.'

She made her way to the front of the office.

'Right. Norm has just informed me Catren has found an address for Rhona Pritchard, and that she owns the chalet Griffiths lives in. Well done, Catren. How are you doing, Frosty?'

'My head's aching from staring at this computer screen,' Winter grumbled.

'I know what you mean,' said Southall. 'It doesn't do any of us any good. But what about Giles Rotherby's bank account? Has he even got one if he hasn't got a fixed address?'

'Oh, he's got one, all right,' said Winter. 'He's had the same account for over twenty years. He just hasn't told the bank he no longer lives on the estate.'

'Do the statements tell us if he has any kind of income?' asked Southall.

'He doesn't appear to be earning what you'd call a regular salary. He gets varying amounts transferred into his account at different times.' He held up a sheet of paper. 'I've printed out a list of payments and dates.'

'Do you know where these payments are coming from?'

'I can tell you they're always from the same account number, but I haven't got as far as tracing it yet.'

'Well, you can leave it for now. One of us can do that.'

Winter's face fell.

'Don't look so worried. I've something more important for you to do.'

Winter's smile returned.

'Catren's going up to Aberystwyth and I'd like you to ride shotgun. She needs your help, and you need the experience.

You're going to check out Griffiths's business and speak to this Rhona Pritchard as she's obviously close to Griffiths.'

Winter glanced nervously at Morgan, then Norman, who smiled and nodded reassuringly.

'Trust me,' said Norman. 'Despite appearances, Catren's bark is much worse than her bite. And she's seriously good at her job.'

'Do I tell this Rhona Pritchard we have CCTV footage of her going into Griffiths's room?' asked Morgan.

'You can guarantee she'll be calling him as soon as you leave, so I'd rather he didn't know about the CCTV if you can help it. However, you're going to be in the driving seat for this one, so it's your call. If you think it's the way to get her to talk, then it might well be worth it,' Southall said.

'Come on, then, Frosty, let's get going,' said Morgan, jingling her car keys. 'I'm driving. You can navigate.'

As soon as they'd left, Southall turned to Lane.

'How are you getting on, Judy? I sometimes worry we take you for granted and dump far too much work on you.'

Lane smiled brightly. 'It's okay. It's nice to know you trust me. I'm sure you wouldn't ask if you didn't think I could handle it.'

'Yes, but you ought to get out of the office more often.'

'I'm perfectly happy to be here. I might be in the background but the way I see it, I'm the hub of it all — everything goes through me, and that's a privilege.'

'But you must say if we're putting too much on you,' insisted Southall. 'We're supposed to be here to help develop your career, not treat you like a workhorse.'

Norman broke the awkward silence that followed. 'Which one of your many jobs have you been doing this morning?'

'I've been looking at Tilly's bank account. I was hoping I might be able to work out who the initials in the diary belong to from payments she's made. All I've managed to do so far is confirm that D and G are Donna and Glynis, but we already knew that.'

'It was always going to be a long shot,' said Norman.

'Have you found out where she gets her income from?' asked Southall.

'I can't at this stage tell you where it comes from, but I can tell you she pays in large sums of cash. It's rarely the same amount twice running, and although there seems to be a payment most weeks, it's never on the same day.'

'What sort of amounts are we talking about?' asked Southall.

'Usually between two and five thousand, but sometimes as high as ten,' Lane said. 'At first glance, her finances appear to be all over the place, but, if you look carefully, there is a pattern within the apparent randomness. For example, she goes supermarket shopping every week—'

'So do half the people in the UK,' said Norman.

'Yes,' agreed Lane. 'But most people go shopping on the same day, to the same store every time, or at least if they go to different shops, they're within the same town. Tilly never pays the same store more than once in any month, and she never shops in the same town either. She goes to supermarkets all over the area, some of which are miles from her home.'

'That's definitely not normal,' said Southall. 'Everyone I know uses the same store every week. They do it for convenience because it's near home and because they know where they can find everything.'

'Exactly,' said Lane. 'And the other thing that happens is that every time she goes shopping, the very next day she pays cash into her account. And every time she pays cash in, she also transfers half that amount back out.'

'Who to?' Southall asked.

'From what Frosty was saying a few minutes ago, I think it could be her brother.'

'Her brother!' echoed Southall.

'We can soon check that out,' said Norman. 'Let me get that list Frosty was working on.' He grabbed it and handed it to Lane, who quickly compared it with her own list.

'No doubt about it,' said Lane. 'It's a perfect match for my list. He's getting half of everything.'

Southall frowned at Norman and shook her head. 'What do you think, Norm?'

'You don't bring in that sort of cash selling Tupperware,' said Norman. 'My guess is sex, drugs, or money laundering. But with Tilly dead, the only person who can really tell us what's been going on is Giles Rotherby.'

'You're right,' said Southall. 'We need to find him asap.'

# CHAPTER 14

It was early afternoon by the time Morgan and Winter neared their destination.

'D'you know your way around Aberystwyth?' asked Morgan.

'Not really. My parents brought me here a few times when I was a kid, but that's about the extent of my knowledge. You?'

'The same,' said Morgan. 'We did a few day trips on the steam train, but that's all. So, we can use the satnav, or you can navigate. Take your pick.'

'I hate the voice on the satnav. I'll use online maps and navigate.' He found a map on his phone and studied it for a moment. 'Does it matter if we go to the business park or the house first?'

'I don't think it matters. Why?'

'We're going to go past Rhona Pritchard's house on the way in, and the business park is at the other end of town.'

'It's a no-brainer then,' said Morgan. 'We'll start with the house.'

Following Winter's instructions, she was soon driving through a relatively new housing estate.

'It's a bit posh,' said Morgan.

'Why, what were you expecting?'

'I dunno, but nothing this grand, that's for sure. What number did you say she lives at?'

'Fifty-three,' said Winter. He glanced at the nearest house number and then pointed ahead. 'It must be down towards the end of this cul-de-sac.'

'I bet there's no one at home,' said Morgan as she identified the correct house and pulled up in the drive.

'Norm said you were quite good at this, but he didn't tell me you were psychic,' said Winter.

'I don't need to be psychic. There's no car on the drive.'

'It could be in the garage.'

'Most people fill their garages with so much junk there's no room for a car.'

'Not everyone does that,' argued Winter.

'We'll see. If I'm right, you can buy dinner.'

'But I bought lunch!' protested Winter.

'Roadside burger bars don't count.'

'Who made up these rules?'

Morgan offered him a wicked grin. 'Me, of course. Try to look at it in a positive light. I mean, how many guys get the chance to buy me lunch and dinner on the same day?'

Winter slapped his forehead. 'Of course. How could I fail to realise how lucky I am?'

'There are plenty who would love to swap places with you.'

'Only if they're masochists,' said Winter. 'I didn't choose to be here, remember? The boss volunteered me.'

Morgan smiled at Winter. 'Now that's more like it. You're beginning to get the hang of this, aren't you?'

'You mean I'm getting better at answering back?'

'Exactly. It's all done in jest. It makes the boring bits of the job pass more quickly. Anyway, now you need to stop arguing and go knock on the door. I'll be right behind you.'

Winter made his way to the front door and rang the doorbell. As he waited, Morgan came up and stood next to him, and hammered on the door with her fist.

'Give them a chance,' said Winter.

'Why? I'm telling you, there's no one at home.'

After a couple of minutes, Winter had to admit defeat.

'Okay, so you were right. There's no one at home.'

'Never mind. We can come back this way later,' said Morgan. 'Let's see if we can find Griffiths's supposed workplace.'

\* \* \*

Barely ten minutes later, they arrived at a small business park.

'I've got to hand it to you, Frosty, you're quite good at navigating.'

'It's only a question of following an arrow on a screen. It's not rocket science.'

'Still, there's plenty of people who can't do it.'

Winter looked around.

'Is this the right place?' he asked.

'It looks like the one I saw online.'

'I'd have expected a wind-turbine business to be situated somewhere a bit more industrial. It looks as if this place is just for small local businesses, not big industry.'

'That's exactly what I thought when I viewed it online,' said Morgan. 'It's why I got so suspicious about it.'

'D'you know where we're going?'

'Unit Twenty-one,' said Morgan. She pointed to a collection of Portakabins a little way ahead. 'It must be one of those.'

There was a small car park in front of them, which was empty of cars. Morgan pulled up and they climbed out.

'There's not even a name outside,' said Winter.

As they neared the door, Morgan glanced in through a window.

'Hang on,' she said. She retraced her steps, took another discreet look through the window, and then scuttled back to join Winter.

'Change of plan,' she said. 'If I'm right about this, I'll buy dinner on the way back.'

'If you're right about what? What's happened?'

'You'll see,' she said, reaching for the door. 'I think we might just have hit the jackpot.'

As they pushed the door open and walked inside, a small, dark-haired woman sitting behind the only desk looked up in surprise.

'Rhona Pritchard?' asked Morgan, showing her warrant card. 'I'm DC Morgan, and this is my colleague, DC Winter. We're investigating the murder of Tilly Rotherby, and we'd like to ask you a few questions.'

Morgan found it difficult to tell which of the two was more surprised — Winter or Pritchard. For a moment, the woman said nothing, and Morgan began to think she might have been mistaken, but then the colour drained from Rhona's face and she knew she'd been right.

'It is Rhona, isn't it?' asked Morgan.

The woman nodded dumbly.

'D'you think you can answer some questions?'

'About Tilly? I didn't know her.'

'We're more interested in events before and after her death. And just so you know, my partner will be taking notes.'

The colour slowly returned to Rhona's face as she regained her composure.

'I don't see how I can help. I didn't go anywhere near her at the weekend.'

'But you stayed at the Seaview Hotel on Saturday night,' said Morgan. 'That's not far away, is it?'

'My husband and I stayed there overnight because we were supposed to be at Tilly's wedding reception. We went to the house but the police wouldn't let anyone through the gates. I really don't see what else I can say about it.'

'You say you didn't know Tilly, yet she invited you to her wedding reception. Did she invite many random strangers?'

'I was invited by her husband, David Griffiths.'

'You mean the guy who lives in your holiday chalet?'

'It's a temporary arrangement. I'm just helping a friend in need.'

'Ah, so David's a friend. But this place is listed as his business address, isn't it?'

'Yes, it is. Is that a problem?'

'The jury's still out on that one,' said Morgan. 'I am curious to know where you fit in, though.'

'I'm David's secretary, and I have a small shareholding in the business, like everyone who works for him.'

'Are there any investors from outside the company?'

'Yes, of course. Why?'

'I'm just curious, that's all. Can you tell me who they are?'

'I don't have a list to hand. David deals with all that stuff.'

'Now, there's a surprise.' Morgan looked around the sparsely furnished office. 'Speaking of everyone who works for the business, where are they all, and how do you fit them all in? It's crowded in here now, with just the three of us.'

'This is a forward-thinking business. Everyone works remotely.'

Morgan nodded. 'Right. Of course. That's very forward thinking.' She turned to Winter. 'Don't you think that's forward thinking?'

'It certainly is,' he agreed, looking up from his notebook. 'Convenient, too.'

Morgan turned back to Rhona. 'This is a bit small for a head office, isn't it? I mean, wind turbines are massive things. Where is your manufacturing plant, or your warehouse?'

'We don't make the turbines here. David has shares in a plant up in Scotland. We order from there and have them delivered to wherever they are needed and then one of our installation teams installs them. David's very cash conscious and likes to save money where he can. This is a much more cost-effective way of operating. Manufacturing and warehousing would be an enormous drain on profits.'

'Oh, right, I see. So, you have installation teams that travel around the world?'

'Exactly.'

Morgan turned to Winter again. 'Efficient, and cost effective,' she said. 'And what was that other thing you said?'

'Convenient.'

'Yes, that's it,' said Morgan, turning back to Rhona. 'It's all very convenient, don't you think?'

Rhona was starting to look a little red in the face. 'I'm not sure I understand what you mean.'

'Who designed your website?' asked Morgan.

'David hired a web designer.'

'I hope the designer didn't charge too much.'

'I wouldn't know. You'd need to speak to our accounts department about that.'

'Have you seen the site?'

'Of course I have. Why do you ask?'

'Because I was looking at it yesterday, and I also looked at other sites in the same field. Did you know your site is the only one that seems to have lifted pages from your competitors?'

Rhona was beginning to fidget. 'As I said, David organised the website. I'm sure he'll get it put right if what you say is true.'

'If you're David's secretary, and a shareholder, you must know all about the business.'

'I don't need to know the nuts and bolts.'

'No, but you must know if it's making a profit.'

'Of course we're making a profit.'

'Are you? I couldn't find any financial records submitted at Companies House.'

'That's not my department.'

'I guess that's the accounts department again, right? So, where is it? And how do I contact the chief accountant?'

'I'm not sure I can give you that information,' said Rhona. 'There are privacy rules we have to follow.'

'There's also a rule that a company's shareholders should be listed at Companies House.'

'What's that supposed to mean?'

'You said you've invested money in this company and that every member of staff is a shareholder, and you also have outside investors.'

'That's right.'

'And yet there are no shareholders listed at Companies House.'

'I'm sure that's just an oversight. David will put it right when I tell him.'

'I hope you're making a list of all these things he has to put right,' said Morgan. 'What's the company turnover like?'

'I'm sorry?'

'Turnover. You know, money coming in,' said Morgan.

'I don't see what that has to do with Tilly Rotherby's death.'

'Have you ever seen what's in the company bank account?' asked Morgan.

'I told you, that's not my depa—'

'Oh, yeah,' said Morgan. 'That's the accounts department, right? What would you say if I told you there's less than a thousand pounds in the account, and that not a single penny has been deposited in the last four months?'

'I'd say you were probably looking at the wrong bank account.'

'Is that right?' asked Morgan. 'What about this plant in Scotland that makes the turbines? Can you tell me where that is?'

By now, Rhona looked utterly miserable. 'I don't know, I believe it's in Aberdeen, but I've never been there.'

'Does it have a name?'

'I'm not sure off the top of my head. Campbell and Stewart, I think.'

'Telephone number?'

'David deals with all the technical stuff.'

'So, you don't know the telephone number of the company that makes your turbines?'

'I don't have it to hand, but I expect I can find it.'

'You're sure this manufacturing plant exists, are you?' asked Morgan.

'Of course it does,' insisted Rhona. 'David spends two or three days a week up there.'

'Does he take you with him when he goes?'

'Well, no. He goes up to work. What would I do there?'

'Tell me, Rhona, how much money have you invested in this company?' Morgan said.

'I don't think that's any of your business.'

'You really don't see what's going on here, do you?'

'I'm not sure what you're getting at.'

'No?' Morgan smiled grimly. 'Well, it's lucky for you we've come along, then. The thing is, it's our job to recognise a scam when we see it, and you appear to be involved in one.'

'You're mistaken. This isn't a scam, it's a very efficiently run business. Okay, David may have been a bit lax here and there, but he's a very busy man.'

'I guess he must be away a lot, overseeing all these turbine installations,' Morgan said.

'He likes to be there when work starts, but he has managers to run the projects.'

'He told us he's away a lot of the time.'

Rhona was regaining some of her composure. 'I already told you he's up and down to Scotland, and sometimes we travel the world finding new projects and investors.'

'We?' said Morgan.

'Well, yes. I'm his secretary. I go with him.'

'So, if he's doing what we think, and he's conning money from people, that makes you an accessory,' Morgan said.

'Of course he's not conning people. I keep telling you, it's all above board.'

'I suppose you know this because you attend when David's meeting his investors?' asked Winter.

'Oh, no. There wouldn't be any point. I've never been one for technical matters.'

'Are you saying you have no idea what happens at these meetings?' Winter said.

Rhona said nothing to this for a few moments. 'I . . . I don't need to know.'

'But you're a shareholder. Surely you have a right to know,' Morgan said.

'I trust David. He knows what he's doing.'

'Yeah,' said Morgan. 'I think DC Winter and I both agree that he knows what he's doing, but I'm not sure you're on the same page.'

Morgan wasn't sure if Rhona's silence meant she'd missed the inference, or if she was choosing to ignore it.

'Who covers your job while you're away, Rhona?' she said.

'We close the office.'

'A busy company like this, running large-scale installation projects, and you close the office?' Morgan said incredulously.

'David handles all the enquiries — he diverts them to his mobile phone.'

'So, what exactly do you do all day?' Morgan said.

'Er, well, I take care of the travel arrangements — book the hotel rooms, that sort of thing.'

'So, really, what you're saying is you're more travel agent than company secretary,' said Morgan.

'And I suppose it's because David is so cost-aware that you book a double room when you travel together?' suggested Winter.

He was taking a punt but the shot hit its mark. Rhona's hand shot up to her mouth and for a second time, the colour drained from her face. For a moment she seemed to have trouble breathing. She took an inhaler from her drawer, put it to her lips and slowly recovered.

'So, what came first?' asked Morgan. 'The job, or the affair?'

'There is no affair.'

'Oh, come on, Rhona. Do we look stupid? You travel with the guy and you share a double room. He lives in your holiday chalet, which is two minutes from your house. How many times a week do you call in at the chalet to check on him?'

'He's my tenant. I'm obliged to make sure he has everything he needs.'

'I'd call what you do going above and beyond any normal obligation,' suggested Morgan.

101

'I don't know what you think you're implying, but you've got this all wrong,' said Rhona.

'Okay, so, if we've got it all wrong, you'll be able to explain why you were caught on CCTV making your way to his bedroom on Saturday night, wearing nothing but a negligee and a smile.'

Rhona's face turned a vivid shade of red, and she seemed to sag in her seat. 'Oh. You know about that. Please don't tell my husband.'

'Let's forget the rip-off business you're involved in for a moment and consider your other problem,' said Morgan.

'Other problem? What other problem?'

'We're investigating the murder of Tilly Rotherby, who, in case you need reminding, was married to David Griffiths.'

Rhona's eyes suddenly blazed. 'She wasn't his wife,' she snapped. 'They weren't married, and they weren't going to be, either. He was going to call the wedding off.'

'According to what he told my boss, they married secretly two weeks ago in a registry office.'

'Rubbish!' she snapped. 'He would have told me.'

'If he had told you, it wouldn't have been a secret, would it?'

Rhona said nothing for a moment. 'David and I have no secrets.'

'It's not just about the sex, then?'

'Trying to make our relationship sound sordid won't work, you know.'

'We don't have to make it sound sordid, Rhona, it is. Or are you suggesting there's something romantic about sneaking away from your sleeping husband in the middle of the night so you can spend an hour in your lover's bed?' Morgan said.

'It's not like that.'

'That's how it looks on CCTV.'

'We have a meaningful relationship,' Rhona said primly.

'We can talk about how meaningful your relationship is later. But, right now, you have a bigger problem.'

'I don't know what you mean.'

'Then let me explain. A young woman was found dead on Sunday morning, and now we find you've been having an affair with her husband, whose bed you shared on the night she died.'

'You can't blame me. I had nothing to do with her death. I never went anywhere near her.'

'Maybe not, but you can see how it looks, right? I mean, we've established that you and David Griffiths are having an affair. Perhaps Tilly found out. You already told us you don't want us to tell your husband about it, so I'm sure you wouldn't have wanted Tilly to tell him, either.'

'You can't seriously think I had anything to do with her death,' Rhona said.

'Why not?'

'Tilly didn't know about the affair.'

'This would be the same affair that a few minutes ago you said wasn't one at all, have I got that right?' asked Morgan.

'You're confusing me now,' said Rhona.

'Okay, perhaps Tilly didn't know about the affair, but she could have figured out the business scam. Maybe she was threatening to spill the beans. Neither you nor David Griffiths would want that to come out, would you? Maybe you were both involved in her death.'

'This is preposterous!'

'Has it occurred to you that men like David Griffiths prey on unhappy women with money?'

Winter had been happy to let Morgan do most of the talking so far, but now he couldn't help himself. 'I hate to say this, Mrs Pritchard, but it's no more preposterous than a man who could pass for thirty-five having an affair with a woman who looks old enough to be his mother.'

Morgan winced.

'How dare you!' Rhona shrieked.

'I have to agree my colleague wasn't being very tactful,' said Morgan, 'but even you must see he has a point.'

Rhona looked daggers at Winter.

'Mind you, I can imagine how good it must have made you feel when this good-looking younger guy started to take an interest in you,' said Morgan.

'You wouldn't understand,' muttered Rhona.

'Sure I would,' said Morgan. 'We see this sort of predatory behaviour all the time — good-looking guys like David Griffiths on the lookout for unhappy older women.'

'I'm not unhappy.'

'Perhaps you aren't now, but I bet you were when he first spotted you. Guys like him can spot an unhappy marriage from miles away.'

'My marriage is not unhappy.'

'Your husband looked totally wrecked on the CCTV. I imagine that if he makes a habit of getting drunk and leaving you to clean up behind him, it can't exactly make for wedded bliss. Maybe you've even thought about leaving him, though you'd have to leave that lovely house, wouldn't you? And the rest. He might be reluctant to share much of it with you in a divorce settlement, especially since you are the guilty party. And, of course, as you get older, the idea of starting over gets scarier . . .'

'So what if my husband does like a drink. He's retired; he's earned the right.'

'And he's loaded, right?' Morgan said. 'That house didn't fall from the sky, did it? Even here in Wales, a place like that is going to be worth a fortune.'

Rhona sniffed. 'Yes, all right, we're comfortable and I admit we don't always see eye to eye, but I've never considered leaving my husband.'

'But then along comes this young guy who takes an interest,' continued Morgan. 'He sweeps you off your feet, makes you feel wanted and suddenly there's a light in your darkness. Better still, he offers you a job, working with him, and even takes you away with him sometimes. Now, for the first time in years, you have something to look forward to every day.'

'It's a very good story, but it's got nothing to do with me,' said Rhona.

'How did you meet Griffiths?' asked Morgan.

'He used to belong to the local golf club. My husband was the club captain at the time, still is. He used to hold these dinners at the club and as the dutiful wife, I had to attend and pretend I was enjoying myself. We met at one of the dinners. He was very attentive, unlike my husband, who was too busy getting drunk to even notice.'

'And you really don't think he saw you as an unhappy wife with money? He would have sized you up the moment he set eyes on you.'

'It wasn't like that.'

'Oh, Rhona, open your eyes. He's only sticking around because you keep giving him money.'

'I haven't given him that much. I just pay a few of the bills. I'll get it back when the company starts to make a profit.'

'What sort of bills?' Morgan asked.

'As a shareholder I agreed to pay the running costs for this place. I let him live in my chalet for free and I pay the travel costs.'

'You pay for him to go up and down to Scotland, and fly all over the world?' Morgan said.

'He takes me with him some of the time.'

'How much d'you think you've given him so far?'

'I don't know. I haven't added it up,' Rhona said.

'Okay, take a guess. Roughly how much?'

'I don't know. Fifty thousand, maybe.'

'Fifty grand! Jesus, Rhona, have you really got that sort of money to throw around?'

'Technically, it's not my money, it's my husband's, but we've always said that whatever we have belongs to both of us.'

'And he doesn't mind that you've lost all this money?'

'He hasn't noticed, so I haven't—'

'He hasn't noticed? How much money does he have?'

'I don't know. Three or four million.'

'You said you were a shareholder in the company. Did you invest money to buy the shares?'

'Yes, of course.'

'And it's all legal and above board? You have paperwork to back up this shareholding?'

'Not yet. There's a delay at the legal department.'

'Oh, yeah, I bet there is,' muttered Winter.

'And is that investment part of the fifty thousand?' asked Morgan.

'Oh, no. That's separate.'

'And how much did you invest?'

'Seventy-five thousand.'

Winter gasped.

'Hang on. Let me get this straight,' said Morgan. 'You're saying that, in total, David Griffiths has taken a hundred and twenty-five grand from you, and you've had nothing back.'

'He hasn't taken it from me. I gave it to him. Anyway, I'll get it back when things settle down and the company's making a good profit.'

'And you really believe this is going to happen?' Morgan said.

'I don't know why you keep suggesting the business is a scam,' said Rhona.

'Well, let me see,' said Morgan. 'Where shall we start? How about your head office is a Portakabin, there's no money in the business bank account and you've never set eyes on anyone else who works for the company. Then there's this imaginary manufacturing plant up in Scotland, which you know nothing about. If I had to guess, I'd say it doesn't even exist.'

'That's rubbish,' hissed Rhona. 'Of course it exists. I'll find the damned phone number for you and prove it.'

She opened the drawer of her desk and rummaged around, finally producing a business card. She slapped it down on the desk.

'Here,' she said. 'Here's your proof. The trouble with you people is you just don't want to listen.'

Winter studied the card and slipped it into his pocket.

'Trust me, Rhona,' Morgan said. 'We really do want to believe you haven't been taken for a ride, but you're not convincing either of us.'

'What do you mean, taken for a ride?'

'You've invested a hundred and twenty-five grand in a company you seem to know nothing about, and you've never had a penny back. Shall I go on?'

Rhona flipped open her laptop and began tapping at the keyboard. 'I've explained how we operate, but as you won't listen to me, let me show you something that will prove we're legitimate.'

She spun the laptop so they could see the screen. Morgan and Winter watched a two-minute promotional video that showed a huge wind farm far out to sea, ending with a spinning logo that came to a stop, revealing the name OffTurbUK.

'There,' said Rhona when the video had finished. 'That's Doordewind. It's a wind farm we built off the coast of Holland.'

'Could we have a copy of that video?' asked Winter.

'What for?'

He looked at Rhona. 'Is there some reason we can't have one?'

'Er, no, I suppose you can have one of our spare copies.'

Reluctantly, Rhona opened another drawer, found a memory stick and handed it to him.

Winter took the memory stick and dropped it into his pocket alongside the card.

'And you've been there and seen this Doordewind, have you?' asked Morgan.

'It was built before I started working here.'

'How long have you worked here?'

'Almost a year. David promised me a job as part of the deal when I invested.'

'And you invested when?'

'Three months before that.'

'And you are yet to see any sort of return on your investment?'

'That's right. You seem to be far more worried about it than me.'

'I just can't understand why you refuse to accept that this whole operation is nothing but smoke and mirrors.'

Rhona laughed. 'Because it isn't. I've just shown you the video. If that's not enough proof, I don't know what is. And at the end of the day, it's my money and I can spend it however I want to.'

'Let's hope your husband sees it that way,' Morgan said.

'Oh, I'm not going to tell him.'

'Well, we will,' said Morgan.

'But you can't!'

'Rhona, we're police officers. If a crime is reported, it's our job to act upon it. And, if you and your husband have been swindled out of a hundred and twenty-five grand, that's a crime, and he has a right to know.'

'There we are, then,' Rhona said. 'We haven't been swindled, so he doesn't need to know.'

'Are you serious? You just told us you've given Griffiths all that money and you've not had a penny back.'

'But I haven't reported a crime,' said Rhona. 'And I'm not going to. I don't understand why, but you're trying to put words into my mouth. You may not have faith in David Griffiths, but I have.'

Morgan sighed. 'It's your choice, Rhona. I just hope you know what you're doing.'

'As you said, it's my choice.'

'We still need you to make a statement about what you were doing on Saturday night.'

'Why?'

'Because a woman is dead, and we need to account for your whereabouts, and those of David Griffiths, between the hours of eight p.m. on Saturday, and eight a.m. on Sunday,' said Morgan.

'But you know David was with me, so how could he have had anything to do with Tilly's death?' said Rhona.

'I'm afraid everyone is a suspect until we prove otherwise, even Saint David Griffiths. Your statement could help prove his innocence. It would be better for you if you came down to Llangwelli police station voluntarily.'

'But I have work to do. When am I supposed to find the time to come to Llangwelli?' Rhona said.

'From what you were saying earlier, Rhona, you don't do any actual work. Besides, if you can close the office to go off on a jolly, what's stopping you closing it for something important like helping with a murder enquiry? Tomorrow morning would be good.'

'I can't possibly do tomorrow. I'll come on Thursday.'

'Just make sure you do,' said Morgan.

\* \* \*

'We could have taken her statement there and then,' said Winter when they were back in their car.

'Yeah, we could,' said Morgan, starting the engine. 'But I want Norm, or the boss, to have a go at her.'

'And I thought you weren't going to tell her about the CCTV,' Winter said.

Morgan smiled. 'I wasn't going to tell her about the secret wedding either, but, wow, didn't she bite when I did?'

'True,' agreed Winter. 'But I couldn't decide if she genuinely didn't know about it, or if she was acting like she didn't.'

'Me neither, which is another reason why I think we need a second opinion. Did you think the whole thing was an act?'

'I doubt it,' said Winter. 'Acting is a skill. I'm afraid Rhona might just be one of the dumbest people I've ever met.'

Morgan pulled a face. 'Don't be too hard on her. A good conman can make an unhappy person believe anything. And, going back to the CCTV, the boss said it was my decision to make, so I made it. Are you saying I was wrong?'

'What if she calls Griffiths now, and they make sure their stories agree?' Winter said.

'The way I see it, that's not a problem,' said Morgan as she made her way out onto the road and headed for home. 'We already have the CCTV footage of what happened in the hotel that night, so they can't deny it. What I'm hoping is that she's going to tell him what we've told her. If I'm right, that will be enough for him to show her his true colours.'

'You think he'll ditch her? But if he does that—'

'Then she'll see what a fool she's been and, after having had a night to think about how he's conned her out of all that money, she might be a little more talkative. That's why I wanted to get her to come to Llangwelli. I think she might crack when faced with Norman and the boss.'

'I hope you're right,' said Winter. 'She seemed well smitten to me. It was like she's under some sort of spell.'

'That's how these guys work,' said Morgan.

'But why don't the women see them for what they are?'

'Because the guys know which ones to pick.'

'It's like a gigolo being paid to satisfy some sad, middle-aged woman,' Winter said.

'I don't think any of them would thank you for saying it, but that's not far from the truth,' said Morgan. 'I mean, look at Rhona. If her husband's captain of a golf club, guess where he spends all his time?'

'On the golf course.'

'Or in the bar at the golf club,' added Morgan.

'So, if she's not interested in golf, they don't see much of each other.'

'Exactly. And I bet when he does come home, he's already had a skinful. On top of that, she has to attend these golf dinners and play hostess. Can you even begin to imagine how dull and boring her life must be? I almost feel sorry for her,' Morgan said.

'Almost?'

'If a marriage is really that bad, I don't see having an affair is the answer,' said Morgan. 'It's a temporary solution at best. She's going to be just as unhappy when she gets out of her lover's bed and goes home. And then there's all the lies and deceit you have to live with. That can't do you any good, can it? I think, if it's that bad, and there are no kids involved, you should just pack your bags and leave.'

'Yeah but look what she'd lose,' Winter said.

'You mean the house and the money? What good is any of that if your life is so miserable? I'd rather start again with nothing.'

'That's easy for you to say, but you're not married. You're also a young woman. Rhona's almost sixty,' Winter said.

'I realise it's scary and it takes guts, but at least you've got a chance at finding happiness.'

'But she thinks she has found happiness,' said Winter.

'Yeah, that's the problem. What she's really found is an illusion that Griffiths has sold her.'

'All I can say is she must be desperate,' Winter said.

'But that's the whole point,' said Morgan. 'He's only been able to sell that dream to her because he's spotted how unhappy she is and how desperate to find an escape. I mean, she's no spring chicken, right?'

'And here's this much younger, nice-looking guy, giving her all his attention,' said Winter. 'Yeah, I suppose I can see what you're saying.'

'You can see how it works now, can't you? Looking at it from the outside, it's obviously a con, but she's so blinded by all the attention that she can't see it. You put it so bluntly you made me cringe, but even then she wouldn't consider the idea that it might be the case.'

'Yeah, I feel bad about that. I was well out of order,' conceded Winter. 'I just couldn't believe she refused to hear what you were saying.'

'Well, now you understand why she wouldn't listen,' said Morgan. 'She's a classic example of a woman in denial.'

'You can say that again!'

'And I wouldn't lose any sleep over what you said. It was a bit of a blunt instrument to hit her with, but I'm sure she won't make a big deal out of it, especially when she realises you were right.'

'Do you think she will?' he said.

'We'll just have to wait and see.'

'What did you think of the video she showed us?' asked Winter.

'I think it's all part of an elaborate con,' said Morgan. 'Wind farms are all the rage, aren't they? Everyone wants to do their bit for the environment, so why not encourage them to invest in a company that builds them?'

Winter fished the memory stick from his pocket. 'That's just what I thought. I mean, did you see the size of it? If it's for real, it must stretch halfway to England.'

'And if Rhona has worked there for a year, and it was built before she started working there, it doesn't add up,' said Morgan. 'I don't know about these things, but I would think it must take years to build something like that, and then you've got the tendering process and all the legal stuff beforehand. Surely it would take the best part of ten years from start to finish, and the company was only formed three years ago.'

'Do you really think Rhona murdered Tilly?' asked Winter.

'We can't ignore the possibility. She has more than one motive. If Tilly found out about the affair, Rhona could have thought she had to be silenced. Or, if Tilly found out about the business being a scam, maybe Griffiths thought he needed to silence her. Anyway, forget all that for now and concentrate on what you want to eat on the way home. I'm buying, remember? Just don't think it's going to happen every time.'

They were heading south. They passed through the town and as they headed out, the houses began to give way to fields and trees. Up ahead, an ornate signpost came into view.

'That must be the golf club,' said Winter.

'Are you thinking what I'm thinking?' asked Morgan.

'Now we know Rhona was having an affair with Griffiths we're going to need her husband to confirm her whereabouts. She was only with Griffiths for an hour. And as we're here . . .'

'That's exactly what I was thinking,' said Morgan, indicating to turn right.

She drove into the car park and crawled around looking for a free space.

'I think we're in luck,' she said, pointing to a Mercedes parked close to the entrance. 'Look, that's reserved for the Club Captain.'

'Let's hope he's still sober enough to talk to us,' said Winter.

* * *

Confident they would find Thomas Pritchard in the bar, Morgan and Winter asked the barman, who pointed out a lean, fit-looking man in his sixties. He was sitting at a table on his own, studying a laptop, sipping from a glass that appeared to contain orange juice.

'Mr Pritchard? My name's DC Morgan and this is my colleague, DC Winter.'

Thomas Pritchard looked up in surprise, but immediately switched on a warm smile.

'Have I done something wrong?' he asked.

'We're investigating the death of Tilly Rotherby.'

'Wasn't she the woman who was going to marry David Griffiths?' he said.

'That's right.'

'I didn't know her, but, still, it was a terrible business, and what a time for it to happen.'

'Would it be possible to ask you a few questions?' Morgan said.

'Yes, of course, if you think I can help.' He indicated the chairs around the table. 'Please, sit down. Can I get you a drink?'

'That's very kind of you,' Morgan said. 'No alcohol while we're on duty but a cup of coffee would be nice.'

Thomas ordered two coffees and settled back in his chair. 'Now then. How can I help?'

'I understand you were invited to the reception.'

'It was my wife who was invited really. As I said, I didn't know Tilly at all, and I barely know David Griffiths. I just sort of tagged along, but in the end the police turned us away at the gate.'

'Can you confirm where you were the night before?'

'Seaview Hotel. We got there sometime between eight and eight thirty. My wife can confirm that.'

'Yes, we've already spoken to your wife,' said Morgan.

'There you are then, she's already told you.'

'And you stayed the night at the hotel?'

'We had a meal in the restaurant, a couple of drinks in the bar and went to bed when it closed. I'm sure the staff will remember me — I had a bit too much to drink.'

'Yes,' said Morgan. 'We've seen the CCTV footage.'

Thomas smiled. 'Just as well I was honest about it, then.'

'And neither you nor your wife left your room again that night?'

'Well, I certainly didn't. I was out cold.'

'What about your wife?'

'I'm afraid you'll have to ask her. Oh, hang on a minute, you already have. What did she say? Or, did you catch her on CCTV, too? I know there's a camera at the back of the rooms.'

'I'm not sure what you mean,' said Morgan, taken by surprise.

'Oh, come now, Ms Morgan, there's no need to be coy. I know all about my wife and David Griffiths.'

'You do?'

'He's not the first, you know. Rhona likes to think that by having affairs with younger men she's striking a major blow for women's independence. But I happen to think that any woman who allows herself to be used in that way is achieving quite the opposite.'

'Exactly how much do you know about David Griffiths, Mr Pritchard?'

'You mean, do I know he's bleeding Rhona's bank account dry? Yes, of course I do.'

'She told us it's your money, but it's in a joint account, and you have no idea she's spending it.'

'I suppose technically it is my money as I earned it, but it's hers to spend. I put half a million in the account for her. When it's gone, so is she.'

114

For a moment Morgan thought she must have misheard. Was that a threat to Rhona's life?

'I'm sorry? What exactly do you mean?'

'It means I've put up with her abuse for too many years. Now I've had enough. I'm about to divorce her.'

'Does she know?'

'I've told her, but I doubt she's taken it on board. The thing you have to understand is that Rhona thinks she has some sort of power over me.'

'You said she abuses you. What did you mean exactly?'

Thomas smiled. 'It's hard to believe, isn't it? Abuse doesn't have to take the form of physical or even verbal violence, Officer. It can take another form which is much more insidious. But I'm sure you don't want to hear about my problems.'

'No, please do go on,' said Morgan.

Thomas took a sip of his orange juice, seeming to consider his words.

'There was a time when I adored Rhona. I would have done anything for her back then. I thought she loved me too, but in retrospect I don't think she ever did. I'm not sure she's capable of really loving anyone.

'As the saying goes, love is blind, and I certainly had stars in my eyes when it began. First, to soften me up, she indulged in a string of small indiscretions. They were the sort of things that most normal people would forgive, and of course, I did just that. I desperately wanted to trust her. But what I didn't realise was that every time I forgave her, I was slowly being programmed to accept her bad behaviour.' Pritchard had a faraway look in his eyes. 'I needed Rhona to reassure me that we were okay and that she loved me, but instead she became more and more emotionally distant.' Pritchard stared almost accusingly at Winter. 'D'you know what happens to someone in that position?'

Winter gaped, caught off-guard.

'When your wants and needs are increasingly ignored like that, you begin to feel unloved and unimportant, and in time your self-esteem slowly withers away. It's a form of progressive manipulation that eats away at an individual until they're just an empty shell of the person they once were. Most people don't even realise what's happening. But there are a few lucky ones who wake up one day and wonder how they ever allowed themselves to get into that position.'

'And the lucky ones get to plot their revenge, right?' asked Morgan.

'It's just a divorce, Detective. I'm not planning to murder her. I've told her what's going to happen when that money's gone. It's up to her whether she wants to believe I'm bluffing.'

'Why don't you just divorce her anyway? Why wait?' Morgan asked.

'Because I want to give her a final chance to sort herself out before the divorce. She could use that money to buy herself a nice house, but it appears she wants to fritter it away on that conman, David Griffiths. Did she tell you how much she's wasted on him?'

'She said about a hundred and twenty-five thous—'

'It's closer to two hundred thousand,' said Thomas. 'I may not use the account, but I have access to it, so I know what she's spending.'

Ignoring Winter's dismayed mutter, Morgan said, 'What can you tell us about Griffiths?'

'I can tell you he's a fraud, but beyond that I neither know nor care.'

'Your wife works for him. Doesn't it bother you that she's complicit in his fraud?'

'Of course it does. I must have told her at least a dozen times that she should walk away from him. The problem is, she chooses not to listen to me on principle.'

A club steward was trying to attract Thomas's attention, gesturing at a man standing at the bar.

'Is there anything else?' asked Thomas. 'I have a visitor waiting.'

'No, I think we're done for now,' said Morgan. 'Thank you for taking the time to speak with us.'

'Not at all,' said Thomas. 'If there's anything else I can help you with, just let me know. You can usually find me here.'

# CHAPTER 15

'How did you get on in Aberystwyth?' Southall asked Morgan the next morning.

'We confirmed our suspicions about David Griffiths and his business. We've still got a couple of things to check out, but I'm convinced he's a conman and his business is totally bogus.'

'What about this Rhona Pritchard woman who owns the chalet?' asked Norman.

'She's a bit more than just a landlady. It turns out she's also his secretary, and a shareholder in his business. She pays the running costs of the Portakabin, his rent for the chalet and even pays for him to travel the world on supposed business trips. She says she's probably put a hundred and twenty-five grand into his business.'

'You mean he's conned her?'

'I tried to tell her it's a scam, but she wouldn't believe me. As far as she's concerned, the sun shines out of his backside. She's convinced she'll get her money back.'

'Has she really got that sort of money to throw away?' asked Norman.

'Technically it's not her money. It's her husband's.'

'Jeez. Have you spoken to him?' Norman said.

'We took a punt on the way back and found him at the golf club.'

'What does he think?'

'Well, this is where it gets interesting. According to her, he hasn't noticed that the money has gone, but when we spoke to him, he said he knows exactly how much she's taken, and it's nearer two hundred grand.'

'He knows about it?' Norman said.

'Oh, yeah. Rhona thinks he's only interested in playing golf and getting smashed, but in fact he's not so dumb as she thinks. He's put half a million into an account she thinks only she uses, and when that's gone he'll divorce her.'

'How much money does the guy have?' Norman said.

'According to Rhona, he's got three or four million, but I get the impression he's got a lot more than that. He also knows about her affair with Griffiths.'

'And he's just letting her fritter all his money away?' asked Norman. 'Why, what's he up to?'

'He told us he's giving her a chance to reform, though he knows she won't.'

'My guess is he wasn't as drunk as he appeared to be on the CCTV footage. I reckon it was an act for Rhona's benefit. He knew she'd left the room to sleep with Griffiths, and he knew we would probably see it on the hotel's CCTV.'

'So, what are we saying? That she's a wealthy, unhappily married woman?' said Southall. 'If so, she's the perfect victim for a creep like Griffiths.'

'I tried to explain it to her, but she didn't want to hear,' said Morgan. 'She even denied they were having sex until I asked her to explain how she came to be on camera at the Seaview Hotel. She changed her tune about the affair after that, but she's still adamant that Griffiths is genuine and has done nothing wrong.'

Southall turned to Winter. 'What did you think, Frosty?'

'Catren's right. Rhona is totally deluded. It's as if Griffiths has put a spell on her. I actually felt a bit sorry for her.'

'We're not really much further forward then,' said Norman.

'I don't think she's a murderer if that's what you mean,' said Morgan. 'She got a bit flustered at times but, overall, she was pretty calm. There was only one thing that seemed to get her all fired up, and that was when I told her Griffiths had married Tilly in secret two weeks ago. She got mad about that. She insisted it didn't happen.'

'She would say that if he's convinced her he's for real,' said Southall. 'She's in denial.'

'People have committed murder for a lot less,' added Norman.

'Yeah, I thought that too,' said Morgan. 'But the more I think about how she reacted, the more I think she really didn't know until I told her.'

Southall turned to Winter. 'What about you, Frosty? Do you agree with Catren?'

'I think I do. Compared with the rest of the interview, she reacted to the marriage as if we'd just jabbed her with a cattle prod.'

'I'm sure she probably knows a lot more than she told us,' said Morgan. 'So, I said she'd have to come in and make a statement. I'm hoping she called Griffiths last night and told him what we said about the business being a scam, and that he then told her where she really stood.'

'And you think that by the time she gets here, she'll have had time to consider. Having realised he's conned her out of all that money, she'll be willing to talk?' asked Norman.

'That's what I'm hoping,' said Morgan. 'And I thought if you and the boss question her, she'll be more forthcoming.'

'Let's just hope they don't both panic and do a runner,' said Norman.

'We'll soon find out,' said Southall. 'I've just told Griffiths Forensics have finished with the farmhouse and he can have it back after midday.'

'Do you want me to go and pick him up?' asked Norman.

'Let's take a chance and wait,' said Southall. 'I'm sure Rhona will have called him last night, so if he was going to run, he would have gone by now. When I spoke to him earlier, I got the impression he couldn't wait to get back in.'

'It's a gamble but as you say, he would have gone by now,' agreed Norman, 'unless there's something he needs to collect from the farmhouse.'

'That's exactly what I'm thinking,' said Southall.

'Perhaps we should have a team watching the house from the road, so we know when he arrives. There's only one way in or out so if he tries to leave, we can grab him.'

'Now you're thinking, Norm,' said Southall.

'Me and Frosty can watch the house,' suggested Morgan. 'We can be outside the main gate by midday and let you know when he arrives and whether or not he leaves.'

'That sounds like a plan,' said Southall. 'In the meantime, Frosty, I want you to find Giles Rotherby's solicitor. And someone needs to check with the registry office. Let's find out if Griffiths and Tilly really did get married in secret.'

\* \* \*

'This wind-turbine factory up in Aberdeen looks to be yet more bullshit,' said Morgan, ten minutes later.

'You mean it doesn't exist?' asked Norman.

'I take the view that if a company doesn't have a website or an online presence of some sort, it's probably a scam.'

'There are some exceptions to that,' said Norman.

'Yeah, maybe, but wind turbines?'

Norman shrugged. 'I can't argue with that. But don't you have a phone number and an address? You should still check those out.'

'I have. The phone number is real enough, although all you get is an answering machine. The address is real, too, but according to the Aberdeen police it's a residential house on a rather posh estate.'

'Any idea who lives there?'

'Apparently, it's owned by a woman called Patty McDonald, a widow with a twelve-year-old daughter.'

'If this whole thing is a scam, maybe Griffiths set up the phone number and then just picked a random address in Aberdeen,' suggested Southall. 'It's careless, because anyone could check it out and see it's not right.'

'Well, even the best cons make mistakes now and then,' said Norman. 'And I don't have Griffiths down as a master of the art.'

'You're right there,' said Morgan. 'I'm surprised none of his so-called investors have seen through him yet.'

There was a brief silence while they considered David Griffiths and his scam.

'Of course, it's possible that's because there's only one investor, and she's so blinkered she never thinks to check up on him,' said Norman.

'Don't you think it's a bit of an elaborate set-up just to con Rhona?' asked Southall.

'Is it really so elaborate?' said Norman. 'I mean, anyone can set up a company and register it at Companies House for less than fifty quid.'

'But aren't there checks?' asked Morgan.

Norman shook his head. 'You'd think so, wouldn't you? But Companies House is just a register. It has no powers to investigate whether a company is real or not. It's always been open to abuse.'

Morgan was thinking about Norman's suggestion. 'And anyone reasonably competent can clone pages from the internet to create a website. A promotional video could easily be copied and given a new soundtrack, and answering services are easy enough to set up. And we all know you can buy mobile phones just about anywhere.'

'That's exactly what I mean,' said Norman. 'It might be fiddly, but it's not that complicated.'

'It would explain why the office is just a cheap old Portakabin, and why Griffiths has told Rhona business calls are diverted to his mobile number,' said Southall.

'So, where does Tilly come into it?' asked Morgan. 'Why did he marry her?'

'Because he thought the estate would provide a more regular source of funds,' suggested Norman.

'But it won't. There are no stud horses and the cottages have been sold,' argued Morgan.

'But we think he didn't know that until we told him,' said Norman. 'Anyway, perhaps he's thinking that with Tilly out of the way, he could sell the whole estate.'

'I've just had a thought,' said Morgan. 'Rhona told us Griffiths used to spend two or three days up in Scotland every week. What if he used that address in Aberdeen because that's where he actually goes?'

'I see what you're getting at,' said Norman. 'Young widow, on her own, quite possibly with money. Jeez, she could easily be another victim!'

Southall had been listening to the conversation with interest. 'Before you two start jumping to conclusions, it might be an idea to confirm that this woman actually knows Griffiths. The fact he uses her address doesn't necessarily mean he goes there, nor does it mean she's another victim.'

'You're right,' agreed Norman.

'The Aberdeen police confirmed it's the correct phone number for that address,' said Morgan. 'Shall I give her a call?'

'I think that would be wise,' said Southall.

* * *

Morgan settled at her desk with a mug of tea and dialled the number in Aberdeen. Almost immediately a soft, slightly accented voice answered.

'Hello.'

'I'm looking for Mrs Patty McDonald,' said Morgan.

'That's me,' said the woman.

'Good morning. My name's Detective Constable Catren Morgan. I'm calling from Llangwelli police in Wales.'

122

'Why would you be calling me all the way from Wales?'

'I'd like to ask you a few questions,' said Morgan. 'Do you know a man called David Griffiths?'

'David? Yes, I know him.'

'Can I ask what your relationship is?'

'Me and David? I suppose you could say we're good friends.'

'Can I ask how good?'

'Do I need to be careful what I say here? He stays here two or three nights a week, but I don't want you thinking I'm some sort of merry widow. I take it you know I'm a widow?'

'Yes,' said Morgan. 'I'm sorry for your loss.'

Patty sighed. 'It's the nature of the job. We always knew there were risks to working as a diver, that's why they get paid so well, and they're so well insured. I couldn't have afforded to stay in this house without the insurance money.'

'Even so, it must be hard to deal with,' said Morgan, feeling rather inadequate.

'It's worse for my daughter. Five years on and she still doesn't understand why he was prepared to do a job that might kill him.'

'And you've not remarried?'

'You mean to David? Good heavens, no. I let him sleep here two or three nights a week, but we're not in love or anything like that. He's good company, and handy for fixing things and cutting the grass. He's even quite good in bed, but he's not the sort of guy anyone would want to marry. Can I ask why you're asking about him? Is he in some sort of trouble?'

'As this is an ongoing inquiry, I'm afraid I can't tell you much.'

'Oh. I see. That means he is, then,' she said. 'Oh well, at least Maisie will be pleased.'

'Maisie?'

'My daughter. She was always afraid David might be trying to replace her dad. I told her it wasn't like that, but she's too young to understand I have needs that aren't quite the same as hers, if you see what I mean.'

'That must have made things difficult when David was there. How did he cope?'

'He was surprisingly okay with it. He seemed to understand Maisie's concern, and he never tried to act the father with her. I got the impression he wasn't mad about kids, so I think deep down he was pleased she hadn't taken a shine to him.'

'Did he ever talk about his business?'

'Not really. I knew he owned a business in Wales, something to do with wind turbines, but he didn't speak about it much.'

'He didn't ask you to invest in the business?'

'You mean did he try to con me out of my husband's insurance money? That was his opening pitch when we first met, but I told him right from the start that if he ever mentioned it again, he'd be out on his ear.'

'You knew the business was a scam?'

'How many business owners can afford to spend three days a week away from it? He didn't even contact the office.'

'We understood he had business connections in your area.'

'Yes, he told me that. He even used to go out every day, but never for long, and he never once took a business call when he was here. That's why I had my suspicions. I phoned his office number one time when he wasn't here, and that secretary — I can't recall her name now—'

'Rhona?'

'That's her, yes, Rhona. If she's the first point of contact for enquiries, it's a wonder they have any customers at all.'

'Don't be too hard on Rhona,' said Morgan. 'I hate to say it but David has actually persuaded her to invest a lot of money in the business, and she's going to get nothing in return.'

'Flattered her into it, did he? I'm sorry he's done that to her, but I can't honestly say I'm surprised. If it wasn't her, it would have been someone else.'

'Did he ever mention a woman called Tilly Rotherby?' asked Morgan.

'I can't recall the name. Who is she? Another one of his scam victims?'

'We haven't quite worked that one out yet. She owns an estate in Wales. We believe David married her a couple of weeks ago.'

'She owns an estate and he married her? This sounds like a pattern, doesn't it? Exactly how many women does he have on the go?'

'That's what we're trying to establish.'

'Does this Tilly know he's only married her for her money?'

'The thing is, Tilly was murdered last Saturday evening.'

'Oh, my God! But you can't honestly think David killed her. A conman, yes, but never a murderer. He's far too gentle to do something like that.'

Morgan had learned all she needed to know, and soon ended the call.

As she explained to Southall and Norman, Patty McDonald had merely confirmed their suspicions without adding anything of significance to their case.

# CHAPTER 16

At ten forty-five the following morning, Morgan took a call.

'I've just had Thomas Pritchard on the phone,' she announced afterwards. 'He woke up this morning to find that Rhona had packed a suitcase and gone.'

Southall frowned. 'Gone where?'

'He says he doesn't know, and he's not sure he really cares, but he thought we should know.'

'What do you think she's up to?' asked Southall.

'I'm sorry, but this is probably my fault,' confessed Morgan. 'I told her she would be an accessory if Griffiths was conning his investors. I'm guessing she finally realised the truth about the business, and now she's panicked and decided to do a runner. Do you want me to try and find her?'

'Hang on. Before you rush off on a wild goose chase, we need to decide where our priorities lie,' Southall said.

'You mean you don't think Rhona murdered Tilly Rotherby?' said Morgan.

'You spoke to her, Catren. Do you think she's capable of murder?'

'Honestly? No, I don't. For a start she's not clever enough.'

'Frosty?'

'I agree with Catren. I don't think Rhona has it in her.'

'Don't forget the hotel CCTV gives her an alibi,' said Norman. 'And if her husband wasn't really asleep, I'm sure he can vouch for her not having left the hotel.' He turned to Southall. 'Do you think Griffiths might have put her up to this in order to create a diversion?'

'I wouldn't put it past him,' said Southall. 'Or perhaps it's just about the money. Rhona's still got over a quarter of a million left in that bank account of hers. A sum like that could be quite handy if he's planning to escape.'

'What are we going to do about Rhona, then?' asked Norman.

'I think we're all agreed she's not a murder suspect, and there's no reason to think she's in any danger,' said Southall. 'On the other hand, she is the victim of a conman, even if she doesn't want to admit it. On that basis she probably needs saving from herself, so let's put out a general alert for her to be detained if seen.'

'We could still pick Griffiths up, couldn't we?' said Norman.

'I just called the hotel,' said Lane. 'He's already left.'

'Crap!' said Norman. They've probably planned to meet up. They could be anywhere by now.'

'Let's not panic,' said Southall. 'I'm sure he'll go to the farmhouse first.'

'You really think he will?' Norman said.

'Don't forget, he doesn't know Rhona's husband has called us. Plus, if she is supposed to be a decoy, he'll be expecting us to follow her. Remember how keen he was to get inside the farmhouse on the day Tilly died. I'm sure there's something in the house he needs to get hold of, so he'll go there first, and meet up with Rhona later.'

'Do you want me to get out there with Frosty?' asked Morgan.

'How are we getting on with the registry office?' Southall asked.

'They say they're happy to speak to me, but I need to catch the registrar between weddings. I was going to go over there this afternoon, but it can wait until tomorrow if you need me for surveillance.'

'What about you, Frosty? Any luck with the solicitor?'

'I've found him, but I've not contacted him yet. I've also got this,' he said, holding up a memory stick. 'Rhona says it features a huge wind farm Griffiths has allegedly built. She said it proves the business is legit. I was going to check it out but I haven't had time yet.'

'Can I ask something?'

They all looked at Lane.

'I know that's the sort of stuff I usually do,' she said. 'But would anyone mind if I go on surveillance for a change?'

Norman exchanged a look with Southall. This was a bold move on the part of Lane, who hadn't ventured out of the office since she was knocked unconscious a couple of months ago.

'I think that's an excellent idea,' said Southall. 'You and Frosty head over to the estate. Watch the gate but try to keep out of sight. Let us know when he arrives, and we'll decide how to proceed when we know he's definitely there.'

'Yeah, cool,' said Morgan. 'Pass that other stuff over here and I'll take a look at it.'

Lane and Winter gathered up their coats and made a hasty exit.

'Shall I get going too?' asked Morgan. 'If I go to the registry office now, I can take a look at Frosty's stuff when I get back.'

'Good idea,' said Southall.

When Morgan had left, Southall raised her eyebrows at Norman.

'What do you make of that?' she asked Norman. 'Is that Judy getting back on the horse after a fall, or is it something else?'

'Well, we've always said Judy does a fantastic job in here, but there's no denying we have doubts about her confidence in the field. Maybe she wants to prove she can work just as well out there. One thing's for sure, Catren didn't seem to

128

mind standing down and letting Judy take her job. I reckon she knew the request was coming.'

'I hope she's not going to do something stupid to try and impress us all.'

'I don't think it's that,' said Norman. 'I think it's much more likely that Catren has been encouraging Judy to get out there and rebuild her confidence.'

# CHAPTER 17

It was three p.m. Lane and Winter had parked a short distance from the main entrance to the Rotherby estate, from where they had a good view of traffic approaching from both directions. At least, it would have been a good view if it wasn't for the sheets of heavy rain, which had begun to fall shortly after their arrival.

Winter had never spent any time alone with Judy Lane before. Intrigued by this attractive yet intensely private young woman, he regarded being cooped up in a car with her for a few hours as an ideal opportunity to get to know her. But Lane had stonewalled even the most mundane of his personal questions and, realising he was getting nowhere fast, Winter took the hint and broadened the scope of their conversation.

But now, after three hours of staring out at the rain, while munching their way through a packet and a half of chocolate Hobnobs, they had exhausted every topic of conversation Winter could think of.

He yawned expansively. 'This is so boring,' he said. 'We don't even know for sure that Griffiths is here.'

'But we both saw that car turn into the drive just as we got here,' said Lane.

'Yes, but we only think Griffiths was the driver. We don't know for sure, do we? We could end up sitting here all night waiting for him to come back out when it wasn't him driving at all, but someone who lives in one of the cottages.'

'But when I asked Norm to check, he told us no one at the cottages owns a white car.'

'He also told us Griffiths doesn't own one either.'

'But he did tell us the car is registered to a car-hire company.'

'But why would Griffiths hire a car?'

'I've been thinking about that,' said Lane. 'He knows we know what car he drives, so perhaps he's hired a different car to throw us off the scent.'

'Okay, but what if it's just a visitor to one of the cottages?'

'Yes, well, there is that possibility, of course. Look, if it's any consolation, I'm just as bored as you.'

'I don't know why they were so sure he was going to rush in, grab something and then rush off again.'

'Because they think he might be going to meet up with Rhona.'

'But if he doesn't care about her, why would he do that?'

'So he can get hold of the rest of her money.'

'But now he's got the estate, does he even need Rhona's money?' Winter said.

'You're assuming Tilly didn't make a will.'

'But who would she leave it to?' he asked.

'I don't know. What about her mysterious brother?'

'We don't even know if he's still around—'

'Hold on. Look!'

A black Mercedes emerged through the rain, indicated a right turn and went in through the gates.

'Was that Griffiths?' asked Winter.

'It wasn't easy to tell through the rain, but I think not. That guy was either bald, or his head was shaved.'

'What do we do?' asked Winter.

'Did you get the registration number?' asked Lane.

'No. I couldn't read it. We're too far away,' said Winter.

'That's why you have the binoculars,' said Lane.

'Yeah, sorry. By the time I remembered, it was too late.'

'Well, wake up. I know surveillance is boring and we do nothing for hours, but you still need to stay alert and be ready when something does happen. If we knew the registration number, we could find out who he was and then maybe we'd know what to do.'

'Right. Yes, I'm sorry,' said Winter sheepishly. 'Should we follow him?'

'Without knowing who he is? I don't know. Let me call Norm. He'll know what to do.'

She put her phone on speaker and waited for Norman to answer.

'Judy. What's going on?'

'As I told you earlier, we think we saw Griffiths driving in as we got here, but we couldn't be sure. But now, just a couple of minutes ago, a black Mercedes turned into the estate. We don't know if we should follow it or wait here.'

'Did you get the registration number?'

'Sorry, we missed it. It's pouring with rain here, and there was too much spray from the cars passing by.'

They heard Norman utter a muffled curse. 'Okay. Let's think about this. What reasons do you think a man in a black Mercedes might have for being there?'

'The two obvious possibilities are that they're meeting Griffiths, or it could be someone innocently visiting one of the cottages. But I'm sure there could be plenty of other reasons as well.'

'Well, if you go down there and the black Mercedes is visiting someone at the cottages, we could be giving Griffiths an excuse to claim we're harassing him.'

'What if we had an excuse for calling in?' Lane said.

'Like what?'

'What if I say it was me who called Animal Welfare, and I just popped in to make sure the horses were being looked after. I'll say we were passing, and we didn't realise the boss had released the house back to him.'

'Do you think he'd fall for that?' Norman asked.

'It's not as if we're going to be asking lots of questions, is it? We just want to make sure he's there. We'll knock on the door, take a quick look at the horses and then leave.'

'And what if he doesn't want you to look at the horses?'

'Then we'll apologise for disturbing him and leave. We'll still know he's there, won't we?'

'Well, yeah,' said Norman. 'But if it was me, I think I would ask myself why I was there, and then apply that to the two possibilities to help me decide what I should do. Having said that, you never know for sure what's going to happen so there's always a good chance that whatever you decide could be wrong.'

Winter and Lane looked at each other, amused.

After a few moments' silence, Winter said, 'You're the boss, Judy, what do you think we should do?'

'I think we should sit tight and see what happens,' said Lane. 'In my opinion it's the least worst option.'

'That works for me,' said Norman. 'Just keep me informed of anything else that happens.'

Lane ended the call.

'Thanks for that,' said Winter. 'I owe you.'

'For what?'

'Not telling Norm about the binoculars.'

'That's okay. Just don't make me have to remind you again.'

'I won't,' he said, brandishing the binoculars. 'I've got them here in my hand, ready and waiting.'

'Good,' said Lane confidently. 'Now we'll carry on sitting here awaiting developments.'

'Boring,' said Winter.

'Yes, but it is what it is. If you want to play action man, perhaps you should think about joining the SAS.'

Winter was beginning to enjoy being with Lane. She was like Catren Morgan without the loudness. He offered her the biscuits. 'Want another Hobnob?'

'Yuck, no. I am well and truly Hobnobbed out. I'll throw up if I eat another one.'

Winter smiled. 'In that case I may as well finish the packet.'

'You'd better not — Jesus, he's a in a hurry.' Lane pointed to the road.

Winter looked up just in time to see the black Mercedes come barrelling out of the estate. He dropped the biscuits and grabbed the binoculars as the car swerved onto the wet road with a loud squeal of tyres and roared off into the distance.

'Bloody hell,' muttered Winter as he frantically adjusted the focus of the binoculars. 'What's set his arse on fire?'

Lane was already calling Norman.

'Judy. I wasn't expecting you to call back so soon.'

'You and me both,' she said. 'I wouldn't have called, but the black Mercedes has just come flying out of the drive. He nearly set his tyres alight taking off down the road. There's no point in trying to follow him. He's already out of sight.'

'Holy crap,' said Norman. 'I don't like the sound of that. Did you get his number this time?'

Winter nodded. He scrawled it down and passed it to Lane, who read it out to Norman.

'I reckon we should go down there and see what's going on,' said Lane.

'I think you're right,' said Norman. 'But use your animal-welfare story and don't stay any longer than you have to. Griffiths thinks we're too dim to figure out what he's up to, so let's make sure it stays that way.'

'Have we figured out what he's up to?' asked Lane.

'Not really,' said Norman. 'It's all guesswork so far but, whatever it is, it's nothing good. Anyway, you get going and I'll get this black Merc checked out. Give me a call when you're done, and I'll come out there and take over so you guys can get off home.'

'Okay, I'll call you back in a while.' Lane ended the call. 'Okay, Frosty, let's go and see if we were right about Griffiths being here.'

Winter drove up to the farmhouse. The white car they had spotted earlier was parked outside.

'Looks like we were right about the car,' said Winter. 'But if he was waiting for a delivery, why is he still here?'

'Perhaps it wasn't a delivery, and he can't find whatever it is he's looking for. Perhaps Tilly had it and she's hidden it. Who knows, maybe that's why she was killed.'

Winter parked the car, and they made their way to the front door. Lane rang the bell. As she did so, the front door swung open.

Lane and Winter glanced at each other.

'Doesn't look good, does it?' he whispered.

Lane pushed the door open and called out, 'Hello. Mr Griffiths? It's the police. Are you there?'

There was no reply.

'Maybe he's down with the horses,' suggested Winter.

'I think we'd better take a look around here before we go to the stables,' said Lane. She took a couple of steps inside and then called out again.

'Hello! Anyone home?'

She waited a few moments, then turned to Winter and shrugged.

'He'll go apeshit if he comes back and finds us wandering around his house,' said Winter.

'Yes, he probably will,' she said. 'But this doesn't feel right to me. You can stand outside and wait if you're worried about upsetting him, but I'm going in.'

Lane headed towards the kitchen. Winter heaved a sigh and followed.

'Look at this,' she said, pointing to the table. 'Car keys, and I'm sure that's the bag he was carrying when he booked into the hotel on Saturday evening.'

There was a mug of black tea by the kettle, with a carton of milk beside it. Lane went over and touched the mug with the back of her hand.

'It's cold,' she said. 'And the tea bag is still in it. Why would he leave it half made?'

'Perhaps something more important occurred to him. Not everyone finds tea as important as you.'

She smiled at this. 'Obviously not, or he'd have come back and made a fresh one. Joking aside, I think we need to check the rest of the house. Something bad has happened here, I can feel it.'

'I'll check upstairs,' said Winter.

A couple of minutes later, they were back in the hallway.

'I don't think anyone's been up there since the forensics team checked it,' said Winter.

'Okay, so what are we saying? He got here, dumped his bag and keys on the table, started to make a cup of tea and then rushed off somewhere.'

'That's how it looks,' agreed Winter.

'Then whatever made him leave must have happened almost as soon as he got here, over three hours ago. We know he didn't leave the estate, so he must be around here somewhere. Let's check the garden and the stables.'

The rain was finally beginning to ease as they made their way across the garden towards the stables.

'You take that side,' said Lane, indicating the row to the left.

They walked slowly, peering into each stable, but neither of them noticed anything out of the ordinary. They entered the American barn.

There were still no horses inside, but the gate to the stall where Tilly had been found was wide open. They peered inside. It was empty.

'How can we have missed him?' asked Winter.

'He's got to be around here somewhere,' said Lane. They went back out into the yard and looked around. Facing them at the far end was the yew hedge with the gate through to the garden. To the right, between the end stable and the hedge, was a gap.

'Is that a path, or just a gap in the hedge?' asked Lane.

'I think it's a path,' said Winter.

'Let's see where it goes.'

They went through the gap and followed the path, which led them along beside the stables. Lane reached the end first. She stopped for a second and stared, before breaking into a run.

'Shit,' she muttered. 'Shit, shit, shit!'

# CHAPTER 18

Norman entered the Mercedes's registration number into his computer. Immediately, a warning flashed up on the screen. Muttering to himself, he hurried across to Southall's office. She seemed to have become less communicative as the day wore on but, as usual, her office door was open.

'How does that work?' he asked.

Southall looked up from her desk. 'How does what work?'

'Someone drove into the Rotherby estate in a black Merc. Five minutes later he came flying out like his arse was on fire. Then, when I run a vehicle check on it, I get an access denied warning.'

'What sort of access denied warning?'

'The sort that's above my pay grade, yours too.'

'That's interesting.'

'I think we're going to need Nathan's help with this one.'

Superintendent Nathan Bain was their boss. Many years ago, he and Norman had worked at the Met. It was Bain who had persuaded Norman to become a police rejoiner.

Southall reached for her phone. 'I'll speak to him now.'

A few minutes later, she was standing by Norman's desk. 'It seems we are forbidden from intercepting the Mercedes or its driver, nor are we to make any enquiries about him or the car.'

'But that's ridiculous! The guy is now connected to our murder inquiry. For all we know it could be him that killed Tilly Rotherby.'

'Apparently, someone is coming to brief us about why this guy is so special.'

'Crap! I hate it when I hear someone tell me that,' said Norman. 'It means this guy is almost certainly a terrorist, a people trafficker or a drug dealer. I don't suppose Nathan knows which it is?'

'He says he doesn't.'

Norman heaved a sigh. 'I suppose it doesn't really make much difference. Whatever this guy is, a small team like us is always going to play second fiddle to that type of operation.'

'It does make you wonder if there isn't a bit more to our murder than we first thought, though,' said Southall. 'Perhaps this explains where Tilly was getting her money.'

'Well, maybe, but I can't see her as any sort of terrorist. And there was never any evidence to suggest she was involved in that people-trafficking operation we stumbled upon. So that just leaves drugs, but I can't see her as your typical drug dealer, can you?'

Before Southall could answer, Norman's phone began to ring.

'Hi, Judy, what's up? I hope this isn't another registration number, because—'

He listened for a moment.

'You've found what? Now, hang on a minute. Whatever has happened, it isn't your fault. We talked it through, remember. I said I was happy with your decision so if it's anyone's fault it's mine. Just take a deep breath and tell me what you've found.'

He listened again.

'Okay,' he said. 'You know what to do, right? Frosty has already called them? That's good. It sounds to me like you have it all under control. We're on our way.' He slammed the receiver down. 'Bollocks!'

'What's the matter?'

'They've just found David Griffiths. He's dead.'

'Are they sure?'

'Oh, yeah, no doubt about it. It looks as if someone bashed his head in.'

'Bugger,' said Southall. 'That's the last thing I expected to happen.'

'You and me both. And it's just our luck that the one man who might know what happened is out of our reach.'

'You mean—'

'Mercedes Man. Judy says they saw the guy drive into the estate and then, a few minutes later, come tearing out like the proverbial bat out of hell. He's got to be our prime suspect.'

'We'd better get down there,' said Southall.

She made for the door so fast Norman had to run to keep up with her. Out in the car park, she threw him the keys.

'You drive,' she said, and jumped into the passenger seat. 'I'll call the duty doctor, Forensics and the pathologist.'

'There's no need to panic,' said Norman, sliding in behind the wheel. 'Lane and Frosty are on the ball. They've already called for a doctor and Forensics. You just need to get hold of Bill Bridger and make sure he knows.'

'Panicking? Who's panicking?' she snapped.

Norman glanced at her set face. 'You know what I mean. It's a figure of speech, we use it all the time. No need to take offence.'

Southall's face turned slightly red. 'It's called following procedure,' she said, somewhat sheepishly.

'I know what following procedure is, Sarah. So do Lane and Frosty. You ought to be pleased that our two youngest detectives have coped so well with such an unexpected situation.'

'Yes, you're right. I'm sorry. It was unnecessary. I shouldn't have snapped at you like that. I hope you'll accept my apology.'

Norman wondered what was up. Southall wasn't usually like this, something must be eating away at her. Normally he'd ask if there was anything he could do to help, but not right now. Maybe later.

'Apology accepted,' he said, putting the car into gear. 'Now, let's go and see what we're dealing with.'

'I'll call Dr Bridger,' said Southall, taking her phone from her pocket. 'And then I'd better let Catren know we need her down at the farmhouse.'

# CHAPTER 19

It was coming up to five p.m. Norman looked dispassionately down at David Griffiths's body, lying face down on the ground behind the stables. Pathologist Bill Bridger was kneeling alongside the body.

'Any idea how long ago he was killed?' asked Norman. 'I'm guessing less than two hours.'

'Hard to narrow it down right now,' said Bridger. 'Being out in the pouring rain will have interfered with normal body cooling. If I had to guess, I'd say anything from a couple of hours to possibly as much as six.'

'Really? But we know the guy was alive around midday.'

'Well, why didn't someone tell me that?' said Bridger. 'Considering this new information, I'll amend that to between two and five hours. I'll be able to say more for certain when I get him to the lab, but that's my first impression.'

Norman sighed. 'So much for wrapping this one up before bedtime then.'

'You know who did it?' Bridger asked.

'We have a suspect in mind, but that huge window of opportunity isn't going to help us,' said Norman.

Bridger grunted. 'As I said, it's just a guess right now.'

'On a positive note, even from here I can see what killed him,' said Norman.

'Yes, I think we can safely say the massive traumas to his head did the job.'

'Any idea what the weapon was?'

Bridger looked up at Norman. 'I'm hoping your detectives or one of my forensic team are going to find it.' Then he winked. 'But I can tell you this much, it was something with a sharp edge. It's nearly taken his head off.'

'Oh, well, there we are, then. That really narrows it down for us.'

Norman turned to Southall, who had been listening in silence to his exchange with Bridger.

'Well, his death is going to make it rather difficult for us to charge him with Tilly Rotherby's murder, isn't it?'

She smiled grimly. 'We can't question him now, that's for sure.'

'I'm sorry if this is spoiling your case,' said Bridger. 'But I'm afraid there's nothing I can do about that. I'm pretty good at finding out what happened to the dead, but I've yet to master the art of bringing them back to life.'

'Pity. I was looking forward to hearing him explain how his dodgy wind-turbine business worked,' said Norman.

Southall sighed. 'The thing is, the dodgy business is all we really had on him, wasn't it? And now this has happened we may have to face the fact that all along I've been chasing the wrong murder suspect.'

'We all thought he was the prime suspect,' said Norman.

'Only if you ignore his cast-iron alibi, which we even have on film.'

'That doesn't mean he couldn't have found some other way to sneak out unseen, or paid someone to do his dirty work for him.'

'Let's be honest, Norm, he might have been a conman, but we've found nothing to suggest he was a killer. Even his girlfriend in Scotland doesn't think he could have done it. No, we need to accept I was wrong and change our focus.'

'There's no "I" in team,' said Norman. 'Isn't that what they used to tell us? I was just as sure it was him.'

'That's as maybe, but the buck has to stop somewhere, and as far as Headquarters is concerned, I'm the boss, therefore it's my responsibility.'

Norman exchanged a glance with Bridger, who seemed to share Norman's view that she was in a particularly crappy mood today.

'I'm going to take a look around,' he said, heading off towards the tack room.

'He's right,' said Bridger, when Norman had moved away. 'Anyone would have focused on Griffiths once they saw how dodgy he was. And, as Norm says, he could easily have paid someone else to carry out the murder.'

'Yes, but could he?' asked Southall testily. 'Hitmen don't come cheap, and Griffiths appears to have had no money of his own. He relied on Rhona Pritchard to fund everything, and she hasn't drawn out enough cash in the last week or so to pay for a hit.'

'I was only saying—'

'Well, don't,' she snapped. 'And when am I going to get those lab results?'

'As you well know, there's a limit to how much I can do in my own lab. Sometimes I have to rely on outside analysis.'

'Yes, I'm aware of that, but why is it taking so long?'

'The results should be here tomorrow, which, for your information, is no later than usual. And, for future reference, biting the head off your pathologist is not a good way to get test results any faster.'

Southall knew she was in the wrong but was unable to come up with an apology that didn't sound insincere. She stalked off after Norman and found him in the tack room.

'The pathologist seems a bit oversensitive today,' she said.

'Are you sure it's him?'

'What's that supposed to mean?'

'I think you know exactly what I mean,' said Norman. 'But I'm not going to get into an argument about it.' Keen to change the subject, he pointed to a yellow sticker affixed to the shelf with the trophies. 'Isn't that a forensic marker?'

Southall walked over to the shelf and stared at it. 'There's nothing there.'

Norman peered over her shoulder. 'I think that's the point. If you look at it from here, there's like a clean patch, almost a circle, in the dust. Something that was on that shelf when we were here the other day is no longer there.'

'Tilly's lucky top hat,' said Southall.

'Yeah, of course. But why would anyone want to take an old top hat?'

'I have no idea.'

'Still, I can't think it's relevant. I mean, it's not likely to be our murder weapon, is it?'

They stood staring at the shelf in awkward silence.

'Are you okay?' asked Norman at last.

'I'm fine,' said Southall.

'Really? Only if you need to talk, you know I'm here, right?'

'That's very sweet of you, Norm. I'm sorry I'm a bit touchy. It's just a bad time of year, you know?'

It took a couple of seconds for Norman to catch on. 'Oh, Jeez. I'm sorry, I completely forgot about that. Maybe you should take a couple of days off.'

'You mean sit at home thinking about the child I lost? I don't think so. Being here keeps my mind occupied.'

'Does Bill know?'

'I prefer not to talk about it.'

'I understand that, but is it fair to keep him in the dark? Maybe you should tell him.'

'You really think so?'

'Look, he's in there now, trying to figure out what he's done to upset you. He's a good guy, and he'd want to be there for you, but he can't understand what you're going through if you don't tell him, right?'

'I don't know . . .'

'It's your choice, but I know what I think you should do,' said Norman. 'And while you do it, I'm going to have a look around outside, beyond where the body was found. The SOCOs should be finished there by now.'

He left the tack room, crossed the yard and headed towards where the body had been found. About twenty yards further on, a couple of white-clad scene-of-crime officers appeared to be marking something on the ground under the shelter of a large tree.

Southall considered what Norman had said for a few seconds, then squared her shoulders and headed after him. Two of Bridger's team were pushing a trolley bearing Griffiths's body across the yard towards a waiting vehicle. Bridger was by the end stable removing his forensic suit. He eyed Southall cautiously as she approached.

'Can you spare a few minutes?' she asked.

'I'm not sure I can. I've got this crabby DI demanding results, and I don't know how she's going to react if I—'

'Please, Bill,' she said. 'I owe you an apology. There's something you need to know. Something I should have told you before.'

\* \* \*

'What have you got?' asked Norman.

One of the SOCOs waved a hand around. 'There are assorted footprints and old cycle tracks all over the place. They've mostly been washed away by the rain so they're not much good. But this tree has offered a bit of shelter from the rain.' He pointed to a marker they had placed on the ground. 'There are some fresh footprints here. They're a bit scuffed and mixed up, but we think we can isolate one or two clear ones.' He pointed to a second marker. 'And there's a nice clear print here that looks like someone may have laid a bike down on its side. And just there,' he pointed to a third marker, 'is a set of big fat bicycle-tyre tracks. Again, the rain's got at them, but under this tree there are enough identifiable marks to suggest they're freshly made. We'll take casts of them of course, but if I had to guess I'd say they belonged to a mountain bike.'

'You mean a kid's bike?'

'Not necessarily. Plenty of adults ride them too. They're great for getting to places cars can't go.'

Norman stared down at the tyre tracks. They were in an area of soft sand under the tree, which was why they had been so easy to spot.

'They lead off across there.' The SOCO pointed behind the stable block.

'Is that a footpath?' asked Norman. 'Only it looks a bit overgrown to me.'

'There are old footpaths like this everywhere,' said the SOCO. 'They get overgrown like that from disuse, and most landowners dislike people walking through their property, but legally they are still a public right of way.'

Norman squinted into the distance. He couldn't see where it went, or even if there really was a path at all.

'This one certainly looks as if it doesn't get used very often,' said the SOCO, pointing into the distance along the back of the stables. 'But you can see it comes from over there, behind the stables.' He turned and indicated in the opposite direction. 'It follows the hedgerow along the back of that field and into those trees.'

Norman stared. Now it had been pointed out to him, he could see the footpath more clearly. It was patchy from lack of use, but it was there all right. 'So, anyone can come and go along this path, and the estate owners can't do a thing to stop them?'

'That's about the size of it.'

'And these tyre marks suggest someone used it to cut across the estate quite recently,' said Norman. He studied the jumble of tyre tracks and footprints for a few more moments. 'And these tracks definitely don't go beyond the stables in the other direction?'

The SOCOs both shook their heads.

'They stop here, where it looks as if someone got off the bike and left it on its side. Then they go back the other way.'

'So, whoever came here came from beyond those trees, stopped under this tree for some reason, and then went back the same way?' Norman asked.

'We think that's what probably happened.'

Norman studied the tracks again. 'I think you're right. Can you guys do me a favour?'

'Sure.'

'My boss is talking with Dr Bridger. When they've finished, can you tell her I've gone exploring? I want to see where this path leads.'

Careful to avoid destroying any remaining tyre tracks, Norman set off along the old footpath.

# CHAPTER 20

Norman followed the path to a small group of trees, the odd tyre track that hadn't been obliterated by the rain indicating that he was heading the right way. He walked through the trees until he came to a T-junction. He stopped and stared. The path adjoining his was obviously more frequently used, making it almost impossible to spot individual tyre tracks.

He studied the tracks on his path and decided the bike he was following had turned right, so he did the same, following the new path for another hundred yards or so. The trees began to give way to smaller bushes and, as the path weaved its way through the shrubs, he could make out a small church to the left, surrounded by neatly tended graves. On the opposite side, a burst of loud quacking suggested a pond that was hidden behind the bushes.

Norman saw a gate that opened into the graveyard. Beyond the church, he made out the roofs of distant houses, and as the shrubs thinned on the opposite side the duck pond came into view. More houses beyond the pond suggested he was on the outskirts of a village.

Inside the churchyard, an elderly, white-haired man was sitting on a bench opposite a large granite headstone. Perched on the bench next to him was what looked like a picnic basket, suggesting he might be a regular visitor. Norman went through the gate and approached the man.

'Hi,' he said. 'You look like you come here a lot.'

'Most days,' said the man. He nodded towards the granite headstone. 'I come here to enjoy the peace, read a book, and have lunch with my wife. Sometimes I end up spending the whole afternoon and evening here, reading or putting the world to rights with her.'

For a second Norman thought the man must be waiting for his wife to arrive, but then he realised what he meant.

'I'm sorry. I didn't mean to intrude.'

'No apologies necessary,' said the man. 'It's not a problem for me. I expect she'd complain if she was here, but she can't now, can she?'

'No, I guess not,' said Norman.

'Don't get me wrong, I loved her to bits, but there's no getting away from the fact that she used to complain a lot. And argue? My God, that woman could start an argument in an empty room. That's why I like coming up here so often, you see. I can say what I like now, and she can't object.'

'I hope it doesn't become an accepted way of achieving marital harmony,' said Norman.

The old man smiled. 'I'd vote for it,' he said. 'We get on much better now than we ever did before.'

Norman studied the man's face. Was he joking? Unsure of how to respond, he decided he'd better get down to business. He produced his warrant card. 'I'm DS Norman.'

'Gareth Jones,' said the man.

Norman shook Jones's hand. 'Would it be okay if I asked you a couple of questions, Gareth?'

'Ask away.'

'We're making enquiries about something that happened not far from here.'

'Is it about that woman at the stables?'

'You know about that, then.'

'I heard it on the radio. It's big news around here, you know.'

'I guess it would be.'

'It happened on Saturday, didn't it?'

'That's right,' said Norman. 'Were you here on Saturday evening?'

'Just the afternoon, I'm afraid.'

'What about earlier today?'

'I was here for lunch as normal and as you can see, I'm still here now.'

'Didn't you get wet?'

'You mean from the rain?' The man pointed to a rolled-up umbrella propped against the headstone. 'This is one of those enormous fishing umbrellas. Keeps me dry as a bone, it does.'

Norman pointed towards the old path. 'Did you notice any unusual activity along the path there?'

'Just some teenager. He came racing down that path on one of those fancy bikes they have now. Going like a bat out of hell he was. I remember because he tossed something into the pond as he passed. It scared the life out of the ducks. They made a hell of a racket.'

'You said "he." Are you sure it was a boy?'

'Can anyone be sure these days? It seems a lot of them aren't sure themselves.'

On any other day, Norman might have enjoyed discussing the problem of today's youth, but he didn't have time for it right now.

'Did you see what he threw in the pond?'

'Sorry, no, but I heard the splash and, as I say, the ducks went crazy.'

'Which way was he heading?'

'From the stables, towards the village. The same way you've just come.'

'Can you recall what time this was?'

'I got here at about half past twelve, and it wasn't long after I arrived.'

'So, you would have seen the teenager on the bike between twelve thirty and one o'clock?'

'Nearer twelve forty-five, I'd say.'

151

'Could you describe him — or her?'

'Oh, I didn't see the face.'

'Okay, what about the height?'

'Difficult to say. They were standing up on the pedals, hunched over the handlebars.'

'What about the clothes?'

'He was wearing one of those hoodie things; black, I think it was. And blue jeans.'

Norman thought most kids in Wales probably dressed just like that.

'I'm not much help, am I?' said Jones. 'Sorry about that.'

'You're doing just fine,' said Norman. 'What about the bike? Can you recall anything about that?'

Jones's face lit up. 'Ah, now there I can help you. The frame of the bike was pillar-box red, and it had those ridiculous fat tyres. I'm told they're for riding off-road.'

'There you go,' said Norman. 'That was very helpful.'

'Do you know, now I think about it, I remember he was riding one-handed.'

'You mean he's disabled?'

'No, no. He had one hand on the handlebars, but he was holding something in the other hand. I couldn't swear to it, but I believe it may have been a top hat.'

'A top hat! Really?'

'Yes, I'm almost certain it was a black top hat.'

'Thank you,' said Norman. 'That's a great help.'

'Really?'

Norman smiled. 'There can't be that many teenage cyclists around here who happen to have a top hat.'

The old man looked inordinately pleased with himself.

'Let's make sure I've got this right,' said Norman. 'At about twelve forty-five, a teenager came past on a red mountain bike, wearing a black hoodie and blue jeans, and holding a top hat. The bike was headed for the village and just before you saw it, you heard a splash from the pond. Is that correct?'

'I reckon so,' said Jones, looking smug. 'I can tell you where the rider probably lives too.'

'You can?'

The old man pointed beyond the church. 'You see that village over there?'

Norman nodded.

'It's called *Nef Anfon*.'

Norman looked puzzled.

Jones smiled. 'It means "heaven-sent".'

'Oh, right.'

'Anyway, in the village there's a small estate of about twenty houses, called Tollgate. It's full of foul-mouthed yobs. I expect he lives in one of them.'

'Now that really is helpful,' said Norman.

'I've always fancied myself as a bit of an armchair detective, you know,' said Jones. 'Helping to solve a big crime.'

'Let's not get carried away,' said Norman. 'There's no law against riding a bike, or owning a top hat, and the chances are this was just some kid racing home for lunch. But if whoever it was came from the direction of the stables, maybe they saw something as they were passing.'

# CHAPTER 21

The following morning, Southall gathered the team together. 'In view of what happened yesterday,' she announced. 'I feel I may have led this investigation on a wild goose chase. I believe I erred in focusing too much on David Griffiths. We know he was operating a scam, but it appears his only victim was Rhona Pritchard. We have nothing to suggest he was violent, and there's no escaping the fact that he had an alibi for the time of Tilly's death.'

'Are we saying Mercedes Man killed Griffiths and Tilly?' asked Winter.

'We can't ignore the possibility,' said Southall. 'It appears he had the opportunity, and we assume he had the means, although, at this stage, we have no idea what his motive would be.'

'You say it "appears" he had the opportunity,' said Lane. 'Are you suggesting there may be some doubt?'

'We're waiting for the pathology results. Because of the rain yesterday, Dr Bridger couldn't give us a definite time of death. It's possible that David Griffiths was dead before the Mercedes arrived on the scene.'

'Is it right that we're not allowed to trace the car?' asked Winter.

'Yes, it is, and it's beyond frustrating,' said Norman. 'We have a red-hot suspect for Griffiths's murder and we can't touch him.'

'Why not?' asked Winter.

'Apparently, there's an undercover operation of some sort going on, and we could blow the whole thing if we start making waves,' said Southall. 'I'm told someone is coming here today to tell us more.'

'Do we know what time this "someone" is going to turn up?' Lane asked.

Southall shook her head. 'No. Just that they're going to be here today. I know it's vague, but it's all I can tell you. In the meantime, let's focus on what we can do. So, did anyone in the cottages see anything?'

'I spoke to all the tenants except the Howells, who weren't at home, and whoever lives at number six,' said Winter. 'No one saw or heard anything.'

'Who does live at number six?' asked Norman. 'We didn't get an answer either, when we went to ask about Tilly.'

'I asked the guy at number five. He says that in the three years he's been there, he can't recall ever seeing or hearing anyone in that house. He thinks whoever lives there must work abroad, or at least be away from home most of the time,' Winter said.

'What about your mountain-bike rider, Norm?' asked Southall.

'Well, I followed some cycle-tyre tracks from close by the murder scene and found a witness who claims that at roughly twelve forty-five he saw a teenager — male or female, he wasn't sure — dressed in a black hoodie and blue jeans tearing along on a red mountain bike with a top hat in their hand. The cyclist was heading away from the scene of the crime.

'Now, this is of particular interest — first, because the rider threw something into a pond they were passing. Secondly, a top hat is missing from the tack room, and third, Jimmy Denman, who used to feed the horses every morning, owns a mountain bike.'

'So, until Dr Bridger gives us an accurate time of death, we have to consider both the mountain-bike rider and Mercedes Man as suspects,' said Southall.

'The witness also told me he thought the bike rider probably lives on a small estate called Tollgate, in a village called Nef Anfon.'

'Hang on a minute,' said Lane, shuffling through some papers on her desk. 'I've come across that name somewhere. Yes, here we are. Number fourteen, Tollgate, Nef Anfon. It's where Jimmy Denman lives.'

'But why would he want to murder Griffiths?' asked Winter.

'We don't know if he did,' said Norman. 'But it might be a good idea to ask him.'

Morgan put her phone down. 'That was the registrar calling back,' she announced. 'She confirms that David Griffiths did marry Tilly two weeks before she died.'

'Griffiths was telling the truth about something, then,' said Norman.

'But the registrar also says there was something odd about it.'

'Odd in what way?' asked Southall.

'She says it was the witnesses.'

'Griffiths did say he'd hijacked them from the previous wedding,' Southall said.

'I told her that, but the registrar says she didn't recognise them from the previous wedding. She got the feeling they were students, and they may even have been paid to be there. Also, she felt the bride was high on drugs. If she hadn't known for sure that bride and groom were both UK citizens, she would have suspected it of being a marriage of convenience.'

'But she let it go ahead anyway?'

'She says that this was all suspicion on her part, and she didn't have sufficient grounds to stop it.'

'I don't suppose there's any way of checking any of this now,' said Southall.

'I asked her that,' said Morgan. 'And she said she'll email the names and addresses of the witnesses.'

'Yeah, but if the whole thing was a set-up, they may have given false names,' said Norman.

'We didn't have Tilly down as a drug taker,' said Southall, 'but maybe we've got that wrong.'

'Or maybe Griffiths drugged her,' suggested Lane. 'He might have planned to marry her, then murder her and inherit the estate.'

'That may well have been his plan, but he can't inherit anything now, can he?' said Norman.

'Do you want me to follow it up?' asked Morgan.

'Yes, but it's no longer a priority,' said Southall.

'Who shall I take with me to see Jimmy Denman?' asked Norman.

'Take Frosty, and let's not mess around anymore,' said Southall. 'We've got two murders on our hands now, so, if you have the slightest suspicion about this boy, arrest him and bring him in.'

As the doors banged shut behind Norman and Winter, Morgan headed to the kitchen to make tea.

Southall smiled at Lane. 'So, how did it go yesterday?'

'I suppose I would have to say not very well, since our suspect was murdered,' said Lane.

'That wasn't anyone's fault, Judy. We had no reason to think Griffiths was at risk. Anyway, that's not what I mean. It's the first time you've been out of the office since you were attacked. I was impressed that you volunteered.'

'I have to start somewhere,' said Lane. 'Let's face it, sitting in a car keeping my eyes open isn't exactly high risk, is it? And it's not as if I was completely on my own.'

'How did you get on with Winter?'

'He's fine, except he never stops talking.'

'He's new, and he hasn't worked with you before. He was probably trying to make an impression,' said Southall. 'Anyway, that shouldn't be a problem for someone who works with Catren. I can't see her staying silent for long.'

Lane laughed. 'Too true. Catren never stops. I suppose I don't notice anymore because I've been working with her for so long.' Lane paused for a moment. 'She told me she spoke to you about her promotion prospects. She'll be moving on if she's successful, won't she?'

'Our team is too small to warrant a second sergeant,' admitted Southall.

Lane sighed. 'Well, I can't deny that I'll miss her, but I'll be pleased as well. She deserves it. Will she be replaced?'

'We don't even know if it's going to happen yet. It's probably months away, but if she does go I hope they will give us someone else. We can barely cope as it is. But it'll most likely be another rookie, like Winter, which means I'll need your experience out in the field rather than in here. Would that be a problem?'

'I've been thinking about that,' said Lane. 'I often feel I don't contribute enough and that I ought to get out more.'

'Judy, by running the office as well as you do, you contribute much more than you realise, but I can't let you do that forever. The issue isn't what you contribute here, it's what you're going to do moving forward. You need to decide if you want to be a detective, or if your skills would be better served in an admin position.'

'You mean you don't think I'm right for the job?'

'On the contrary, I think you have a lot of the skills necessary to eventually become a high-ranking office manager running major incidents, but to achieve that, you first need to prove your investigative abilities.'

'Oh, right. I see what you're getting at.'

'I understand how you must feel after being attacked,' said Southall. 'It would undermine anyone's confidence. But, if you want to fulfil your true potential, you must address your issues. We can help you with that, if you want us to, but if you feel they're too great to overcome, then you will have to decide where your career is going in the long term.'

'Are you going to fire me?'

'Don't be ridiculous. Of course I'm not. You're a valued member of this team. However, Llangwelli is a tiny station and sooner or later the powers that be will close it down. So, before that happens, I'd like to know that everyone is equipped for the next step on their chosen career path. I'm just asking you to decide what that's going to be, so we can make sure we're offering the best help we can.'

'So, I don't have to decide right now?'

'No, but I'd like you to think about it.'

## CHAPTER 22

'Remind me what we know about Jimmy Denman,' said Norman.

Beside him on the passenger seat, Winter opened the slim folder on his lap and read from the first page.

'James Denman, eighteen years old, lives at home with his mother, Megan. Father's whereabouts unknown. Never been in trouble so he's no criminal record. Went to school in Carmarthen, recently started an apprenticeship as a motor mechanic, also in Carmarthen.'

'Not exactly your average teenage tearaway then,' said Norman.

'Is that what you were expecting?' Winter asked.

'I have no expectation one way or the other,' said Norman. 'It's what I was told by my witness. Is this road getting narrower, or is it my imagination?'

'This is Wales, Sarge,' said Winter. 'Nearly all the rural roads are narrow, and they've been like it for so long they can't be widened.'

Up ahead, a sign at the side of the now truly narrow lane welcomed them to the village of Nef Anfon, though the tiny collection of expensive-looking residences barely even qualified as a hamlet. It looked pleasant enough, though Norman couldn't help wondering what might lie hidden behind the quaint exteriors.

'Here we go — Tollgate.' Norman slowed the car and turned into a small close of semi-detached houses. 'What number are we looking for?'

'Fourteen,' said Winter. 'Ah, there it is.'

Norman parked outside number fourteen and stared up at the house. Then he looked at the others. This quiet close seemed an unlikely setting for a teenage murderer.

'When I spoke to the old guy yesterday, he gave me the impression that Tollgate was a rundown estate full of criminals.'

'It looks nice enough to me,' said Winter. 'I think old people label anyone under thirty as a tearaway simply because they don't conform to their old-fashioned ideas of how young people should be.'

Norman turned to Winter. 'Not every old person thinks like that, surely. It's a bit of a generalisation.'

Winter smiled.

'Yeah, you're right. I have to admit you seem to be one of those old guys who doesn't see a tearaway in every young person you meet.'

Norman grinned. 'Lucky for you I'm not touchy about my age. A little respect for your elders wouldn't go amiss, though, especially when this particular elder has the car keys. It's a long walk back to the station.'

'Good point,' conceded Winter. 'I withdraw my observation.'

'Wise move,' said Norman, opening his car door. 'Now let's see what young Jimmy has to say for himself.'

The front garden was neat and tidy, with a rose climbing over the small porch. Norman rang the doorbell and, while they waited, took a quick look around the side.

'It's here,' he said. 'A red mountain bike, leaning against the house.'

A moment later, the door was opened by a red-faced woman wearing a flowery apron.

'Yes?'

'Mrs Megan Denman?' asked Norman. She nodded. 'Good morning. I'm DS Norman and this is DC Winter. We're from Llangwelli police. We'd like a word with Jimmy Denman if possible.'

'Well, I'm sorry, but it's not possible. I'm busy, so if you don't mind—'

Norman put his foot in the door before she could close it. 'Mrs Denman. I appreciate you're busy, but so are we. We wouldn't have come out here if it wasn't important. We do need to speak with Jimmy.'

'What about?'

'We'd rather talk to him if you don't mind.'

'Well, you can't. He's not here. He's at work.'

'Where would that be?' asked Winter, notebook and pencil at the ready.

'He's an apprentice at Davy Jones. It's a garage in Carmarthen.'

Winter scribbled the name in his book.

'Perhaps you can answer a couple of questions,' said Norman.

'Make it quick,' she said. 'I'm off to work in a minute.'

'Can you tell us where Jimmy was yesterday?'

'He was here, in bed, all day.'

'Teenagers and their beds, eh?' said Norman. 'Why was he at home? Did he have a day off?'

'No, he was sick.'

'Oh, I see. But he had you to look after him, right?'

'I was at work. How do you think I manage to keep a roof over our heads?'

'Right, yeah, of course. So, Jimmy's okay today?'

'He wouldn't have gone back to work otherwise, would he? Poor love, he's been bad for a few days.'

'Can I ask how he gets to work?'

'Sorry?'

'How does Jimmy get to work? Does he have a car?'

'Bus.'

'Oh, right. Does Jimmy still work as a stable lad at Tilly Rotherby's stables?'

'You mean that dead woman? He did until he got his proper job.'

'And when was that?' Norman asked.

'He started a month ago. He was supposed to stop doing the horses when he started the job, but she took advantage of his good nature and persuaded him to keep on doing them while she found someone to take over.'

'Most people would have said no,' said Winter. 'How come he agreed?'

'Well, Jimmy's not most people. He's far too trusting. It makes him easily led,' she said.

'Oh, I see,' said Winter. 'Sorry. I didn't mean to—'

'Don't worry, I'm used to people putting him down, calling him the village idiot. Well, he's not.'

'You were telling us about his job, and the horses,' said Norman.

'He missed his bus one morning because of those horses and was late for work. His boss told him he had to be there on time every day, or else. Well, you can't carry on like that, can you? So he stopped going down to the stables.'

'When was that?'

'End of last week. He's still going to do some evenings though.'

'Can you tell me where Jimmy was on Saturday evening?' Norman asked.

Megan narrowed her eyes. 'What d'you want to know that for? This isn't about her, is it? That Tilly? You can't think—'

'It's just routine, Mrs Denman. We're trying to account for anyone who knew Tilly so we can eliminate them from our enquiries.'

'Well, you can eliminate my Jimmy straight away. He was with me on Saturday evening. We went to see a James Bond film, then we caught the last bus home.'

'Which cinema did you go to?' asked Winter.

'The one in Carmarthen of course.'

'What time did the film start?' Winter asked.

'Seven thirty, I believe it was.'

Winter added this information to his notes.

'Now, if you've finished, I have to go to work and I don't want to be late.' She began to push at the door.

'Yep, I think we're all done here for now,' said Norman. 'Thank you for your time.'

He had barely finished speaking when the door slammed in his face.

'Charming,' said Winter, as they walked back to their car.

'She's scared, that's all,' said Norman. 'Imagine being a single mum with a teenage son. He's never been in trouble with the police, but it could be that he just hasn't been caught. Now, suppose you're his mum. You know he's up to something, but you don't know what it is. Then two detectives turn up on your doorstep asking questions about your son's whereabouts on the night someone was killed. Wouldn't you be a tad defensive?'

'I hadn't thought of it like that,' said Winter, getting into the passenger seat. 'I didn't realise I was supposed to feel sorry for everyone we speak to.'

'I don't feel sorry for her,' said Norman as he started the car. 'I'm just offering a possible explanation for her attitude. Understanding why she might respond that way doesn't mean I believe everything she told us.'

'You think she was telling porkies? It can't all have been lies, can it?'

They began to head out of the village.

'Where should we go now? asked Norman.

'Davy Jones's garage in Carmarthen?'

'Is the correct answer,' said Norman. 'And on the way there you can tell me what you think of what she told us.'

Winter flipped open his notebook and set it on his knee. 'He has a red mountain bike, but he doesn't have an alibi for yesterday. His mum might believe he was in bed all day but she was at work, so he could have been anywhere.'

'Correct,' said Norman.

'She said Jimmy still does the horses some evenings. I understood Carys Howells does the evenings.'

'And what does that tell us?'

'Jimmy's telling his mum he's at the stables but he's somewhere else?'

'Yes, it could be that, or it could be Carys who's telling her mum lies, and Jimmy is standing in for her.'

'What if Carys was lying when she said she hardly knew Jimmy? What if Carys and Jimmy are seeing each other and they meet at the stables?' Winter said excitedly.

'That's definitely another possibility,' said Norman. 'I like the way you're thinking.'

'Are you suggesting the two of them killed Tilly Rotherby and David Griffiths?'

'What I'm suggesting is that they might be up to something, and for all we know, it could have some bearing on one, or both, murders. On the other hand, as you suggested, they could simply be two horny teenagers who use the stables as somewhere convenient to meet, away from their parents. Anything else?'

'I'm not sure there is a James Bond film on at the moment, is there?'

'I have no idea. Anyway, you'll find out when you check her story, right? They must have CCTV in the cinema foyer.'

'It's already on my to-do list,' said Winter.

\* \* \*

Davy Jones Garage Ltd, was a huge car dealership with no less than four different car franchises, and enough service bays to repair a dozen cars at once.

'I've never got my head around the idea of having four different car makers on the same forecourt,' said Norman as he searched for a parking space. 'I mean, look, there are four different versions of each type of car. It's like the dealer is competing with himself!'

'I think it's called consolidation,' explained Winter. 'The dealers with the most money can afford to buy into more than one franchise. If you think of the car buyers as fish, it's like using a bigger net to catch those fish. You're offering the buyer more choice in one place.'

'I get the idea,' said Norman. 'But if you follow that to its logical conclusion, you're going to end up with one massive dealership selling every make of car. We all know the bigger these places get, the more impersonal they become. And what about the customer who doesn't like the dealer with all the cars? Where's their choice?'

Winter shrugged. 'It's supposed to be good business practice. Bigger is better.'

'Is that right?' said Norman, as he eased their car into a space and turned off the engine. 'The thing is, there comes a point when you make things so big and impersonal you put people off, and then they turn to the internet. Yes, it's just as impersonal, but it's a heck of a lot more convenient.'

'And that's business done the Norman way, is it?'

'I just don't think bigger is necessarily better. In my opinion, it was better when everything was smaller.'

'No, really?' said Winter. 'I would never have guessed.'

'Okay, I'll step down from my soapbox now. As we're here, I suppose we should probably do what we came to do and see if we can find Jimmy Denman.'

Five minutes later they were back in the car.

'Oh, well, at least now we know he's a twenty-four-carat liar, and we haven't even spoken to him,' said Winter. 'D'you think his mum knows?'

'I think Jimmy's mum knows he's in some sort of trouble, but I doubt she knows what that is. My guess is he doesn't tell her anything and that's why she's so scared.'

'Do you think she knows where he is right now?'

'I have no doubt she'd be prepared to lie to protect him, but my gut tells me she has no idea he isn't at work today, or why.'

'Do you think he's been pretending to be sick to avoid telling her he's lost his job?' Winter asked.

'I reckon so, and I can understand why. She's going to go spare when she finds out he got fired less than a month into his apprenticeship.'

'What now?' asked Winter.

'Drop me off at the railway station and I'll get a train back to Llangwelli,' said Norman. 'You take the car and check out the cinema.'

'I don't mind getting the train back,' said Winter. 'I can walk to the cinema from here. It's not far. You should have the car. I might be hours going through the CCTV and it won't be much use to anyone if you're needed in a hurry and you're stuck on a train.'

Norman grinned. 'I was kinda hoping you'd say that. I'll see you later, Frosty.'

# CHAPTER 23

'So, where is he?' asked Southall. Norman was just going into the office.

'That's a good question. His mother says he's at work, but when we checked, his boss said they fired him last week. Have we got a definite time of death for Griffiths yet?'

'We'll know later this afternoon,' Southall said.

'Denman's still in the frame, then?' Norman asked.

'We certainly can't rule him out yet. Where's Frosty? Is he okay?'

'Denman's mother told us they were at the movies on Saturday. Frosty's over at the cinema now, checking her story.'

'Do you think Denman could have killed Tilly?' she asked.

'I dunno. I'm probably barking up the wrong tree, but he has no alibi for yesterday and he's been off sick since the weekend. Now, he could simply be pretending to be ill because he's scared to tell his mother he's lost his job. But there could be a more sinister reason. Don't forget, he knows the horses and he knows his way around the stables.'

'You think he's lying low because of what he's done?'

'Maybe he's in shock. Or perhaps you're right and he's just hiding.'

'Does he have a motive for the two murders?' Southall asked.

'We won't find that out until we question him,' Norman said.

'Sorry to butt in,' said Morgan, 'but I finally managed to track down Joe Lyndall.'

'Who's he?' asked Norman.

'He's retired now, but he was Giles Rotherby's solicitor back when Tilly inherited the estate.'

'He was the guy handling the legal action?'

'That's the one. He didn't want to speak to me at first, but once I told him what we were investigating, he was a bit more willing to help. He says Giles came to him in a rage after the will was read because he had expected to inherit the estate but instead found he'd been written right out of it and left with nothing.'

'Lyndall prepared the case?' Southall asked.

'Yes, but by the time he got everything ready, Giles told him to forget it and didn't want to take it any further.'

'Does he know why Giles changed his mind?'

'He doesn't know for sure and nothing was ever stated in writing, but his understanding is that Tilly offered Giles a deal,' Morgan said.

'A deal?'

'As Lyndall understands it, Tilly also felt Giles had been treated badly and she agreed to let him share the farmhouse and run the estate.'

'I thought there was an estate manager running things back then?' Southall said.

'Lyndall believes the manager was relieved of his duties so Giles could take over.'

'Is he sure about that?' Southall asked.

'He wasn't the family solicitor so, no, he doesn't know for sure, but that's how he remembers it.'

'I suppose there was nothing to stop Tilly doing that if the will didn't stipulate that Giles had to stay away,' said Southall.

'It seems very generous, though, considering her brother was supposedly a pariah and lived up in London most of the time.'

'Maybe she felt guilty about him being kicked out of his flat when the old man died,' suggested Norman.

'Did Mr Lyndall know anything else?' asked Southall.

'He did come up with another bit of information that may be relevant. When he first started to prepare his case, he asked Giles if he knew any reason why his father may have chosen to write him out of the will. Giles admitted that he likes a bet. Apparently, while he was living in London, he ran up debts at two casinos, which his father had to clear.'

'That would be a damned good reason not to let him get his hands on the estate,' said Norman.

'And, subsequently, his father arranged for Giles to be banned from every casino in town for life,' Morgan said.

'Wow! The old man must have had a bit of clout if he could arrange that,' said Norman.

'It was probably a deal,' suggested Southall. 'I'll pay my son's debt, but only if you ban him.'

'Yeah, you could be right,' said Norman. 'I suppose that's one way to frustrate a compulsive gambler.'

Morgan pulled a face. 'Well, if that was the plan, it didn't frustrate him for long. According to Lyndall, Giles got over his frustration by turning his attention from casinos to the gee-gees and ran up some enormous debts with the sort of bookies it's probably best advised to steer well clear of.'

'Did Lyndall know who the bookies were?'

'Rotherby never actually named them, but Lyndall says his best guess is that it's the Crowther brothers in Bristol.'

'Do we know anything about them?' asked Norman.

'Zilch,' said Morgan. 'Do you want me to see what I can find out?'

'Yes, please. Call Bristol. Someone there must know all the bookies in their area,' said Southall.

Morgan made a note.

'I'd really like to speak to Giles Rotherby,' said Southall. 'If he had a deal that gave him what he wanted, why did he fall out with Tilly and move out four years ago?'

'Maybe he didn't fall out with Tilly,' said Norman. 'If he owes money to the wrong people, that would be a very good reason to drop off the radar.'

'You're right,' said Southall. 'And if he needs money to pay off his debts, it gives him an excellent motive for murder.'

'The more we talk about Giles Rotherby, the more I wonder if he's our killer,' said Norman.

'You agree we should give up on Griffiths being the killer?' asked Southall.

'As you said this morning, we know where Griffiths was when Tilly died because we have him on CCTV,' said Norman. 'But we have no idea where Giles was.'

'We have no idea where he is now, come to that,' said Morgan, gloomily.

'I said I'd been focusing on the wrong man,' said Southall.

'I'll say it again,' said Norman. 'We had to make him a priority, especially when he turned out to be such a fraud. We had no reason to suspect Tilly's brother.'

Southall sighed. 'Yes, I suppose you're right, but now, thanks to Catren, we've got plenty of reason.'

'So, now we have three suspects,' said Morgan. 'Giles Rotherby, Jimmy Denman and Mercedes Man.'

'There's nothing like narrowing it down, is there?' said Norman. He suddenly realised someone was missing. 'Where's Judy?'

'She wanted to go to the ATM,' said Southall. 'So, I suggested she collect some sandwiches on her way back. I think we could all do with a break for lunch.'

'Now that sounds like a plan,' said Norman.

# CHAPTER 24

'I've just spoken to a DS Gerry Rowley at Bristol,' Morgan told Norman. 'Apparently, he's already got his eye on the Crowther brothers. According to him they own a chain of betting shops, a casino in the centre of Bristol and a fair-sized online operation.'

'Are they legit?' asked Norman.

'DS Rowley says they are on the surface, but there have been questions about how they go about collecting their debts, and there have been a few questionable business acquisitions.'

'Questionable how?'

'The manner in which they were acquired. One day something will belong to them that wasn't even up for sale the day before.'

'But no one ever complains, right?' said Norman. 'It sounds to me like that's how they're collecting debts. Are there any unexplained deaths linked to them?'

'Rowley said they've had their suspicions about one or two people who've gone missing over the years, but there has never been enough evidence to pin anything on the brothers. The feeling is that they'd rather acquire a business than have a dead body on their hands.'

'That figures,' said Norman. 'Dead bodies can attract a lot of unwanted attention.'

'I did learn something that might be relevant to us, though. When Gerry Rowley was telling me about these questionable business acquisitions, he offered a few examples. Apparently, the brothers got their hands on some stud horses a few months ago.'

Norman's eyes widened. 'Really! Now there's a coincidence.'

'Just a bit,' said Morgan. 'I asked if they'd ever come across a guy called Giles Rotherby, who we believe may owe the brothers a sizeable amount, but Rowley said the name didn't ring any bells.'

'That would have been too much to hope for, wouldn't it?' said Norman.

'It wasn't all bad news, though. It turns out Gerry's on speaking terms with the brothers. I had to sweet-talk him a bit, but in the end he offered to find out where the Crowthers got their stud horses from.'

Norman smiled. 'And does "Gerry" think they'll tell him?'

'He says they will if it's legit. I also persuaded him to run Giles Rotherby through their system. It's a long shot, but I thought it was worth a go.'

'Well, that's great, though I'm not sure I want to know how you managed to sweet-talk "Gerry" into offering all that help.'

Morgan grinned. 'I put on my best sexy voice and agreed to go for a drink with him next time I'm in Bristol.'

'I was afraid it might be something like that.'

'I was fostering better cooperation between branches. You could call it international cooperation.'

'Yeah, right. I think you'll find working with branches in England isn't actually classed as international cooperation.'

'Well, perhaps it should be,' said Morgan. 'Anyway, I'm a big girl, Norm, and you're not my dad.'

'That's probably a good thing. I'm sure if I'd been your father, my hair would have turned grey years ago.'

'Trust me, Norm, you'd have been bald, never mind grey. Anyway, you don't have to worry. There's zero chance of me going over the bridge to Bristol for a date with some guy I've never even set eyes on, even if we are both in the police.'

'Okay, you win,' said Norman. 'Now, go and find the boss. I'm sure she'll love to hear what your friend Gerry told you.'

# CHAPTER 25

'We have some news on the mobile phone — the one that was taped to the back of that food manger in the stables,' said Southall. 'It appears that the calls and a text on it were sent from a single unregistered number.'

'Did they find out who owns it?' asked Winter.

'It's unregistered, but the text seemed to be meant for Tilly and it does have her fingerprints all over it.'

'Why would Tilly have a burner phone?' asked Winter.

'Now that,' said Norman, 'is a good question. If we can find out why, we might well have another motive for her murder.'

'What about the brother? Are we still interested in him?' asked Morgan.

'He's a strong possibility,' said Southall. 'But right now, we have no idea where he is.'

'And now, because of the burner phone, you're saying we might have another possibility?' asked Morgan.

'We can't ignore it,' said Norman. 'But at the moment we don't know who sent the message and called her. And unless they're foolish enough to switch their phone on, we can't know where they are.'

'If whoever owns it knows Tilly is dead, I suspect that particular phone will have been destroyed by now, so we're unlikely to get a location,' said Southall. 'However, we do know the text message was a threat, and we do know that Tilly was handling large sums of money.'

'Burner phones, threats and big money,' said Morgan. 'Are we saying she was money laundering and tried to cheat someone?'

'That's possible,' said Norman.

'What about sex?' suggested Winter. 'Or drugs?'

'My feeling is there's too much money involved for this to be sex, unless it's on a huge scale,' said Norman. 'I'm more inclined to think it's drugs.'

'I think we need to look at both drugs and money laundering,' said Southall. 'But we mustn't ignore Giles Rotherby, and don't forget Jimmy Denman could be involved in some way.'

Morgan's phone began to ring. She snatched it up and listened, nodding.

'That was Gerry Rowley from Bristol,' she said when she put the receiver down. 'He's spoken to the Crowther brothers about the stud horses. They claim they made a legal agreement, eighteen months ago, to take Tilly's stud horses as surety against what her brother owed. They say Giles and Tilly had twelve months to clear the debt, but never did, so for the last six months, the horses have belonged to the Crowthers.'

'And does Gerry think Tilly and her brother were coerced?' Or was it all legal?' Norman asked.

'He thinks it's unlikely the brothers had to stoop that low. They did have a reputation years ago, but no evidence that they used violence was ever found, and although they're not averse to pushing boundaries when they can get away with it, they've been squeaky clean for years.'

'I don't think they were ever in the frame for our murders anyway, were they?' said Southall. 'Their gripe was with Giles, not Tilly. Besides, if they had acquired the horses legitimately, and the beasts were already in their possession, what would they gain by killing her?'

# CHAPTER 26

The doors swung open and, like a character from a Western, a stranger strode in. Tall and swarthy, his head shaven, he was wearing a rather snappy suit, his open-necked shirt a brilliant white. Perched on the top of his head, a pair of aviator sunglasses completed the look.

Norman and Morgan were huddled over a desk at the back of the room, picking out sandwiches from a bag Lane had just brought in.

'He looks like a heavy,' muttered Morgan.

'If you ask me, he looks like a twat with those sunglasses perched on his head,' said Norman. 'Why do people wear the damned things when there's no sun? Is it supposed to ward off the rain?'

'It's supposed to look cool,' said Morgan.

'Not to me it doesn't.'

'Can I help you?' called Southall from her office doorway.

'DI Hayward,' the man announced. 'I'm looking for the boss.'

'That's me,' Southall said.

He looked Southall up and down, frowning.

'Is there a problem?' she asked.

'No, no. It's just that I was expecting someone a lot older.'

'I'm not sure if I should be flattered or insulted,' said Southall. 'Isn't being in charge about rank, not age? You're a DI yourself, and you're not exactly a pensioner, are you?'

'No, what I mean is, I was led to expect some old fart who's apparently made a career out of lodging complaints.'

'Arrogant bastard,' muttered Norman.

'If you mean Superintendent Bain, he made a complaint on our behalf. He did so because you are obstructing our murder investigation. If you think he makes a habit of complaining, I can call him down from his office and you can tell him yourself.' Southall stood with her arms folded.

Hayward smiled. 'Feisty and loyal. I like that in a girl.'

'Woman,' she said without returning his smile. 'I may be young for my rank, but I stopped being a girl some time ago.'

'Sorry, I didn't mean to offend you, but it's hard not to, it seems. Do you want to hear what I've got to say, or shall I leave now?'

'If you mean do I want you to explain why we can't arrest a murder suspect, then, yes, I do, but I'd prefer to hear it without being patronised,' Southall said.

'Can we go into your office?' Hayward said.

'I don't think that will be necessary. My team should understand what's going on.'

Hayward smirked. 'What? Four of you? You can hardly call that a team, can you?'

'Are you from Region by any chance?' Southall said.

'As a matter of fact, I am.'

'Then you're in no position to judge my team, DI Hayward. I think if you compare our success rates with those of the much larger teams at Region, you'll find we're equally effective, if not more so.'

Hayward's smile softened, became more friendly. 'To be honest, when describing the detectives over there, the words "hands," "own arse," "find" and "couldn't" spring to mind.'

Southall remained unsmiling. 'But not where you're concerned, naturally.'

'Oh, no, not me. I'm from the drug squad.'

'Yes, we guessed you might be.' She turned to the team. 'Okay, everyone, this is DI Hayward. He's from the regional drug squad. He's here to explain why we can't touch Mercedes Man.'

All eyes focused on Hayward.

'Mercedes Man?' Hayward asked. 'Who's he?'

'Explain, Norm,' said Southall.

'We had a house under surveillance yesterday and saw a black Mercedes enter and then a few minutes later come flying out again at speed. When we went to the house to investigate, we found the man we'd been watching dead. Naturally, we'd like to interview the driver of the Mercedes — Mercedes Man — as he's a prime suspect in the killing.'

Hayward was smiling again. 'I can assure you that "Mercedes Man" is not your killer.'

'How can you be so certain?' Southall said.

'Because Mercedes Man is me. Yes, I did drive the Mercedes to the house and, yes, I did come across the body, but the guy was already dead when I got there.'

'How come you knew to go to the stables?' Southall asked.

'Because there was no one at the house.'

'So, why flee the scene?' Norman said.

'Do you guys know anything about undercover work?'

'Not a great deal,' admitted Norman.

'But you do understand the risks people who go under-cover face?'

'Well, yeah, of course.'

'Okay. So, let me tell you what I can. I'm currently working undercover, and I've managed to infiltrate a gang run by a guy called Rocco Lombardo. It's taken me a year, but I'm now so deeply embedded they employ me as a gofer.'

'If you don't mind me saying, you look more like a heavy,' said Morgan.

Hayward grinned. 'If you don't mind me saying, you probably watch too many movies. I do understand what you mean though. I dress like this to blend in with the other guys.'

'Rocco Lombardo sounds like some old mafia godfather,' said Winter.

'That's more or less what he is,' said Hayward.

'And he deals drugs?' asked Norman.

'He's got his fingers in many pies. Drug dealing is just one of them.'

'So why were you at the farmhouse yesterday?' asked Norman.

'Because Tilly Rotherby isn't answering her phone,' Hayward said.

'I take it you're referring to the burner phone we found hidden in the stables?' Norman said.

'Ah! So you guys found it. That explains why it was missing then,' said Hayward.

'Tilly hasn't been answering because she's dead,' said Norman.

'Yes, you know that, and I know that, but the people I work for don't. And if I'd told them before going to the farmhouse, they might have started to wonder how I knew.'

'You came knowing she was dead?' Norman asked.

'You have to understand, these people are for real. They don't trust anyone, not even their own.'

'So they don't trust you, even though you work for them?'

'Exactly. It's how they've stayed in business for so long. In fact, they're so paranoid there's even a tracker on the car I drive. So, with that in mind, when I was told to come down here and find out what was going on, I couldn't risk not coming.'

'Are you saying Tilly had the burner phone because she was involved in drugs?' asked Morgan.

'No way. Rocco is Tilly's sugar daddy.'

'How old is this guy?' Norman said.'

'Sixty-six.'

'And you're saying he gives her money to have sex with him? Doesn't that make her a prostitute?' asked Winter.

'Rocco doesn't see it like that.'

'But that's how it is,' Winter said.

'It doesn't matter how it is,' said Hayward. 'The point is, Rocco wanted to know why Tilly wasn't answering her phone, and he sent me to find out.'

'For God's sake,' snapped Southall. 'Why didn't someone tell us this was going on in our patch? We've wasted days trying to find a motive for Tilly's death, and now you tell us she was being paid for sex by a bloody drug dealer!'

'This sort of stuff is mentioned on a need-to-know basis,' said Hayward.

'But when you knew Tilly was dead, surely you realised we had a need to know.'

'Yes, I get that, but you must understand why we don't want you buggering up our operation.'

'What about our bloody operation? What about the two murders on our patch?' Southall said.

'Trust me, they're nothing to do with Rocco.'

'Jeez, you sound as if you're actually on his side,' said Norman.

'Of course I'm not, but I can't have you guys blowing my cover for no good reason.'

'Isn't murder reason enough?' said Norman.

'In different circumstances I might agree with you, but after months of painstaking work, we're finally getting close to shutting down a major distribution ring.'

'Wait a minute,' said Norman. 'Was Tilly part of a money-laundering operation? Let me get this straight. Rocco was giving her lots of cash that she changed, keeping a share for herself.'

Hayward smiled. 'Something like that.'

'Did she get greedy?'

'I promise you, these guys don't bother murdering small fry like Tilly Rotherby.'

'Why not, if she owed them money?' asked Morgan.

Hayward raised an eyebrow. 'Because it wouldn't be worth the hassle for a measly five grand?'

'So, why were you sent down here?' Norman asked.

'As I said, to find out why Tilly hadn't paid in. She was usually very reliable, and all at once she missed a payment and wasn't answering her phone. We had to consider the possibility that you guys had arrested her. If that was the case she'd lose her contract.'

'Contract?'

'As far as Rocco is concerned, he has a business deal with her, and she's not the only one. There's a lot of money to launder and it has to be spread around in small lots.'

'So, if one of these women drops out, you guys don't actually lose much, and you can afford it anyway,' said Norman.

'Yeah, that's sort of how it works. And the good thing is it means we don't have to beat anyone up if they don't pay.'

'You almost manage to make it sound like an ethical business,' said Norman.

'Look, mate, you can sneer all you like, but if we don't shut Rocco down, we'll have drug dealers popping up all over the place.'

'I take it all your communications are done using burner phones,' Norman said.

'Like the one you said you found,' Hayward added.

'We've been waiting for another message so we can track where it's coming from,' Southall said.

'You realise that won't happen, don't you?' Hayward said. 'When they find out Tilly's dead, any burner phones connected to her will disappear.'

'Apart from the one we have,' Norman said.

'Yes, but I've already made sure you can't use that.'

'Because it will jeopardise your operation, right?' asked Norman.

Hayward smiled. 'Now you're starting to see how this works.'

'And you're sure Tilly wasn't dealing?'

Hayward shook his head. 'Trust me, Rocco doesn't allow it.'

Norman frowned. 'Is this all we're going to get?'

'I'm afraid so.' Hayward looked at his watch. 'I need to get going. I told them I was going to my uncle's funeral, but I mustn't stay away too long. I can't afford to push my luck.'

With a cheery wave of his hand, Hayward was gone.

'Are we sure we can trust him?' said Norman. 'He's a serving police officer so he's hardly going to admit he killed David Griffiths, is he? As far as I'm concerned, he's not in the clear unless Bill Bridger says the time of death doesn't fit.'

Just as Norman was speaking, the doors flew open.

'Did someone mention my name?' asked Bridger.

# CHAPTER 27

'I would put David Griffiths's time of death at between mid-day and one p.m.,' said Bridger, setting his case down on the front desk.

'That rules out Mercedes Man then,' said Southall.

'So, he was telling the truth,' said Morgan.

'I have to admit I would have liked it to be Hayward,' said Norman. 'But at least this eliminates one of our three suspects.'

'As I said at the scene,' Bridger continued, 'his death was due to multiple traumas to the head. We haven't found the murder weapon yet, but I can tell you we're looking for something metallic, probably a spade, or a shovel.'

'Were there any defensive wounds?' Norman asked.

'Nothing on his hands or arms.'

Norman nodded. 'Does that mean someone crept up behind him and hit him with a shovel?'

'I don't think it was quite like that,' Bridger said. 'There was a separate wound to his skull, which wasn't caused by the shovel. I compared the wound with the cut on Tilly Rotherby's head and there are similarities, which make me think the same object was used in both attacks.'

'Are you saying they were both struck with the same weapon?' Norman asked.

'Not exactly. I've spent a lot of time analysing Tilly's wound, but it was only yesterday, after seeing the wound on David Griffiths's head, that I finally understood what happened. You will recall me saying that Tilly's wound had been inflicted post-mortem, and you all know there was a horse in the stall where she was found. I now believe the horse kicked her. He would have been spooked when the body was dumped in the stable and—'

'Would have been prancing around all over the place,' said Morgan.

'Exactly. I believe that, in his panic, the poor thing got a bit too close to her head and his shoe caught it, cutting into the flesh.'

'And you think David Griffiths was hit with another horseshoe?' said Norman.

'There were plenty of old horseshoes lying around,' said Southall.

'And some of those ponies are cobs,' said Morgan. 'They have large feet, so some of those old horseshoes are pretty big.'

'That's right,' said Bridger. 'I believe someone threw one of those old shoes at Griffiths and caught just the right spot on his head to stun him. It may even have rendered him unconscious.'

'And once he was down, they attacked him with the shovel,' suggested Norman.

'That's my guess,' said Bridger.

'My witness told me Jimmy Denman threw something into the duck pond opposite the church,' said Norman.

'That would explain why we didn't find a murder weapon on site,' said Bridger.

'I'll see if I can get some divers to that pond,' said Norman. 'Maybe we'll find Griffiths's mobile phone in there too.'

'We need to find Jimmy Denman, urgently,' said Southall.

'I have a question,' said Morgan. 'If Tilly was unconscious when she was strangled, and she wasn't knocked out by the blow to her head, what did happen?'

'That was next on my list,' said Bridger. 'We finally got the toxicology report back and it shows there were traces of pentobarbital in her blood.'

'That's a barbiturate, isn't it?' asked Norman.

Bridger nodded. 'This particular barbiturate is used to euthanise horses, but in much smaller doses it's also used as a recreational drug.'

'So she wouldn't have needed a massive amount to knock her out?' asked Morgan.

'I'm guessing someone must have stabbed her with a hypodermic syringe. I do check for puncture marks as a matter of course when I do a post-mortem, but I have to admit I missed this one. However, once I knew she had been drugged, I looked again and finally found a tiny puncture mark on her thigh. It was in the centre of a bruise, which is why I didn't spot it first time around.'

'Could she have been on horseback when she was injected?' asked Southall.

'It would make her thigh an easy target,' said Bridger.

'And it would explain why we never found a separate murder scene,' said Norman. 'How long would it take to knock her out?'

'I've seen it used to kill a horse,' said Morgan. 'The poor thing keeled over in a matter of seconds.'

'She wouldn't have stayed conscious for long, even if it was intended to kill her and the perpetrator got the dose wrong. And if she did fall from a horse, she wouldn't have been able to put up much of a fight.'

'So, we think someone drugged Tilly but got the dose wrong,' said Southall. 'Then, realising she wasn't dead, they strangled her with a rein and strung her up.'

'That sounds about right,' said Bridger.

'Did Forensics find any of the drug on site?' asked Norman.

'We found the sort of everyday remedies you'd expect to find at a stable, but no pentobarbital,' said Bridger.

'The killer came prepared then,' said Norman.

'We need to check the local veterinary surgeries,' said Southall.

'I'll get on to it right away,' said Morgan.

'Are there any puncture marks on Griffiths's body?' asked Norman.

'I checked extra thoroughly,' said Bridger, 'and I didn't find any.'

'I wouldn't have expected you to,' said Southall. 'My feeling is that Griffiths's murder was quite different. Tilly's death was planned. The killer might have got the dose wrong, but the whole set-up was pretty elaborate. David Griffiths's murder seems to have been spontaneous — a sudden frenzied attack.'

'We still haven't identified all of the fingerprints we've found in the farmhouse and the tack room and around the stables,' said Bridger. 'We've eliminated Tilly Rotherby, David Griffiths and Carys Howells, but there are half a dozen other prints.'

'Don't forget Tilly used to teach disadvantaged kids to ride,' said Morgan.

'And Jimmy Denman used to work there, so his prints will be all over the place,' said Norman.

'Have you finished, Dr Bridger?' asked Southall.

'Yes, I think that's all I have for you.'

'Still no results from the DNA samples?'

'Apparently there's a backlog, but I've been told I should expect them tomorrow.'

'Tell them to see if there's a guy called Rocco Lombardo on the national database and to compare our sample against his.'

'Rocco who?' said Bridger. 'He sounds like some sort of godfather.'

'Something like that,' said Norman.

'You're joking, right?' said Bridger. 'Last I heard, the mafia weren't involved in this case.'

'Apparently Rocco was Tilly's sugar daddy.'

'Well, why wasn't I told?' snapped Bridger indignantly.

'Calm down,' said Southall. 'The reason you weren't told about Rocco is because we only learned about him less than an hour ago ourselves.'

'If you think he was with her before she died, I assume he is now your prime suspect,' Bridger said.

'According to our source, Rocco wasn't aware Tilly was dead, and he doesn't go around murdering people.'

'Do you believe this "source"?' Bridger said.

'We're keeping our minds open,' said Southall.

'There's an element of doubt because this guy is under-cover, so he has good reason to want to keep away from Rocco,' added Norman.

'On the other hand, if Rocco Lombardo has been around for years without ever having been arrested, he's obviously very careful,' said Southall.

'Murdering Tilly and then sending someone down a couple of days later to check doesn't sound like the actions of a careful man to me. Although it could be an elaborate double bluff, I suppose,' said Bridger.

'I can't see it,' said Southall. 'Why would he risk it?'

Bridger looked at his watch. 'Well, I can't stand around here all day. I've got a body to dissect.'

He picked up his case and stormed from the room.

'Looks like we pissed him off good and proper,' said Norman.

'Does he really think we were keeping Rocco's existence from him?' asked Morgan.

'He'll be fine,' said Southall. 'He'll have calmed down by the time he's back at his lab, then he'll realise he overre-acted. He's just annoyed we know something he doesn't.'

# CHAPTER 28

Following Bill Bridger's departure, the office was a scene of quiet industry. At five p.m., Lane called Norman over to her desk.

'Now we know Tilly was definitely involved in money laundering, I've taken another look at her bank account. Only this time I've gone back a bit further and filtered out the large cash payments.'

'And did you miss anything from the rest?' asked Norman.

'It's not so much what I missed as what isn't there.'

Norman sat down. 'Okay, Judy, you have my full attention.'

'Tilly owned six cottages with tenants paying a monthly rent. From our earlier enquiries, we know the names of five of the tenants, so, going back over the last three years, I can identify who is making the payments. It was easy to find those made by the tenants at numbers two, three, four and five.'

'And one and six?'

'I've only gone back five years but, as far as I can make out, no one has paid rent for number six in the last four years, which is the time she was raking in money from her sugar daddy.'

'And you think this is suspicious?' Norman said.

'Don't you?'

'If no one lives there, it would explain why no one ever answers the door,' said Norman.

'I admit it looks like no one lives there on paper, but when we tried that house and got no answer, I looked through the windows. There wasn't anything special inside, but I didn't think it looked like a house that had been empty for several years.'

'Perhaps the new owners tidied it up,' Norman said.

'Hmm, yes, perhaps,' said Lane.

'You're not convinced?' asked Norman.

'I think there's something funny about the set-up in both end cottages.'

'Go on,' encouraged Norman. 'I'm listening.'

'I'm guessing the end houses would cost more than the mid-terrace ones because they have one more bedroom, and the gardens are much bigger.'

'That figures.'

'Right. Well, there's another, slightly higher, monthly payment that stopped just over two years ago. I don't recognise the name, so I'm guessing it must have been paid by the tenant in number one before Ffion Howells moved in. And, sure enough, Ffion paid in the exact same amount in January and February 2021.'

'I don't see the problem,' said Norman.

'That is the problem. Since then, Ffion has never made another payment.'

'You mean Ffion owes two years' rent? I can't believe Tilly would allow that. According to Ffion, they didn't get on because of something that happened years ago.'

'You did say you thought she was being a little economical with the truth when she told you about that. Perhaps the real reason they didn't get on was because she owed Tilly money.'

'Now that's an idea,' said Norman. 'And, if Tilly was hassling her for the money she owed, that could give Ffion a motive for murder.'

'Or is it possible she was living there rent-free for a reason?' asked Lane.

'How come? You think she was blackmailing Tilly?'

'What if Ffion knew about the money laundering?' Lane said.

'That could explain why she had such a low opinion of Tilly. We thought at the time that we'd need to speak to her again. This has given us something to get our teeth into,' Norman said.

'Do you want me to carry on with this line of enquiry?' Lane asked.

'What have you got in mind?'

'I was thinking I might try to speak to the new owners about the cottages, but I don't want to go off on a tangent if you think it'll be a waste of time.'

'Let's run it by the boss and see what she says.' Norman's mobile phone was ringing. 'Yo, this is Norm.'

'It's Frosty. Unless Jimmy Denman has the power of invisibility, he wasn't at the cinema with his mother. There is a James Bond film on, and CCTV confirms Mrs Denman was there just as she said, but the person with her wasn't Jimmy. It was another woman of about the same age. I'm guessing they're friends.'

'I was right. She is scared, and she was covering for him.'

'It looks that way,' said Winter.

'Where are you now?'

'I'm on my way to the station. There's a train due in about ten minutes.'

'What time does the train get to Llangwelli?' Norman asked.

'I should be there in about thirty minutes.'

'Okay, I'll pick you up,' said Norman. 'I need to bring you up to speed with what's happened this afternoon.'

'What have I missed?' asked Winter.

'It's a long story, but we now know Mercedes Man isn't one of our murder suspects. I'll fill you in on the details later.'

# CHAPTER 29

'Are you making any progress with the veterinary angle, Catren?' asked Southall.

'I was just coming to see you about that,' said Morgan. 'There are three veterinary surgeries within a few miles of the estate. One of those only deals with small animals, so I ruled them out, but the remaining two deal with farm livestock. I thought they would be more likely to use what we're looking for, so I went to see them.

'They both keep pentobarbital on site, but while every-day drugs are kept in a normal refrigerator, heavy-duty drugs like that are kept in locked refrigerators. When I asked if I could check their stock, they produced detailed records showing every drug they have on site — when it was last used, who used it, and so on. Nothing is obviously missing from either of them.'

'The problem is that the drug doesn't have to come from a local vet,' said Norman. 'It could easily have been stolen from any surgery in the UK, and then sold online through the dark web.'

'That's exactly what I was thinking,' said Southall. 'But Catren said "nothing is obviously missing".' She smiled at Morgan. 'Come on then, let's hear it.'

'The second surgery I visited has three vets on site, and one senior vet called Hywell Davies who does all the farm visits. He's the one who'd come out if I had a sick horse needing treatment. When I was checking the drug store, the young vet showing me how the system works told me Mr Davies always carries a syringe loaded with pentobarbital in a small, locked refrigerator in his Land Rover for emergencies.'

Southall frowned. 'So?'

'Apparently, Mr Davies is getting on a bit and can be a bit lax when it comes to paperwork and the safekeeping of drugs. He's supposed to return the syringe to the main store every night, but he has been known to keep the same syringe in his vehicle for a week or more. If he's challenged about it, he always argues that if he gets called out in the night it's better to have it with him and not have to waste time coming to the surgery to get it.'

'Typical. These old guys act like they're still back in the past,' said Norman. 'Does he ever record anything in that drugs logbook?'

'He never used to, but someone from DEFRA came around and raised merry hell about the way they kept their records. After that, one of the younger vets now holds the key to the drugs safe. No one can take out any drug without the key, and the key holder always insists the logbook must be filled in correctly.'

'So, Davies can't just help himself whenever he feels like it,' said Southall. 'Thank goodness for that.'

'Even so, their system is not infallible,' said Morgan. 'I'm told Davies once destroyed a horse and forgot to tell anyone back at the surgery. It was only when the owner phoned to ask why she hadn't been sent a bill that they realised what he'd done.'

'And he hadn't asked for a replacement syringe?' Norman asked.

'Apparently not.'

'Jeez!' said Norman. 'How can they allow someone like that to handle dangerous drugs?'

'Are you saying they don't actually know if he still has an emergency syringe?' asked Southall.

'According to the drugs logbook, he signed for a replacement emergency syringe two weeks ago because he'd used the one he had to destroy a lame horse. But there's no record of him returning this one every night, nor of him using it, or replacing it.'

'Just hearing this is scaring the crap out of me,' said Norman. 'They need to do something about him. Can't they get rid of him, or at least stop him having access to drugs?'

'They would love to stop him but it's his practice and he's their employer, so there's not much the staff can do.'

'Did you check to see if the syringe was in the Land Rover?' asked Southall.

'He was out doing farm visits. I tried to call his mobile, but some of these farms are so remote there's no signal. I was going to wait, but they told me he often stays for dinner at the more remote farms, so there's no telling what time he'll get back.'

'We need to find out if he's got that syringe,' said Southall.

'His routine is to be on site by seven every morning, and to be on the road by eight. I'm happy to be there in the morning to greet him. Fancy an early start, Norm?'

'Is that okay?' Norman asked Southall.

'Yes, of course.'

'Right. I'd better get going,' said Norman. 'I have to collect Frosty from the railway station. Is there anything else for us to do tonight?'

'I don't think so. I suggest we call it a day, so we can all get some rest,' said Southall.

# CHAPTER 30

Norman had just picked Winter up from the railway station when he received a call from an unknown number.

'Is that Detective Sergeant Norman?'

'Speaking.'

'This is Megan Denman. When you left my house this morning you said I should call this number if I needed to speak to someone.'

'That's right. What can I do for you, Megan?'

'It's about my son, Jimmy. He's gone missing.'

'Gone missing? When?'

'He went off to work this morning like I told you, and he's not come home. I've tried calling his mobile but it goes straight to voicemail. I called the garage, and they told me he doesn't work there anymore, they'd let him go.'

'Ah, yeah. I wondered if you knew about that.'

'You mean you knew? Why didn't you tell me?'

'We only found out after we left you this morning and went looking for Jimmy.'

'You could have let me know.'

'I'm sorry, Megan, but I think it should be Jimmy who tells his mother what he's doing, don't you?'

'But I don't understand what's going on. I've tried all his friends and no one seems to have seen him. Where is he, Mr Norman? He's never done anything like this before.'

'How about if I come over to your house and help you figure out where he's gone. Will that do?'

'If you wouldn't mind. I'm worried sick.'

'You hang on in there, Megan. I'll be with you as quick as I can.'

Norman ended the call.

'You look worried,' said Winter. 'Anything I can do to help?'

'That was Megan Denman. Her son Jimmy has gone missing.'

'That doesn't sound like the actions of an innocent man, does it?' said Winter. 'Do you think we rattled his cage by turning up at his house this morning?'

'I don't think this is our doing. He wasn't there this morning, and his mother says she hasn't seen or spoken to him, so how could he know we were asking after him?'

'Good point,' said Winter. 'Unless he was nearby and saw us.'

'No, I don't think it's that. I reckon he knows what happened to David Griffiths. It could be he saw something, or maybe he's involved in the murder in some way. Don't forget we have a witness who says he threw something in that duck pond.'

'You mean you think he planned this and he's on the run?'

'I think it's more likely he's scared shitless, and he's run away because he doesn't know what else to do. I just hope he doesn't go and do something stupid.'

'You think he will?' Winter said.

'We're not talking about a hardened criminal here. Jimmy's just a naive kid. If I'm right, and he is involved, maybe he's just realised how much trouble he's in.' Norman started the car. 'I'll drop you off on the way.'

'There's no need to do that,' said Winter. 'I was with you this morning, and I'd like to come with you. I have no plans for tonight, so why not make myself useful? If you don't mind, of course?'

Norman put the car into gear and pulled away. 'Are you kidding? Of course, I don't mind.'

* * *

As Norman had predicted, it began to rain as soon as they left the station, and by the time they reached the village of Nef Anfon it was raining so hard the drains were struggling to cope, making it difficult to negotiate what was now a partially flooded lane.

'I could easily fall in love with this country if didn't rain so much,' said Norman, peering through the windscreen. 'And don't tell me it's the price we pay for everything being so green.'

Winter smiled. 'If you don't mind me asking, why did you come here?'

'Because, for once in my life, Lady Luck was smiling on me. I had reached a point where I felt my life was going nowhere, and I needed a change. Then, out of the blue, a guy I worked with years ago offered me the opportunity to make a new start.'

'It wasn't a hankering for the green valleys and torrential rain, then?' Winter said with a grin.

'To tell you the truth, I'd never even been here for a holiday, so I had no idea what Wales was going to be like. All I can tell you is when I crossed the bridge from England, I felt like I'd come home. It was as if I'd been reborn.'

'You don't fancy a return to city life, then?'

'I left London a long time ago and I wouldn't go back, even if you paid me.'

'Really?'

'I guess you're another one like Catren who can't wait to get away, right?'

'I haven't really given it that much thought,' said Winter. 'But I imagine things would be a bit more exciting in a city.'

'I suppose it is, if you enjoy playing sardines at a hundred miles an hour.'

'Is that Detective Sergeant Cynical speaking?'

Norman smiled. 'Yeah, you're probably right about that. Perhaps it's my age, but I'll be quite happy never to set foot in another city.'

They were outside Megan Denman's house by now. Before Norman even drew to a halt, her front door was thrown open. They could see her waiting just inside.

'She's going to be scared, stressed, and possibly even abusive, so we need to play it gently and cut her a bit of slack,' said Norman as he opened the car door.

'Right. Softly, softly. Got it,' said Winter.

The rain seemed to be on their side for a minute or two and, much to Norman's surprise, they managed to make it to the house without getting completely soaked.

'How are you doing, Megan?' asked Norman, once they were inside.

'I don't know. I don't seem to be able to think straight. I've never had to deal with anything like this before.'

They were in a big open-plan kitchen-diner. Norman indicated the dining table. 'How about we sit down while Winter makes us all a cup of tea?'

Obediently, Winter filled the kettle and began searching the cupboards for mugs and teabags.

'Jimmy's never done anything like this before,' Megan said, lowering herself heavily onto a chair. 'I can't understand what's happening. Why has he got his phone switched off? He never does that.'

'Has he fallen out with any of his friends? Is he in trouble with anyone?'

'Of course he's not in any trouble.'

'Okay, can you think of anyone he knows who might be a bad influence? Maybe someone has got him involved in something he shouldn't.'

198

'The only bad influence is that Carys who works at the stables.'

'Carys Howells?' Norman said in surprise.

'I don't know what her surname is, I just know she works at the stables.'

'Why do you say she's a bad influence?'

'She's turned his head, that's what she's done. He used to be a hard worker until he met her. Now she's all he thinks about. He walks around with his head in the clouds most of the time.'

'Is she his girlfriend?' Norman asked.

'Girlfriend? Huh! He thinks she is, but I know her type. She's just using him.'

'Using him for what?' Norman said.

'I don't know, but she's definitely got him under a spell.'

This sounded to Norman like it was Megan's pet project. He attempted to steer the conversation elsewhere. 'Do you think Jimmy might be avoiding you for any reason?'

'Avoiding me? Why would he want to do that?'

'Well, if it was me, I wouldn't be looking forward to telling my mum I'd lost my job.'

'Well, yes, he knows I'll be angry about that, but he wouldn't run away over it. He knows I never stay angry with him for long. Like any teenager he's not perfect, but he's a good boy.'

Norman sighed. He had been hoping Jimmy's disappearance might have persuaded her to tell the truth. 'When we spoke earlier today, you told us Jimmy was with you at the cinema on Saturday evening.'

'Yes, that's right, but what's that got to do with anything?'

'It's not true, is it?'

'Of course it is. Jimmy loves James Bond.'

'Yeah, Jimmy might well love James Bond,' said Norman, 'but we checked with the cinema. We know you were there with your friend, but Jimmy wasn't with you.'

Megan opened her mouth, but Norman cut her off.

'Don't try to deny it, Megan. They have CCTV at the cinema.'

Winter placed three mugs of tea on the table and pulled up a chair. 'Sorry, Mrs Denman,' he said. 'But I went to the cinema earlier and checked the CCTV. Jimmy wasn't there watching James Bond or anyone else.'

Megan's face turned red.

'Look, I understand he's your son, and I get that you want to protect him,' said Norman. 'But we believe he may have got himself into some serious trouble, and that's why he's missing.'

'Trouble? What sort of trouble? Surely you can't think he had anything to do with that Rotherby woman's death?'

'Right now, we're more concerned about Jimmy's possible involvement in the death of her husband, David Griffiths.'

'That's ridiculous. Jimmy's just a kid. He wouldn't kill anyone. He won't even tread on an ant if he can help it.'

'Well, I hate to tell you this, Megan, but I have a witness who saw Jimmy riding away from the scene shortly after Griffiths was killed. The witness also told me Jimmy threw something in the duck pond as he passed.'

'Threw what?'

'We won't know that until the divers have finished dredging the pond.'

'I'm sure you've got this all wrong,' said Megan. 'I know he's up to something, but I can't believe it's murder.'

'I really hope I am wrong,' said Norman. 'But I'm afraid the evidence against Jimmy is growing, and he can't tell us what really happened unless we find him.'

'I can't deny he's been behaving strangely these past few days. I did wonder if perhaps he was on drugs. It seems half his mates are. There was a rumour doing the rounds that the Rotherby woman was supplying, but when I asked Jimmy about it, he said it was rubbish, she was far too posh — as if that makes any difference.'

'Have you ever seen him with any drugs?'

'Never. I even searched his room, but I didn't find anything. Though if he has any, he's not going to leave them where I can find them, is he?'

'Can we take a look in his room?' asked Norman.

'I suppose so. If you think it will help.'

'Maybe we'll see something that will give us a clue to where he might be.'

'I'll show you which room it is.'

Megan led them upstairs and opened a door. 'I'll leave you to it, then. I'll be down in the kitchen.'

Norman and Winter slipped on latex gloves and began poking around.

'What did you make of what she said about Carys Howells?' asked Winter, getting down on his knees and peering under the bed.

'Megan's a single mum, right? That means her Jimmy is likely to be a bit of a mummy's boy. Naturally, she's going to dislike any girl Jimmy takes a shine to,' Norman said.

'It did sound a bit like a broken record, didn't it?'

'The way I see it, Jimmy's an impressionable eighteen-year-old asked to show this cute kid the ropes. Of course his head is in the clouds. I'm sure mine would be if I was his age and I found myself working with someone as cute and self-assured as Carys.'

'I see what you mean,' said Winter, sitting back on his heels. Apart from a lot of dust and a well-used pair of slippers he had found nothing under the bed. He got to his feet and turned his attention to the wardrobe.

'Norm,' he called.

'I've found nothing in any of the drawers,' Norman was saying.

'Norm. Look.' Winter pointed at the top of the wardrobe. 'Is that what I think it is?'

'It certainly looks like it,' said Norman. 'If it is hers, it'll have M R embroidered on the inside lining.'

Winter lifted the top hat down from the wardrobe and looked inside. 'M R.'

'Crap,' said Norman.

'Isn't this the sort of thing we were hoping to find?' Winter asked.

'Yeah, of course,' said Norman. 'But I was really hoping we weren't going to find anything incriminating. I guess I feel a bit sorry for his mother. She's really struggling to get her head around all this, and I can only see it getting worse.'

'What do you want to do with the hat?' Winter asked.

'We'll have to take it away, but first we'd better ask Megan if she knows anything about it.'

They trooped back down the stairs, Winter carrying the top hat as if it were the crown jewels.

'Can you tell us where Jimmy got this top hat?' asked Norman.

'I've never seen it before,' said Megan.

'Are you sure? Only it was on top of Jimmy's wardrobe.'

'Well, it wasn't there a couple of days ago. I don't know where he got it from. Does it matter?'

'This top hat is identical to one that has gone missing from the tack room at the Rotherby stables.'

'Are you suggesting he stole it? What would he want a top hat for?'

'I was hoping you might be able to tell us that,' said Norman.

'Just because he has something, it doesn't mean he stole it.'

'It has the initials M R, for Matilda Rotherby, embroidered in the lining. It's Tilly's top hat.'

'So? He used to work for her. She could have given it to him, couldn't she?'

'You're forgetting Tilly Rotherby is dead. It went missing after she died, on the same day David Griffiths was killed.'

Megan seemed to sag, and Norman was sure she was going to burst into tears, when the house telephone began to ring. She rushed to answer it.

'Hallo?'

She turned her back on them and listened for a moment, then she put her hand over the mouthpiece and glanced back.

'It's Jimmy,' she hissed.

'Find out where he is,' said Norman. 'It doesn't matter where — we can take you to him.'

There followed a frustrating couple of minutes as Norman tried to keep up with the conversation. He could just about make out Megan's side of it, and the odd comment she relayed to them, but he could only guess at what Jimmy was saying.

'Jimmy says he's sorry,' she called over her shoulder.

'Sorry for what?' asked Norman, but Megan had turned her back once more.

'He says he didn't know this was going to happen.'

Norman turned to Winter and whispered, 'Do you think he's talking about the murder?'

Winter shrugged. 'I guess he must be, but which one? Or is it both?'

'He says it was supposed to be a laugh.' Megan turned to face them. 'He would never have got involved if he'd known what— Bugger! He's hung up!' She glared at the two detectives. 'This is all your fault.'

'I understand you need someone to blame,' said Norman, 'but turning on us isn't going to help Jimmy, is it? Did he say where he is?'

'He said he was heading for the old lighthouse near Llangwelli harbour.'

Norman's insides ran cold. There had been a suicide from the beach at Llangwelli not so long ago that had been a hot topic of conversation in the local chat rooms. Built on a rocky outcrop, the old lighthouse wasn't the tallest around, but more than one sick person had suggested it was high enough, and the landing would be hard enough, for a prospective suicide to end their life there.

'Did he say why he was going to the lighthouse?' he asked.

'No, he didn't, but I can only think of one reason for going there at this time of night. It's not as if you can enjoy the view when it's dark.'

'Did he sound okay?'

Norman had been impressed with the way Megan had managed to keep it together so far, but now the enormity of the situation seemed to overwhelm her and she began to crumple. Tears spilled from her eyes.

'No,' she said. 'He sounded frightened, and sort of desperate.'

'How desperate? I mean—'

Megan turned glassy eyes on him. 'If you mean enough to do something silly, then, yes, I think he might.'

'Then, what are we waiting for?' Norman said. 'Let's get down there.'

# CHAPTER 31

Norman started the car and activated the blue lights and siren.

'Hang on tight,' he said as the car shot forward. 'Frosty, call DI Southall and tell her what's going on.'

Winter made the call. 'She's organising support, and then she'll be on her way.'

As he ended the call and glanced out of the window, Winter was surprised to find how far they had already travelled, and, as the journey unfolded, he grew increasingly impressed with Norman's driving skill. Despite the speed and the narrow lanes and tight bends, not once did he feel unsafe. Who'd have thought an old geezer like Norm could handle a car like a rally driver?

'There are two torches in the boot,' Norman told Winter as he brought the car to a halt. 'You grab the heavy-duty one and I'll have the small one.'

Winter raced around to the back of the car.

'What do you want me to do?' asked Megan.

'Honestly? I'd like you to stay here,' said Norman. 'But I understand no mother's going to do that when her son's in danger. Our first priority is to keep Jimmy safe. That's all that matters right now. Just be careful, trust me and DC Winter to do our job, and try not to endanger yourself.'

Fortunately, the rain had stopped, but there was still plenty of cloud cover. As they jogged towards the lighthouse, just enough dim moonlight filtered through the gloom to enable them to see their way.

No longer functioning, the lighthouse had been turned into a tourist attraction. There was a now a viewing platform in place of the old beacon, which provided a spectacular view out to sea and across the estuary to the distant hills. The viewing platform was reached via a spiral staircase on the inside, but there was also a vertical fire-escape ladder attached to the outside.

As they neared the foot of the lighthouse, Winter stopped and aimed his torch beam at the fire escape.

'Is that Jimmy climbing up there?' asked Norman.

Winter followed his pointing finger. Sure enough, a tiny figure could be seen nearing the top of the ladder.

'Is that my Jimmy?' panted Megan, coming up behind them.

'I think so,' said Norman.

Megan looked at the fencing around the lighthouse. 'How are we going to get to the ladder?'

'Not "we", Megan,' said Norman. 'I can't allow you to go near that ladder. You must stay back here.'

'But that's my boy up there!'

'Trust me, Megan, and do as I say. I'm not going up there to arrest Jimmy, I'm going to persuade him to come down. Whatever he's done doesn't matter for now. Believe me, I just want him to be safe. The thing is, when he gets back down here, he's going to need his mum. That's why I need you to stay safe. Do you understand?'

'Yes. Of course. But how are you going to get in?'

'What's the plan, Norm?' asked Winter. 'Are we going to wait for back-up?'

Norman took Winter aside and lowered his voice. 'We don't know how desperate Jimmy is, so I don't think we can wait.'

'What are you suggesting? Do you want me to go up there?'

'Of course I'm not asking you. I'm going.'

'No offence, Norm, but I'm a lot younger than you and, without wishing to be rude, you're not exactly in peak physical condition.'

'You're right on both counts, Frosty, but how many suicides have you talked down? I've dealt with situations like this before and, believe me, experience really helps.'

'So, what do I do?'

'You stay down here, shine that big torch on the ladder so I can see what I'm doing, and make sure Megan stays well back.'

Taking the smaller torch, Norman made his way around to the far side of the safety fence. Just as he had suspected, someone had cut a hole in the fence, which luckily looked big enough for him to squeeze through. He cursed as he snagged his jacket, but that was his only mishap and within minutes, he was standing at the bottom of the fire-escape ladder looking up.

As soon as Winter saw the familiar figure of his colleague reach the foot of the ladder, he shone his torch at it. Norman took a breath. Ladders had never been his favourite thing and what had, from a distance, appeared to be a relatively short climb suddenly took on the aspect of a mini-Everest.

'Holy crap,' he muttered to himself. 'Why the hell am I doing this? Okay, Norm, I'm doing it because there's a kid up there with a mother waiting below, and both need my help. And standing here like a dummy isn't helping either of them. And what about Faye? What would she think if she could see you now? Come on, Norm. You can do this!'

Taking a firm grip of the ladder, Norman began to climb. In the distance he could hear the faint sound of approaching sirens.

Megan pointed at Norman as he began his slow ascent.

'What does he think he's doing?' she asked Winter.

'He's going to try and reason with Jimmy.'

'He's taking his time.'

'We can't all be mountain goats.'

'Well, he needs to get a move on. Jimmy's in danger.'

'I appreciate you're under a lot of stress right now, Mrs Denman, but if you don't mind me saying, I think you're being very ungrateful.'

'Of course I'm stressed. How do you expect me to be? My Jimmy's just climbed to the top of that lighthouse and could be about to end his life.'

'I'd expect a little gratitude from you because there's a man up there risking his neck for your son, who he doesn't even know, and all you can do is complain that he isn't going fast enough.'

'Well, he isn't. Why doesn't he go faster?'

Winter counted to ten. 'I'm guessing it's because he's getting on a bit, he doesn't like heights and he's scared shitless.'

'Why is he doing it, then? You're young, why didn't you go?'

'I offered, but he's my boss, and he's looking out for me. He feels if anyone is going to risk their life it should be him, and not me.'

'This is no time for playing at being a bloody hero. My Jimmy could get hurt.'

'For God's sake, open your eyes, Mrs Denman. Can't you see? He isn't playing at being a bloody hero. He is one!'

Winter had raised his voice to almost a shout. In the sudden silence that followed his outburst, they could hear the sirens, which were now much closer. However, Megan Denman couldn't stay quiet for long.

'That's not being a hero. It's what he gets paid for, isn't it?'

'I suppose he would need to wear his underpants on the outside of his trousers for someone like you to be convinced, wouldn't he?'

'Well, you've got to admit, he's not exactly James Bond.'

'No, he isn't. James Bond is a fictional character, whereas that man up there is a flesh-and-blood hero.'

Norman was nearing the top of the ladder as the first emergency vehicles began to arrive. First on the scene was Sarah Southall, followed shortly by the fire service, an ambulance and several patrol cars. Southall briefly explained the situation, before heading for the source of the torch beam illuminating the ladder.

'Where's Norm?' she asked Winter.

He pointed. 'You see that backside near the top?'

'He's up there? What's he doing climbing that thing? He hates ladders.'

'He's trying t—'

'If my Jimmy jumps, there's going to be trouble,' shouted Megan from behind them. 'This is all your fault. If your lot hadn't come calling—'

Southall took a step towards her.

'Stop right there, Mrs Denman,' she growled. 'Before you start blaming us, you should ask yourself why we wanted to speak to Jimmy in the first place. Then you might wonder why Jimmy was running away when he didn't even know we were looking for him. I appreciate you're his mother, but don't you think that's rather suspicious?'

'My Jimmy never murdered anyone.'

'I don't recall saying he did murder someone. The thing is, we're the police and it's our job to investigate suspicious behaviour, especially when it follows a murder.'

'You've got no right speaking to me like that—'

'And another thing,' snapped Southall. 'We've got half the bloody rescue services for miles around making their way here to try and help your son and right now, one of my officers is risking his life to try and help him. So, how about you show a little appreciation instead of complaining all the time?'

She called to one of the uniformed PCs. 'Constable, can you make sure Mrs Denman gets seen by a paramedic? She seems to be in shock.'

The PC led a surprisingly compliant Megan Denman towards the waiting ambulances.

'I'm sorry, Frosty. You shouldn't have heard me speaking to a member of the public like that,' said Southall.

'Who? Me?' said Winter. 'I didn't hear a thing, though you should know I think she got what she deserved. She's been like that ever since we got here.'

Southall pointed to the lighthouse. 'So, what exactly is going on up there?'

'Jimmy's up there and Norm's gone after him to try and talk him down.'

'Is Jimmy going to jump?'

'He hasn't said as much, but his mum seems to think he might.'

'And Norm didn't think to wait for help?'

'He thought it would take too long and Jimmy might jump before they got here.'

There was a sudden flurry of activity as several fire officers arrived on the scene and began inflating huge mattresses to place all around the base of the lighthouse. Behind them, a fire engine was being manoeuvred towards the lighthouse so they could raise a turntable ladder up to the viewing platform. A huge floodlight suddenly burst into life and lit up the top of the ladder in a brilliant glare.

'I guess that makes my torch a bit obsolete,' said Winter, switching it off.

'Who is that?' asked one of the fire crew, pointing at Norman. 'Is that the guy threatening to jump?'

'No. That's my sergeant,' said Southall.

'Is he stuck?'

'I suspect he may well be,' said Southall. 'He doesn't normally do ladders.'

'Bloody fool. What did he go up there for?'

'He's trying to rescue the boy who is threatening to jump,' said Southall.

'That's our job. It's why we're here.'

'Yes, we know that, but you weren't here twenty minutes ago when the boy climbed the ladder, were you? He may well be a fool in your eyes, but DS Norman is not the sort of man to stand back and watch an eighteen-year-old throw himself from the top of a lighthouse without trying to help.'

'But he's not helping, is he?'

'We don't know that, do we?' said Southall. 'Maybe if he'd stood back and watched, as you seem to be suggesting he should have, you'd be scraping up bits of the boy's body and wouldn't need to set up all that equipment. Would you have preferred that?'

'Well, no, of course not.'

'Well, there we are then,' said Southall, turning back to watch Norman's progress.

\* \* \*

Up at the top of the ladder, Norman was now at eye level with the viewing platform. In the harsh light of the fire-service spotlight, his knuckles were white. He seemed to have lost the ability to move, or even turn his head, so his knuckles were all he could see. He was sweating profusely, partly because of the exertion, but mostly due to the paralysing fear that now gripped him.

'Jimmy,' he called, his voice shaky. 'My name's Norm. I know you're up here, so how about you come over and speak to me?'

There was a sound from the viewing platform, just to the left of Norman's head.

'I'm right here,' said a voice.

'Jeez, Jimmy, you could have warned me you were that close. You scared the crap out of me.'

'Come on, you looked terrified all the way up. I was watching you. Man, you are so slow.'

'Yeah, well, in case you hadn't worked it out, ladders aren't really my thing.'

'So why did you come up here if it makes you so scared?'

'Because your mother's down there and she's worried sick about you.'

'She's here?'

211

'Yes, she is, and she's terrified you're about to jump.'

'Yeah, well . . . I'm thinking about it.'

'Why would you want to do a thing like that? With all those rocks down there, it can't end well,' Norman said, still unable to move.

'That's what I'm hoping,' said Jimmy.

'There's no guarantee you'll be killed. And anyway, don't you think that's a coward's way out?'

'Who are you calling a coward? You're the one who's clinging to that ladder shitting himself.'

'Yes, Jimmy, I am scared, but I still climbed up here to try and help you, right?'

'I don't get what you're saying.'

'What I'm saying is I have a responsibility to try and help you, so, even though I'm terrified, I came up here anyway. Does that make me a coward?'

'So I'm supposed to think you're some sort of hero, then, am I?'

'I'm not suggesting that.'

'Good. Because I think it makes you an idiot.'

Despite the situation, Norman couldn't help his lips curving in the ghost of a smile.

'Yeah, I guess that's another way of looking at it. On the other hand, the way I see it I accepted the responsibility that goes with my job, which is to try to protect members of the public from harm. So here I am, whatever might happen as a result.'

'But whatever happens, you won't end up in prison, will you?' Jimmy said.

'No, that's true. I haven't done anything that would get me sent to prison. But, even if I had, I'd like to think I'm big enough to accept responsibility for it,' said Norman. 'And I'd much prefer prison to being dead.'

'But why risk your life for me? You don't even know me.'

'I just told you, it's part of my job, and I know your mother loves you. She won't want anything to happen to you.'

'She won't love me when she finds out what I've done.'

'Are you sure of that? What have you done anyway? Why do you think you're going to end up in prison?'

'I didn't kill that guy by the stables. I found him lying there, and I panicked.'

'Well, you won't get put in prison for finding him.'

'But I took his phone.'

'Why did you do that?'

'Like I said, I panicked. I wasn't thinking right. It was just there, next to him, so I picked it up. I thought I could use it.'

'Did you know the guy?'

'Yeah. He was a shit.'

Norman decided that if he was going to persuade Jimmy not to jump, focusing on the magnitude of what he'd done probably wasn't the best way to go about it.

'I've spent some time with your mum. I believe her when she tells me you're a good kid. She's proud of you. And I can promise you, she cares about you far more than you realise. I reckon she'll always be there for you, whatever you've done.'

'But what if you're wrong? Then what happens? If I jump, I won't have to worry about it, will I?'

'Don't you think that's a rather selfish attitude?'

'Selfish?'

'Yeah, selfish. Maybe you're right. If you jump you'll die and you won't have to worry about anything, but what about your mum? How do you think she's going to feel?'

'I dunno. I haven't thought about that.'

'Then let me tell you how she'll feel. She'll think she failed you, and it will haunt her for the rest of her life. Does she really deserve that, after all she's done for you?'

All at once, Jimmy noticed the flurry of activity at the base of the lighthouse. 'What are all those people doing down there?' he asked.

'That'll be the fire service. I would imagine they're surrounding us with inflatable mattresses so if you do jump, you won't get hurt.'

Jimmy leaned over the safety rail for a better look. 'They've surrounded the place.'

As Jimmy spoke, Norman glanced down and was immediately overcome with dizziness. 'Holy shit!' he muttered, tightening his grip on the ladder. His legs began to shake.

'Wow!' said Jimmy. 'You really are scared, aren't you?'

'Put it this way,' said Norman. 'If I grip this ladder any tighter, I'm going to either bend it, or break my fingers.'

'So, why don't you climb up here on the platform?'

'Yeah, that would be much better, wouldn't it? Problem is, I can't move.'

'You're kidding me.'

'I wish I was, but from where I'm standing — or hanging on — it really isn't funny at all. Please, Jimmy, could you help me?'

'Why would I want to help the police?'

'Because, underneath it all, I'm a person just like you, and just like your mother. I know your mother wouldn't turn her back on someone in trouble, and I'm sure she raised you to want to help others too.'

While Jimmy considered this, Norman prayed he was right, and whatever mistakes Jimmy had made, underneath it all, he was just a scared kid.

Finally, Jimmy knelt at the top of the ladder and held out his hand. 'Hold on to my hand.'

'That means me letting go,' said Norman. 'I'm not sure I can do that.'

'You only have to let go with one hand.'

'That sounds like one too many.'

'Look, if we're going to get you up here, you're going to have to take my hand.'

'That's easy for you to say.'

'You only need to climb about four more steps and you'll be level with this platform. Then it's just one step sideways.'

'Jimmy, if it was that easy, I'd have done it by now.'

'Look, I really do want to help you, but I can't do it unless you trust me.'

'It's not that I don't trust you. I'm not sure I trust myself.'

Jimmy bent forward and took hold of Norman's wrists.

'Jeez, careful,' said Norman. 'You're going to squeeze the blood out of my hands.'

'At least you know I've got hold of you real tight, right? So, now I'm going to hold on to you while you release your right hand, and then I'm going to help you slide your hand up the ladder. When we've done that, we're going to do the same with the other hand, and then you're going to take a step up.'

'I'm not sure I can.'

'Yes, you can. It's just one small step. Come on, try it, before your hands go numb.'

As Norman relaxed his grip, Jimmy slowly eased his right hand up the ladder.

'Right, now keep hold with that hand and we'll do the same with the other one.' Painfully slowly, they repeated the procedure.

'Are you married, Norm?'

'What? That seems a weird question to ask at a time like this.'

'Yeah, but why not? It's a weird situation, right?'

'Well, you're right there. It certainly is.'

'Anyway, are you?'

'Am I what?'

'Married?'

'No, I'm not married.'

'I didn't think so.'

'Really? Why's that?'

'Because I can't imagine any woman putting up with your complaining.'

'Complaining?'

'That's all you've done since you got up here. If you'd just kept climbing up the ladder instead of stopping to complain about how scared you were, you wouldn't have got stuck.'

Before Norman could think of a reply, Jimmy took his arm. 'Now, take a step to your left and you'll be on the platform.'

For the first time in what seemed like hours, Norman took his eyes from the ladder. He was surprised to find he was now level with Jimmy.

'You're not going to fall,' said Jimmy.

'Jeez, are you sure about that? Because I feel really dizzy every time I look down.'

'There's an easy solution to that — don't look down!' Jimmy gave Norman's arm a gentle tug. 'Come on, Norm, you're nearly there. Just one step to the side and you can sit down.'

Norman took a deep breath, closed his eyes, stepped off the ladder and collapsed in a heap. He felt like crying with relief, but pulled himself together.

'Thanks, Jimmy. I think you may have just saved my life. For a minute there I thought I was going to be stuck on that ladder until my hands went numb and I fell.'

'I couldn't leave you there, could I? What good is a fire escape if there's some old fart blocking it?'

Norman smiled. 'That's a good point.' He cleared his throat. 'I hope you understand I can't let this make any difference to what happens, right? I mean, I can put a good word in, but if you did what you said—'

'Yeah, I know,' said Jimmy, looking over the safety rail. 'But there's not much point jumping now, is there? They've got so many of those mattress things set up, I'll probably bounce right back up here again.'

They sat in silence for a few seconds, while Norman, keen to keep Jimmy talking, thought of something to say.

'I do have a girlfriend,' he said. 'She doesn't tell me I complain all the time.'

'Perhaps she's being polite,' said Jimmy. 'My girlfriend's a bit like my mum. She's always putting me right.'

Norman would have liked to continue the conversation, but was interrupted by the grating sound of the fire-service ladder, rising majestically into the air. Two fire officers stood on the platform.

'Ahoy there,' called one. 'Stay right where you are. We'll have you down in no time.'

* * *

It was almost ten pm. Jimmy Denman had been taken away to be observed and assessed overnight, and the fire service had packed up their equipment. Only a solitary ambulance remained on site. In the back, Norman had just been given the all-clear by one of the paramedics.

'I hope you're not going to make a habit of this,' she said. 'Scaling ladders after potential suicides is not a great idea at your age, especially when you're scared of heights.'

Norman rolled his eyes. 'Fancy you saying that. Do you know, I've heard the very same thing from three different fire officers and two of my colleagues. Even the young guy I was trying to rescue told me I was an idiot. I'd rather not have to hear it again if you don't mind.'

'Perhaps if you take the message on board, you won't have to hear it again,' said the paramedic.

'Are you telling me you wouldn't have done the same thing?'

The paramedic smiled. 'Of course I would.'

'Well, there we are then,' said Norman.

Southall, who had been waiting by her car, came over to the ambulance. 'Can I take him home now?'

'Sure you can,' said the paramedic. As Norman got stiffly to his feet, she said to Southall, 'The only thing I could find wrong with him is this stubborn streak he has, but I don't have the means to treat chronic disorders like that.'

'We are aware of that,' said Southall. 'But it's very much a work in progress.'

'Rather you than me.'

'Hey, have I suddenly become invisible?' asked Norman. 'I'm right here, you know.'

'Well, you might as well not be. We know you're not listening,' said Southall, 'because you never do.'

The paramedic was still laughing as Southall led Norman towards her car.

'If you want me to retire, just say the word,' said Norman.

'Oh, please! Do you really need to be quite so melodramatic? I've already told you I don't want that, but I do want you to look after yourself. I can't afford to lose you, Norm. You're what holds this team together.'

Embarrassed by the compliment, Norman changed the subject. 'I appreciate you waiting, Sarah, but you don't need to drive me home. I've got my car here.'

'No, you haven't. I told Frosty to take it back to the station. I'll take you home now, and you can collect your car in the morning.'

'I have an early start with Catren,' he said. 'Is she going to pick me up?'

'I've changed that now. You need a good rest, so Frosty is going with Catren. I'll pick you up in the morning.'

'You don't need to worry. I'll sleep just fine. I can still go with Catren.'

'I want you there in the morning when I interview Jimmy Denman.'

'Is he going to be okay to interview so soon?'

'I don't know yet. He's on suicide watch overnight and he'll be assessed in the morning.'

'Okay, but don't worry about picking me up, it's miles out of your way,' said Norman. 'I can make my own way in.'

'It's not miles out of my way. And, anyway, that's what I'm going to do.'

'There's really no need.'

'Anyone would think you didn't want me coming to your house.'

'It's not that, I just don't think there's any need for you to—'

'I'm sorry, Norm, but I think there is. Hopefully, we're going to be allowed to interview Jimmy Denman first thing, and I want you there with me.'

'Look, I'm fine, Sarah. There's no need to make a fuss.'

'I'm not making a fuss. I promised Faye I'd make—'

'You spoke to Faye?'

'She called me. She said she'd been expecting you hours ago and when you didn't call, she got worried. I take it you had a date?'

'Er, yeah, in a manner of speaking,' said Norman. 'You're right, I should have called her. Is she mad at me?'

'Of course not. She understands how unpredictable this job can be. Anyway, I explained what had happened and told her I'd make sure you got home safely.'

'You told her I was up on top of the lighthouse?'

'No, I didn't mention that bit. I just said you were trying to persuade someone not to kill himself and you didn't have your phone with you. Then I called her back to let her know everything had worked out okay and no one had been hurt.'

'I see. Right. Thank you.'

'I take it things are working out for you two if you're still dating?'

Southall was fishing again. Norman stared out of the window, hoping they were close to home.

'Er, yeah, I guess you could say we're, um, ticking along.'

'Good. I like Faye.'

'Yeah, me too.'

After ten minutes spent stonewalling Southall's questions, they were finally approaching Norman's house.

'You can drop me off here and save yourself some time,' he said. 'I can walk up the lane.'

'It's no trouble,' said Southall. 'We're almost there now.'

Southall turned into the lane leading up to Norman's cottage and into his drive. She had intended to park in front of the cottage but another car was already there — Faye Delaney's. Faye had obviously let herself in and made herself at home. The curtains were drawn and the lights were on.

'Your house looks very cosy, Norm.'

'Yeah, it's just how I imagined a cottage in the country would be, you know?'

Norman opened the car door and stepped out. As he did so the front door opened and, silhouetted against the warm light from the hallway, a woman waved a greeting.

'I'll be on my way,' said Southall. 'It looks as if someone's waiting for you. I'll see you in the morning.'

Norman waited until Southall had driven away before rushing towards the door. Faye ran to meet him and he wrapped his arms around her, hugging her tight. He began to cry.

'Jeez, you wouldn't believe the shitty evening I've had,' he mumbled. 'I got stuck near the top of a ladder, and all I kept thinking was how I longed to be here with you.'

'Hush now,' she said, gently stroking his hair. 'It's all right. You're here with me now.'

For a minute or two, he couldn't bring himself to let go of her, but finally his sobs began to subside and he released his hold just enough to look into her face.

'I'm sorry,' he said. 'You must think me pretty wet, crying like this.'

Tenderly, she placed a finger on his lips. 'Shush, silly. Sometimes we all need a good cry. It's nothing to be ashamed of. Come on, let's go inside and you can tell me all about it.'

# CHAPTER 32

At precisely six thirty the following morning, Winter settled into the passenger seat of Morgan's car.

'You should have seen Norm last night,' he said. 'He was awesome!'

'I'm sorry I missed it. I heard he was a bit of a hero.'

'Hero? Superhero more like it. He was crapping himself but he still insisted on climbing that ladder.'

Smiling, Morgan put the car into gear. 'Yeah, he's like that. Sort of a cross between a hero and an idiot.'

'I feel bad about it, though,' said Winter. 'I didn't even know he's scared of heights.'

'I've heard he's not good with boats either,' said Morgan. 'Or horses, or cattle, or sheep. In fact, now I come to think of it, he's shit scared of lots of things. It never stops him doing his job, though. And you have to admire anyone who's prepared to carry on regardless. Don't tell him, but he's been a hero of mine almost from the day I first met him.'

'Yeah, he's not bad for an old guy, is he?'

'He's the best DS I've come across, and I've worked with a few. Many of them were complete morons.'

They drove on in silence for a couple of minutes.

'What's this vet's place like, then?' asked Winter.

'It's based at an old farm. The barns and stables have been adapted to house large animals in individual pens, and they have their office and a dedicated small-animal clinic in the farmhouse.'

'And what about this old guy, Davies?'

'I haven't met him,' said Morgan. 'But talking to one of the other vets yesterday, I got the impression he's a crabby old sod.'

'Oh, great. Just what we need to ruin our day before it's even started.'

'Don't worry, it'll be fine,' said Morgan. 'If he gets shirty, I'm sure we'll be able to find plenty of reasons to hold him up and waste his time.'

* * *

They pulled into the surgery car park, beside what they assumed to be Hywell Davies's Land Rover and two other cars. Morgan got out and peered through the Land Rover windows.

'It's tidier than I expected,' she said, before walking around to the rear. The back window was thick with grime, so she fished a latex glove from her pocket and cleared a small patch.

'This must be the drug safe in the back here,' she told Winter as he joined her.

'Can I help you?' boomed a voice. An older man in a tweed jacket bustled towards them.

'We're looking for Mr Hywell Davies,' said Morgan.

'And you are?'

Morgan produced her warrant card. 'DC Morgan and DC Winter from Llangwelli police.'

'Really? And what do you want?'

'I understand you keep a syringe of pentobarbital in your vehicle.'

'Of course I do. I'm a vet.'

'Could I ask you to show us the syringe, Mr Davies?'

'Show it to you? Why?'

222

'Why wouldn't you want to?' asked Morgan.

'Look, can't this wait? I'm a busy man. I don't have time to waste—'

'We're quite busy too, sir, but we could probably make time to check over your Land Rover.'

'The front tyres are almost bald for a start,' said Winter.

Davies looked down his nose at Winter. 'The chief constable happens to be a friend of mine, you know.'

'I'm sure he is, sir, but even he would take a dim view of one of his friends obstructing a murder investigation,' Morgan said.

'Murder? What murder? I've never heard of anything so ridiculous in my life.'

'I think you'll find the victim's family don't think it's ridiculous,' said Morgan.

'But what has this murder got to do with me?'

'This isn't personal to you, sir,' said Morgan. 'We're checking every business in the area that stocks pentobarbital to make sure none has gone missing. According to your drug logbook, you keep a syringe in your vehicle. All I'm asking is for you to open the drug safe in the back of your Land Rover so we can make sure it's there. Is that too much to ask?'

'As I said, I'm very busy—'

'Those back tyres don't look too healthy either,' observed Winter.

'What? My back tyres are fine.'

Winter shook his head. 'They look marginal at best. Still, I'm sure I've got a tyre gauge in the back of my car. It might take a while to find it, but—'

'All right. You've made your point, Detective Constable whatever your name is.'

Winter beamed. 'Winter, sir. DC Winter.'

'This is nothing but bloody impertinence.'

'Just doing our job, sir,' said Morgan.

'As should I.'

'And if you'd done as I asked in the first place, you could have been on your way by now.'

Grumbling and cursing, Hywell Davies opened the back door of his Land Rover, leaned inside, unlocked the drug safe, threw the lid open and stepped back.

'There,' he snapped. 'See for yourself.'

Morgan peered inside. 'It's empty.'

'I suppose you think this is funny,' snarled Davies.

'Do I look as if I'm laughing?' asked Morgan. 'Is my partner laughing?'

'But it must be there.' Davies pushed his way past Morgan and reached in. He stopped. 'But it was there. I put it there myself.'

'And you're sure you haven't used it?' asked Morgan.

'Of course I haven't bloody well used it. Do you think I'm stupid?'

'So, where is it?' asked Winter.

'Well, it's, er, it's . . . I don't know. Gone.'

'Gone?' echoed Winter. 'What do you mean, it's gone? Gone where?'

'I, er, I don't know.'

'Oh dear,' said Morgan. 'This isn't very good, is it? I wonder what your friend the chief constable is going to say.'

'It looks like we're going to have to waste a bit more of your time,' added Winter.

Davies turned and began to walk away.

'Just a minute, Mr Davies. Where are you going?' Morgan called.

'I need a replacement syringe of pentobarbital.'

'I don't think so,' said Morgan. 'Not until we find out where the last one went.'

'I haven't got time for this.'

'Well, I'm afraid you're going to have to make time,' she said. 'Unless you'd prefer it if we arrested you.'

'Arrest me? I've never heard anything so ridiculous in my life.'

'Obstructing a murder inquiry is a very serious offence, Mr Davies,' said Morgan. 'But it won't be necessary to arrest you if you agree to answer our questions.'

## CHAPTER 33

At seven fifteen that morning, Southall parked up in front of Norman's cottage. Faye Delaney's car was still there. She got out of her car and headed for the front door, noticing that the garden seemed to have undergone something of a transformation since she'd last been here.

The front door opened as she approached, and Norman appeared. 'Morning, Sarah. You're early.'

'Morning, Norm. You okay after last night?'

'I'm fine.'

Southall nodded towards the garden. 'I thought you said you weren't much of a gardener.'

'Enthusiastic, but ham-fisted amateur would best describe my horticultural abilities.'

'Don't put yourself down, Norm. It's looking much tidier than when I was last here.'

'Yeah, but none of that's down to me.'

'Really? Have you found a gardener?'

'I suppose I have, in a manner of speaking.'

'I see Faye's left her car here,' said Southall, with a sly grin.

'You don't miss much, do you? It's no wonder you've made inspector already.'

225

'Oh, come on, Norm. I think it's great you two are dating. I'm pleased for both of you.'

'Have we got time for coffee?' he asked.

She smiled again. 'I thought you'd never ask.'

'Why don't you come in? There's coffee in the kitchen. Faye will be down in a minute.'

Norman couldn't help smiling. He knew Southall had been itching to find out if he and Faye had got together. He'd spent weeks evading her questions.

'Your house seems different somehow,' she said.

Faye joined them in the kitchen.

'Yeah,' said Norman. 'A woman's touch. She's turned my house into a home.'

Southall stared from Norman to Faye, and back again, comprehension beginning to dawn. Faye drew close to Norman, who put an arm around her.

'You've moved in?' Southall asked her.

Faye nodded enthusiastically. 'Just over a week ago.'

'Oh, that's wonderful news,' said Southall. 'I'm so pleased for both of you. So, this is what you've been so tight-lipped about?'

Norman grinned. 'What? Me? I could have sworn I told you.'

Southall turned to Faye. 'He knows damn well he didn't. Getting anything out of him is like trying to draw blood from a stone.'

'Maybe that's because you keep fishing. You always drop sly hints and never ask a direct question,' said Norman.

* * *

Coffee finished, Southall and Norman set off for work. 'Now I understand why your garden's looking so pretty,' said Southall.

Norman smiled. 'Faye loves gardening. She works part time and spends most of the rest of her day here. And when I'm home she teaches me what to do.'

'And you kept it all a secret. You sly old devil.'

'I'm not usually this lucky, you see. I didn't say anything because I was afraid of tempting fate,' he said.

'I think Faye would tell you there's a little more to it than luck, Norm.'

'Yeah, well, let's hope you're right.'

'Oh, I am,' said Southall. 'I'm sure of it.'

'Anyway, setting aside my private life for a minute, I've been thinking about those houses of Tilly's, especially that empty one, number six.'

'You have a theory about it?'

'I reckon she was keeping that house empty for a reason. Okay, maybe she wasn't dealing drugs, as Hayward said, but what if her brother Giles was?'

'And he uses that house to store them,' finished Southall. 'Yes, you're right. It'd make perfect sense to keep the drugs some distance from the farmhouse in case it was ever raided.'

'I also got to wondering how someone like Tilly got involved with this Rocco character in the first place,' said Norman. 'What if Giles introduced them?'

'I take it you have worked out why,' Southall said.

'I'm beginning to think brother Giles must have had some sort of hold over her. He was written out of the will, supposedly because of his gambling habit, and yet she brought him home to run the estate. A few years later, he runs up a huge debt with the Crowthers and what happens? Tilly hands over the stud horses to pay the debt.'

'You're suggesting Giles got her into drug dealing?'

'Or, maybe they weren't dealing, but Giles is into drugs. Tilly kept Rocco happy to pay for his habit.'

Southall frowned. 'We've nothing to suggest he's a drug addict.'

'Not yet, but we know he has used them, and we can see from his gambling that he's the addictive type. Heck, maybe it goes back years and was why he left university after just a term. Or perhaps he ran up a debt and Rocco asked for Tilly as a way of paying it off.'

'But didn't Hayward say Tilly was getting paid by Rocco?' Southall said. 'That doesn't quite gel with your debt idea.'

'Maybe Rocco actually liked Tilly and thought she'd be better off without her brother, so Giles killed her.'

'You seem really to have got the bit between your teeth, Norm.'

'The thing is, we have Jimmy Denman in the frame for killing David Griffiths, or, if he didn't do it, I'm sure he knows who did. But we're all agreed it's unlikely the same person killed Tilly.'

'It's not impossible, but extremely unlikely,' Southall said.

'Right. So, who does that leave? We'd all like it to be David Griffiths, but there's no getting around his alibi.'

'We still have no idea why he left the hotel so early,' said Southall.

'Yeah, but we're unlikely to find out where he was going now he's dead, and, anyway, Tilly was murdered hours before that, so wherever he was going, he wasn't going to kill her. I might be persuaded that Rhona Pritchard has a motive but again, CCTV puts her at the hotel, and from what Catren and Frosty said, she hasn't got it in her.'

'What about Ffion Howells?' Southall asked.

'Ffion is a definite possibility. She made it clear she had no time for Tilly, and there's definitely something odd about the fact she hasn't paid any rent for the best part of two years. Still, we know where we can find her when we want to question her. The one that really bugs me is Giles Rotherby. I mean, where is he, and where has he been hiding for the last four years?'

Southall pulled into her parking space at Llangwelli police station. 'You think he could have been at number six all this time?'

'Remember when we searched the farmhouse and found all those clothes in a locked wardrobe? They weren't the right size for David Griffiths, and you suggested they might belong to Giles,' Norman said.

'That's right. I thought Tilly might be keeping them safe for him.'

'What if she wasn't just keeping them safe, but he'd actually been living in the farmhouse all along?'

'You mean hiding in plain sight?'

'Yeah, using house number six as a bolthole. If anyone came to the farmhouse, he could have sneaked out the back way and gone to number six.'

'Do you really think he could have kept that up for four years?' she said. 'He'd have to be incredibly lucky to get away with it for that long.'

Norman considered for a moment. Then he sighed. 'Yeah, maybe you're right. When you put it like that it is pretty unlikely, isn't it?'

'Then again, he must be hiding somewhere, and we shouldn't forget he's a gambler,' she said thoughtfully.

Now Norman was sceptical. 'Yeah, but we know how successful he was at gambling. Not.'

'But isn't gambling all about the thrill of the risk?'

'You mean you think I could be right?' Norman said, getting out of the car.

Southall followed suit. She smiled at Norman across the roof of the car. 'I certainly think we should take a look. Even if Giles isn't there, we might find something that will tell us where he is. I'll ask Judy to get us a search warrant while we're interviewing Jimmy Denman.'

# CHAPTER 34

'I finally managed to speak with the new owners after you'd all gone yesterday,' said Lane. 'They're nice people, only too happy to help. According to them, Tilly didn't sell the houses; she signed them over because she thought it was too expensive to renovate them. All the buyers had to do was pay the legal fees.'

'Does that sound likely?' asked Southall.

'Do you mean is it likely she gave the houses away, or is it likely they're going to be too expensive to renovate?' asked Norman.

'Both sound unlikely to me,' said Southall. 'I can't believe the renovations would cost more than the value of the houses.'

'I agree,' said Norman. 'Even if you had to rent them out for another five years, anything after that is profit.'

'There were a couple of interesting clauses in the hand-over agreement,' said Lane. 'Apparently, the tenant in house number one was to be allowed to stay rent-free for the next twelve months.'

'That's the house where Ffion Howells lives, right?' asked Norman.

'Correct,' said Lane.

'We need to find out what Ffion knew about Tilly,' said Southall. 'It must have been something big to give her that much leverage.'

'It sounds to me like she could have figured out that Giles was doing drugs,' said Norman.

'You said there were a couple of clauses in the agreement, Judy,' said Southall. 'What's the other one?'

'That one concerns number six, which must stay empty for six months from the date the houses were signed over.'

'Why?' asked Southall.

'They don't know why, and as they were getting six cottages for next to nothing, they decided it wasn't worth arguing about.'

'There you go,' said Norman to Southall. 'That's the house we were just talking about in the car.'

'Am I missing something?' asked Lane.

'Norm thinks that number six could be Giles Rotherby's drug store.'

'It would explain why there's no tenant,' said Lane.

Norman smiled. 'Looks as if we're all on the same wavelength, then.'

'Right. Judy,' said Southall. 'While we find out when we can interview Jimmy Denman, I'd like you to see if you can get us a warrant to search number six urgently.'

'Will we need one?' asked Lane. 'If the house is empty, couldn't we just ask the owners if we can have a look inside? They said to let them know if there's anything they can do to help find Tilly's killer, and it's not as if we're going to be invading anyone's privacy, is it?

'You're right,' said Southall. 'If the owner grants us access to the house, we won't need a warrant.'

'And it would save us a shedload of time waiting for one,' added Norman.

'Give them a call, Judy, and ask if they're willing to let us go in,' Southall said.

'No problem,' said Lane.

Southall turned to Norman. 'I'll find out when we can speak to Jimmy.'

'Looks like I'm making the teas, then,' said Norman, heading for the kitchen.

A few minutes later, he emerged from the kitchen carrying three mugs of tea.

'Change of plan,' said Southall. 'We can't speak to Jimmy until this afternoon.'

'So, what's the new plan?'

'Judy just spoke to the owners of house number six. They're willing to let us have a key to the house so we can have a look around.'

'When do we leave?' he said.

'I think we can probably drink our tea first.'

# CHAPTER 35

'Do you think we should have brought a few more bodies?' asked Southall as she parked the car.

Norman looked thoughtfully at the house. 'Catren and Frosty are coming, aren't they?'

'That's what Judy said when she called a few minutes ago.'

'They'll be here soon, and we've no reason to think we're in any danger, right?' Norman said.

Southall nodded. 'There's nothing to suggest it.'

'Well,' said Norman 'My feeling is that if Giles Rotherby did murder Tilly, he'll be long gone. He won't have hung around waiting for us to find him.'

'And if he didn't kill her?'

'Then why would he be hiding?'

Still, Southall hesitated. 'If there's a stash of drugs in there, he might think it's worth protecting.'

'That's if there is one. If what Hayward said about Tilly was true, we're not going to find any drugs at all.'

'Yes, that's the other possibility,' said Southall, reaching for the door handle. 'Come on then, Norm, let's do it.'

Southall led the way to the front door, which unlocked easily. She pushed it open and turned to Norman, listening hard. Norman shook his head. Silence. There was no one inside.

Southall stepped through the door and crossed the hallway. An open door led off to the right and she peered in. She saw two armchairs and a small table, but nothing to indicate that anyone had been there recently.

Norman headed for a closed door, which he assumed would lead to the kitchen. Cautiously, he pushed the door open, waited a couple of seconds and stepped through. It was a kitchen all right, and empty. He opened one or two cupboards and drawers, but found nothing.

Southall paused on the small landing at the top of the stairs to get her bearings. The creaking of the floorboards as she climbed would have been a warning to anyone hiding up here. There were two doors ahead of her and one to her right. She had just opened the first door and stepped inside when she heard footsteps.

Before she could react, someone hurled themselves across the landing, barged into her back and sent her sprawling in a heap on the floor. The footsteps receded, heading down the stairs.

'Norm!' she yelled. 'He's coming downstairs.'

Norman opened a door on the far side of the kitchen, which led through to a bathroom. Now, for the first time, he found evidence of someone's presence. He stepped across to examine the items when he heard footsteps pounding down the stairs and then Southall's shout.

Norman raced back through the kitchen, but Giles Rotherby was at the bottom of the stairs and through the hallway before he had a chance to stop him. He flung the front door open and was gone in a flash. Norman knew he'd never catch the younger man, so he went upstairs to see if Southall needed help.

Outside in the lane, Morgan and Winter had just arrived. Morgan was following Winter towards the front door of number six when suddenly it burst open and Rotherby ran past, taking Winter by surprise. Rotherby tried to force his way past Morgan but she had other ideas. She stuck out a foot, causing him to trip, stumble, and finally crash, face down, to the ground. Before he could draw breath, Morgan had his hands drawn up behind his back.

'Going somewhere, Mr Rotherby?' she asked. Winter caught up with them and clipped handcuffs to his wrists.

'Good morning, Giles,' said Southall, as Winter and Morgan helped him to his feet. 'My, aren't you the elusive one!'

Rotherby stared sullenly up at Southall. 'I've done nothing wrong, and I've got nothing to say.'

'You've done nothing wrong? Really? Then why have you been hiding here since your sister Tilly was murdered?'

Rotherby's eyes filled with tears. 'Because I knew you'd assume I killed her.'

'Oh? Why would we assume that?'

'Because you'd know I had been written out of my father's will. You'd assume I killed Tilly so I could get my hands on the estate.'

'And did you?' Southall said.

'No, I did not,' he said, vehemently. 'I loved my sister. I would never hurt her.'

As Southall stared at him, a tear trickled slowly down his cheek.

'We'll talk about this back at the police station,' said Southall. She turned to Winter. 'A patrol car is on the way. When it gets here, take him back to Llangwelli and book him in.' Addressing Morgan, she said, 'Catren, get Forensics out here. I want them to take this place apart, brick by brick if necessary.'

# CHAPTER 36

From the front window of number six, Norman and Morgan watched Giles Rotherby being driven away. Winter followed in Morgan's car, in order to book Rotherby in and make sure he was locked safely in a cell.

'So, Hywell Davies admits he's missing a syringe full of pentobarbital?' Southall asked Morgan.

'He couldn't deny it once he'd opened that drug safe and it wasn't there.'

'Have you charged him?' asked Norman.

'I haven't yet, but I told him I'd be back, and I'm not going to let him off lightly.'

'I should hope not,' said Norman. 'How come he didn't miss it? Doesn't he care?'

'Oh, trust me, he cares — now we're involved,' said Morgan.

'What's he like?' asked Southall.

'He's a spikey old sod and he made it obvious he objected to people as young as me and Frosty lecturing him on drug safety. But I think his biggest problem is that he's living in the past and he's not as sharp as he used to be.'

'You mean he should have retired years ago,' said Norman.

'The young vet I spoke to says they've been trying to get him to retire for the last three years, but he owns the place and he doesn't want to let go. Now, they're hoping that when the shit hits the fan, they'll finally be able to persuade him it's time to go.'

'Let's hope a criminal charge will help push him in the right direction,' said Southall. 'We can't afford to have people like him wandering around the countryside shedding lethal drugs all over the place.'

'And you're sure there's no connection between him and Tilly Rotherby?' asked Norman.

'There's no record of them ever treating any of her horses,' said Morgan. 'Davies admits he's come across Tilly at various horse shows over the years, but he claims he barely knows her.'

'Do you believe him?' asked Southall.

'Yes, I do,' said Morgan.

'If there's no connection, what are we saying?' asked Norman. 'That someone with a grudge against Tilly just happened to stumble upon Davies when his drug safe was open?'

'It's funny you should ask that,' said Morgan. 'You haven't heard the best bit yet.'

'Best bit?' said Southall. 'What best bit?'

'Well, if you're looking for a connection between Tilly and Hywell Davies's veterinary practice, I think Frosty may have found one for you.'

'And how has he done that?' asked Norman.

'Because when we were in the office, Frosty kept his eyes open while I was doing the talking. He saw the work rota for the veterinary nurses pinned up on a noticeboard. One of them is Ffion Howells.'

'Holy crap!' said Norman.

'She works for the vet?' asked Southall. 'Jesus Christ, Norm. Why didn't we know that before?'

'I don't think we had any reason to ask,' said Norman. 'If you remember, it was her daughter we were interested in, because she found the body.'

'Bloody hell. I can't believe we missed that,' said Southall angrily. 'And she really didn't like Tilly, did she?'

'I'm guessing you want to bring her in before she finds out we know about the syringe, right?' said Norman.

'She's not going to know about the syringe yet,' said Morgan. 'According to the rota, she's on leave this week.'

Southall craned her neck and peered along the lane. 'Her car is outside her house. We don't need to bring her in, we can speak to her right now. Catren, you stay here and wait for Forensics. Norm, with me.'

She stormed from the house, Norman following in her wake.

# CHAPTER 37

From Ffion Howells's expression, it was clear she wasn't exactly over the moon to find the detectives on her doorstep once more.

'Oh. It's you lot again. What do you want now?'

'We'd like to ask you a few more questions,' said Southall.

'I've already told you what happened the morning Tilly died.'

'Yes,' said Southall. 'But now I want to talk about something else.'

'Like what?'

'Can we come in?'

'I suppose so.'

Ffion followed them into the tiny lounge.

'I'd offer you coffee,' she said, 'but I wouldn't want you to think you're welcome.'

'That's okay, Ffion, you made it clear how you felt last time we were here.'

Ffion looked pointedly at her wristwatch. 'Can we get on with this? I have to be somewhere.'

'It won't take long,' said Southall. 'I just wanted to tell you we know about the syringe of pentobarbital.'

Ffion looked blank. 'The what?'

'The syringe of pentobarbital that's gone missing from the drug safe in the back of Hywell Davies's Land Rover.'

'It's not the first time the old fool has lost one,' said Ffion. 'He's probably used it to put someone's horse down and forgotten to replace it. He's done that before.'

'Are you saying you didn't take it?'

'Me? Of course I didn't take it. Why would I? I'm a nurse, not a vet. I don't handle dangerous drugs like that.'

'Do you ever go out on the road with Mr Davies?' Southall asked.

Ffion guffawed. 'Not on your life. Have you seen the way he drives? Being a passenger of his isn't for the faint-hearted I can tell you. It's like being on a rollercoaster. A teenager might enjoy it, but not me. Anyway, I work in the small-animal side of the practice, and we don't go out on the road. People bring their pets to the surgery.'

'What can you tell me about Giles Rotherby?' Southall asked.

'Giles? Well, I last saw him years ago when I used to go to horse shows.'

'And your father shared the driving with Tilly's father?'

'Yes. Sometimes Giles would tag along. He was every teenage girl's wet dream back then, but as I said, I haven't seen him in years.'

'You haven't seen him around these cottages, or the estate?' Southall asked.

'Not since I've been living here, no.'

'What about David Griffiths?'

'What about him? He's dead, isn't he? Or are you asking me if I killed him?'

'Did you?'

'Of course not.'

'Where were you on the day he was murdered?'

'I was at work. You can check if you want.'

'Do you know a young man called Jimmy Denman?'

'I know *of* him. He was the boy who worked at the stables, but you already know that. If that was a trick question and I was supposed to slip up, I'm afraid you're wasting your time. I don't know anything about him. Now, unless you have any more questions, I'd like to go out.'

Southall would have liked to continue questioning her, but she knew they didn't have sufficient grounds — yet.

'We'll get out of your hair now, Ms Howells, but we'll be back, I'm sure.'

'You can come back as many times as you like. I've got nothing to hide.'

\* \* \*

'Do we believe her?' asked Norman as they returned to Southall's car. 'I thought she seemed genuinely baffled when you mentioned the missing syringe. If she was acting, it was a brilliant performance. She certainly had me fooled.'

'I hate to say it, but I have to agree with you,' said Southall.

'We can always check what she said about working with small animals and not having access to dangerous drugs,' said Norman.

'Yes, do that when we get back, please,' said Southall.

'What about the rest of it?' said Norman. 'Do we seriously believe that for two years she's been living a few doors down from Rotherby and never set eyes on him?'

'We don't have much choice, Norm. We must accept it, because right now we can't prove otherwise.'

# CHAPTER 38

Much to Southall's annoyance, they weren't permitted to interview Jimmy at the secure unit, so they had to wait while he was driven the fifteen miles to Llangwelli. Now, at long last they were settled in an interview room sitting across the table from Jimmy and a duty solicitor.

'How are you today, Jimmy?' asked Norman.

'All right, I think. My head's a lot clearer today.'

'Good.' Norman indicated Southall. 'This is my boss, DI Southall. She's going to ask you some questions. Is that okay?'

Jimmy nodded.

'Now then, Jimmy,' said Southall. 'When we went to your house, we found Tilly Rotherby's top hat on top of your wardrobe.'

'That's right.'

'Why have you got it?'

'She won't need it now, will she?'

'Did you take it, or did someone give it to you?' Southall asked.

'Tilly let me try it on once. She said I looked good in it. So, I took it.'

'I see,' said Southall. 'Yesterday, when you were up on the lighthouse, you told Sergeant Norman you found David

Griffiths lying on the ground, and that he was already dead. Is that right?'

The solicitor leaned forward to intervene, but Jimmy raised a hand to silence him.

'It's okay,' he told the solicitor. 'I know what you advised, but I'm not going to do that "no comment" stuff.' He looked Southall in the eye. 'Yeah, that's right.'

'Did you see who killed him, Jimmy?'

'No.'

'You told Sergeant Norman you didn't like Mr Griffiths.'

'That's right. He was a shit.'

'Why do you say that?'

'He was mean and nasty.'

'Nasty to you?'

'No, not to me. Her. He attacked her.'

'Her? Who, Jimmy? Who did he attack?'

'I can't tell you that.'

'Why not?'

'I just can't. She didn't kill him, so there's no need for her to be involved.'

'It would really help if we knew who she was,' Southall said.

Jimmy turned to his solicitor. 'Is this where I say, "no comment"?'

'I already told you that you can answer "no comment" whenever you want,' said the solicitor.

Southall decided to come at this another way. 'You said you saw David Griffiths attack a woman. Was it Tilly Rotherby?'

'It was my girlfriend. He attacked her by the stables, so I picked up an old horseshoe and threw it at him to stop him.'

'Did the horseshoe hit him?' Southall asked.

'Yeah. On the back of his head.'

'Then what did you do?'

'I took his phone.'

'Why did you take his phone?'

'I don't know. I thought I could use it, but on the way home I realised it was wrong of me, so I threw it in the pond.'

243

'Which pond?'

'The duck pond at Nef Anfon.'

'That's where you live, isn't it?' Southall said.

'Yeah. I pass it on the way home.'

'Where in the pond did you throw it? At the edge? Right in the middle?'

'I'm not sure. I didn't stop, I just slowed down and lobbed it in when I got close enough.'

A knock was heard at the door. Norman went to see who it was.

'Sorry to interrupt,' Lane said. 'But we've had a call from the divers down at the duck pond and I thought you should know what they said.'

'Have they found anything?' asked Norman.

Lane smiled. 'In amongst all sorts of junk, they came across a mobile phone.'

'Jimmy says he found the one belonging to Griffiths and threw it into the pond,' said Norman. 'Do they think they can salvage anything from it?'

'They say it's doubtful, but they've sent it straight to the tech guys to do what they can,' Lane said.

'I don't suppose they found a shovel?' Norman asked.

'Not yet, but so far they've only covered a small area. They'll call again if they find anything significant.'

'Okay, thank you.' Norman beckoned to Southall. 'Can I have a word, boss?'

They went out into the corridor, where Norman told her of the find.

'Should we stop the interview until they've finished searching the pond?' he asked.

'What do you think of what we've heard so far? Is he confused, or is he trying to confuse us?' Southall said.

'He's definitely not telling us the truth,' said Norman. 'I'm beginning to think he was there when Griffiths died, or he saw what happened. I reckon when he said his head's a lot clearer, what he really meant was he'd got his story straight. But I have no idea how much of it is fantasy and how much is real.'

'What about this woman he mentioned? Does he mean Carys?'

'I couldn't get a name out of him,' said Norman.

'Well, whoever he means, was she really there, and, if so, is he covering for her?' Southall asked.

'We both know there's no way a single blow from a horseshoe could have killed Griffiths. On the other hand, I find it hard to believe that the kid who helped me at the top of that ladder is capable of battering a man to death with a shovel. I think either there was someone with him, or he saw the murder take place.'

'But who would he call his girlfriend if it's not Carys?' Southall asked.

Norman shrugged. 'I dunno. He did tell me he has a girl-friend when we were up on that tower, but he seems to be a bit of a fantasist, so I wouldn't put too much weight on the idea.'

'But you agree he's trying to throw us off the scent?' she asked.

'Oh, yeah, for sure.'

'We need some incontrovertible evidence to hit him with,' Southall said.

'Maybe when Forensics come back to us with the shoe casts they took, we'll have a better idea,' Norman suggested.

'You're right. Let's call a halt now and wait for the divers to finish and the shoe casts to come back. It's not as if we don't have anyone else to question, is it? Let's see what Giles Rotherby has to say for himself.'

# CHAPTER 39

'Now then, Mr Rotherby,' said Southall. 'I'd like to know why you were excluded from your father's will.'

'I don't think that's any of your business.'

'Actually, everything's my business when I'm investigating two murders, especially when it may provide you with a motive for at least one of those murders.'

'I've already told you I didn't kill my sister.'

'It may surprise you, but most murderers insist on their innocence,' said Southall. 'That's why we spend so much time gathering evidence. The first thing we look at is motive. I believe your father's will gives you a powerful motive, which is why I'd like to know why he made his decision. Now, I understand you have a gambling habit, and I suspect you also have a drug habit. Which one was it?'

Rotherby turned to his solicitor, who nodded. 'If you must know, I got someone pregnant.'

'Was this before you were kicked out of university?'

'It was after, and I wasn't kicked out. I left. They are not the same things.'

'Okay, so why did you drop out? Was it the gambling, or the drugs?'

'If you must know, I missed home — and, yes, I turned to drugs. Before I knew it, I was a heroin addict. The old man said I had to leave uni and go into rehab, or he'd stop my allowance.'

'What happened after rehab?' Southall asked.

'When I came out, he insisted I went to live in his London flat.'

'Wouldn't that have left you open to even greater temptation?' she asked.

'I had a bloody nanny keeping an eye on me. I only got away from her when I came home to the estate.'

'What about the gambling? When did that start?' Southall asked.

Rotherby sighed. 'I'm afraid I have an addictive personality. Once I quit one habit, it was only a matter of time before I found another.'

'What about this nanny? Didn't she know?'

'She couldn't stay awake all day and all night, and there are plenty of drugs to help people sleep if you know where to get them.'

'You used to drug your nanny so you could go to the casino?' Southall asked.

'That's right.'

'So, tell me about this girl you got pregnant.'

'I'd rather not. I promised I'd never tell, and I never have.'

'So, how did your father know? Who told him?' Southall asked.

'I don't think anyone told him,' Rotherby said. 'He just worked it out somehow. I won't tell you her name, but she was a friend of the family, you see.'

'Didn't you deny it?' Southall asked.

'You didn't know the old man. There was no point in denying something once he'd decided you were guilty.'

'And that's when he decided to write you out of the will?'

'He claimed it was the final straw. He banned me from the estate, too. He said I was a disgrace to the family name.'

'And after the will was read?'

'Tilly invited me back to run the estate.'

'That was very generous of her. Presumably, she didn't think you were a disgrace to the family name.'

'Tilly thought the old man had treated me very badly. She couldn't change his will, but she could invite me to come back where I belonged.'

'And you lived on the estate with her for ten years, is that right?'

Rotherby nodded. 'About that, yes.'

'And then you had to go into hiding because you ran up another gambling debt.'

Rotherby's eyes widened.

'We know about the Crowther brothers taking the stud horses,' said Southall.

'It was the only way out of it,' said Rotherby, who had the grace to look ashamed. 'I didn't have any cash left.'

'Because you'd gambled it all away before you ran up the debt?'

'Yes.'

'When did you go back to drugs?'

'I honestly tried really hard not to, but, in the end, I couldn't resist.'

'Did you run up another debt?' asked Norman. 'Is that how you and Tilly came to be involved with Rocco?'

Again, Rotherby looked startled. 'So you know about that?'

'Yeah, we know,' said Norman.

'There's not much point me denying it then,' said Rotherby.

'None whatsoever,' said Norman. 'The way we see it, you've been a constant drain on the estate's funds. I imagine Tilly would have been pretty upset with you blowing all her money after she was kind enough to bring you back to run the estate. And then, just to top things off, when all the

248

money was gone, she was forced to sell herself to Rocco to settle yet another of your debts.'

'It wasn't like that.'

'Then, tell us. What was it like, Giles? I mean, Rocco's a London boy and we're almost as far west from there as you can get. How come he hooked up with Tilly all the way out here? Or are you telling me she met Rocco by chance and fell in love with him?'

Rotherby looked away.

'No, of course not,' continued Norman. 'You offered her to Rocco to pay off your debt, didn't you?'

Rotherby stared down at the table.

'Now, I reckon that would have made Tilly so angry that she was ready to kick you out again, but you killed her before she could do it.'

Rotherby looked aghast. 'Me? Kill Tilly? I told you, I loved her. I would never hurt a single hair on her head.'

'Oh, come on, Rotherby. You have motive and living on the estate, you had plenty of opportunity. With the stables so close, you also had the means.'

'I didn't kill her, I didn't, I didn't!'

As Rotherby dissolved into tears and buried his head in his hands, Norman exchanged a look with Southall and raised his eyebrows. Southall addressed the solicitor.

'Obviously we won't be releasing Mr Rotherby,' she said, 'but I think we might take a break.'

Norman ended the interview, switched off the recorder and followed Southall back to the office.

* * *

'Dr Bridger called with the DNA results,' said Lane when they got back to their office.

'Is it going to help us?' asked Southall.

'I don't think so. The DNA recovered from the semen doesn't match any of our suspects.'

'What about Rocco Lombardo?' Southall asked.

'It could have been him, but he's not on the national database so they can't say one way or the other.'

'There you are,' said Southall. 'I said he must have been careful to have got away with it all these years.'

# CHAPTER 40

Norman and Winter had taken the opportunity to stretch their legs and grab a sandwich while they waited. When they got back to the office, Lane had news for them.

'Norm, we've had a report from Forensics about the footprints they found near where Griffiths died,' she said. 'And I've just had an update from the divers. Which do you want first?'

'Tell me about the divers.'

'They weren't getting anywhere close to the path, so they widened the search to the banks. They finally found your shovel, thirty yards away, caught up in some reeds and only partially submerged.'

'Is there blood on the blade?' asked Norman.

'The blade was underwater, but they think they'll be able to recover traces of blood from it. However, the handle was dry, so it should be possible to find fingerprints on it. It's already on its way to the lab and they've promised to get the results to us asap.'

'If there is enough blood to match David Griffiths's, any fingerprints on the handle must belong to the killer,' said Norman.

'But if they're Jimmy's, that means he killed Griffiths,' said Winter.

'If Jimmy's prints are the only ones on that handle, I'll eat my hat,' said Norman.

Winter looked puzzled.

'Norm doesn't believe the same person could possibly have thrown the shovel and the phone, if they're that far apart,' Lane explained.

'Really?' said Winter. 'But didn't the witness state that whoever was on that bike threw two items into the pond?'

'Yeah,' said Norman. 'But what if those two things were Griffiths's mobile phone and the horseshoe Jimmy hit him with?'

'The divers say the shovel was just too far away for the same person to have thrown both. They reckon the only way the rider could have done it is if he threw the shovel in among the reeds and then chucked the phone in the pond as he rode past.'

'I followed the tracks left by that bike,' said Norman. 'And they didn't leave the path at any point. Besides, the path only gets close to the pond in one place, where I believe he threw the phone from. And I'm sure I didn't see any reeds near there.'

'You see, there is another possibility, Frosty,' said Lane. 'You think Jimmy is covering for someone. Now, what if that someone offered to dispose of the shovel?'

'But why dump it in the reeds?' asked Winter. 'Wouldn't it be better to take it somewhere completely different? Or at least make sure it went into deep water?'

'Of course it would,' said Norman. 'But I think what Judy is suggesting is that the person Jimmy's covering for wanted us to find it.'

'Why?' asked Winter.

'Because I think there's a possibility that Jimmy's being framed,' said Lane.

'Think about it,' Norman said. 'Jimmy has already admitted to being at the murder scene and to taking Griffiths's phone and throwing it into the pond. Finding the shovel in the same pond is compelling evidence that he's also the murderer, especially if his fingerprints are on the shovel.'

'And if he insists this other person was there and they deny it, it's their word against his,' added Lane.

'And the chances are they've prepared an alibi,' said Norman.

'Okay, so who is the person framing him?' asked Winter.

'Well, if it's a man, it could be Rotherby,' said Norman.

'And if it's a woman?'

'I don't know.'

'Ffion Howells?' suggested Lane.

'But why would she want Griffiths dead, and why would Jimmy cover for her?' asked Winter. 'Are you suggesting they're having an affair?'

'It wouldn't be the first odd relationship in this case,' said Lane.

Norman thought for a moment.

'Now you come to mention it, when I was up on the lighthouse platform with Jimmy, he did say something about his girlfriend being like his mum.'

'Ffion's just about old enough to be his mother,' said Lane.

'He probably meant she nagged him, like his mother does,' said Winter.

Norman considered again. 'I think Frosty's right,' he said, finally. 'Now, if you said he was having an affair with Carys, I could believe that, but Ffion? I don't think so.'

'Hang on a minute, Norm,' said Winter. 'Do you remember when we first went to Jimmy's house, his mum told us he had stopped doing the horses in the mornings but was still going some evenings?'

'That's right,' said Norman. 'And you said you thought Carys did evenings.'

'And then we decided that maybe Jimmy and Carys were two horny teenagers using the stables as an excuse to meet up away from the prying eyes of their parents.'

'I find that a lot easier to believe than the idea of Ffion being his girlfriend,' said Norman.

'Well, with any luck the fingerprints on the shovel will tell us who he's protecting,' said Lane.

'Talking of forensics,' said Norman. 'What's in that report?'

'Shoe sizes,' said Lane, handing him a copy of the report. 'Trainers, size eleven and wellies size four.'

'The eleven must be Jimmy's, and the size four has to be a woman, right?'

'It could be me,' said Lane. 'I'm size four.'

Norman laughed. 'Well, we could arrest you, except you don't have a motive, and I don't believe you could batter anyone to death. But it does suggest a woman was there with Jimmy when David Griffiths was murdered. We need someone to get over to Ffion Howells's place and check her shoe size.'

'I'll go,' said Lane. 'But what if there's no one there?'

'You won't need to go inside the house. They keep their wellington boots outside in the porch. Call me when you have the answer.'

'Won't you be interviewing?' Lane asked.

'Yes, but don't worry about that.'

# CHAPTER 41

A short time later, Norman and Winter again faced Jimmy in the interview room.

'What shoe size are you, Jimmy?' asked Norman.

Jimmy stuck a leg out from under the table. 'Size eleven, that's me.'

'Nice trainers,' said Norman. 'I bet they have fancy soles.'

Jimmy turned up his foot to show Norman.

'Cool,' said Norman. 'Do you wear them all the time?'

Jimmy looked puzzled. 'Mostly. Why?'

'No reason,' said Norman. 'I just wondered. Did I already tell you we've got casts of footprints from the crime scene? They look just like the soles of your trainers.'

'Well, so what?' said Jimmy. 'I already said I was there.'

'Oh, yeah, that's right. You did,' said Norman. 'Don't you think it's time you started to tell the truth about what happened while you were there?'

'I have told the truth.'

'I don't think you have,' said Norman. 'I think you've given us one or two bits that might be true, but we know it's not the whole story. The thing is, when you stand up in court, you have to tell the whole truth, so you might as well start now.'

'I've told you what happened. I've nothing more to say.'

'You'll have to help me out here, Jimmy. When you say you've told us what happened, do you mean that you don't know who killed David Griffiths, you just found him lying there, or the story where you threw a horseshoe at him and knocked him down?'

Jimmy's eyes darted from Norman to Winter and back again. 'The horseshoe one,' he muttered.

'You should understand that we're not going to stop investigating just because you said that,' continued Norman. 'We'll be asking you a lot more questions before we've finished.'

'But I've told you everything I know.'

'Yeah,' said Norman. 'But I'm afraid it's not that simple, and we're not that stupid. You see, we know there was someone else with you around the time Griffiths was murdered, and we know—'

'I already told you there was someone else.'

'Yes, but you didn't tell us who. Well, we now have a pretty good idea of who it was, but we just need to know for sure.'

'But it doesn't matter.'

'It matters to us, Jimmy, because she's a murder suspect. For starters, she wears size four shoes. That's already beginning to narrow it down. I reckon by the end of today, we'll have worked it out.'

'Well, you won't hear it from me.'

'When we were up on that lighthouse viewing platform, you told me you had a girlfriend,' said Norman. 'I believe it's her you're protecting. Am I right?'

'No comment.'

'Okay, I'll make a suggestion and you tell me if I'm right,' said Norman. 'My guess is she's an older woman, about the same age as your mum, and that's why you don't want to say who it is. Well?'

As Norman had expected, Jimmy couldn't suppress a smirk.

'No comment.'

'No? Let's try another one then. This mystery girlfriend of yours said she was going to hide the shovel.'

Jimmy's smile faded. 'Shovel? What shovel?'

'Not smiling now, are you, Jimmy? I must have guessed that one right.'

The solicitor coughed.

'No comment.'

'Now I expect you're wondering how I knew that,' continued Norman. 'The thing is, we found a shovel just like the one that was used to kill David Griffiths in the very same pond you threw the phone in. To be honest, it confused me at first, because I thought it was such a dumb thing for you to do.'

'I don't know anything about any shovel.'

'The other guys were sure you must have thrown it in the pond, but then I heard it had been found some distance away from where you threw the mobile phone. In fact, it was so far away, none of us could work out how you could possibly have thrown it that far. Another odd thing was that the shovel was half out of the water, which made it easy to find.'

Norman watched the confusion growing on Jimmy's face for a few seconds before he continued. 'But I got to wondering why you would have done that, when the sensible thing would have been to hide it somewhere else, or at least make sure it went into deep water. I mean, leaving it where we could find it is a stupid thing to do, right? But I know you're not stupid, Jimmy, and I finally realised there was only one explanation that made any sense. You see, I reckon someone else dumped that shovel in the duck pond, and they wanted to make sure we found it.'

Jimmy began to chew his bottom lip and, as Norman paused to let him absorb this latest piece of news, he turned to his solicitor.

'I don't understand why he keeps on about this shovel. I don't know anything about it.'

Just at that moment, Norman's mobile phone began to ring. 'Sorry, I have to take this call,' he muttered, getting to his feet. He suspended the interview and stepped out of the room.

Winter looked pointedly at Jimmy. 'That'll be the call we've been waiting for.'

'What call?'

'The one that's going to tell us who your girlfriend is.'

A line of perspiration appeared on Jimmy's top lip, and by the time Norman returned to his seat, Jimmy looked very pale indeed.

'How about that, Jimmy?' said Norman. 'Your girlfriend does wear size four. That means we can put her at the crime scene with you.'

This seemed to be enough for Jimmy. 'All right, so she was there. But she didn't kill him. It was the horseshoe I threw that did it.'

'Come on, Jimmy. We all know the horseshoe might have knocked him out, but it couldn't have killed him.'

'Yes, it did. I threw it, it hit his head, and he dropped dead.'

'You realise that when we speak to her, she's going to deny having been there.'

'What? Why?' Jimmy said.

'It's why she dumped the shovel where we could find it. She's going to say she was never there when Griffiths was killed, so it'll be your word against hers. She's framing you, Jimmy.'

'That's bullshit. She wouldn't do that to me.'

Norman removed a photograph from the folder he'd brought with him and set it down in front of Jimmy. He looked down at the photo and then up at Norman, his eyes wide.

'Ugh. What's that?' Jimmy said.

'You don't know?'

'It's horrible,' Jimmy said, sounding genuinely revulsed.

'That's because it's a photograph of David Griffiths's head when we found him. Are you still saying you did *that* with a horseshoe?'

'That's not right,' said Jimmy, his eyes wide with panic. 'Where's all that blood come from?'

'Now do you see why we're talking about a shovel, Jimmy? David Griffiths wasn't killed by the horseshoe you threw, he was battered to death with a shovel and I think it was your girlfriend that did it.'

'No. She couldn't do anything like that. Someone else must have done it.'

'She's going to say you did it, Jimmy. Are you going to let her do that?'

Jimmy slumped back in his chair.

'Don't tell me,' said Norman. 'She said she loved you, right? Did you really believe that? We'll be speaking to her real soon, and when she denies having been there, you'll see I'm right.'

'I'm not saying another word,' Jimmy said.

'I'd like to speak with my client,' said the solicitor.

'I think that's an excellent idea,' said Norman. 'See if you can talk some sense into him.'

# CHAPTER 42

At seven that evening, Ffion Howells opened her front door to find Southall and Norman standing in her porch. She rolled her eyes.

'I don't believe it. You two again? Whose death are you trying to pin on me now?'

'Nice to see you too, Ffion,' said Norman.

'Trust me, we'd rather not have to come at all,' said Southall. 'But we just follow the evidence, and I'm afraid it keeps leading back here.'

'This is harassment,' Ffion said.

'It might well be if only we didn't have a good reason for it.'

'Good reason? What good reason?'

Norman pointed to the two pairs of boots standing side by side near the door.

'Are these your boots out here?' Norman said.

'What do you think?'

'That's not helping, Ffion,' said Southall.

'Well, it's a stupid question. They're in my porch, so they're not likely to belong to anyone else, are they?'

'So, that's a pair of wellies each for you and Carys,' said Norman. 'Which one of you owns the mucker boots?'

'They belong to Carys. She wears them when she's doing the horses.'

'They both look the same size. Four, is it?'

'So? Why the interest in our footwear?'

'If you let us come in, we'll explain,' said Southall.

Grudgingly, Ffion stepped aside for them.

'What's this all about?' she demanded, following them into the lounge.

'We found footprints in the wet sand where David Griffiths was murdered,' explained Southall.

'Oh, so that's it. Well, don't even begin to think it was me. I was at work all day.'

'Yes, we know. We checked,' said Norman.

'Actually, we weren't thinking of you,' said Southall. 'It was Carys we wanted to have a word with.'

'Don't be absurd. She was at school.'

'We checked that too,' said Norman.

'Well, there you are then.'

'She wasn't there. All day.'

Ffion stared at them. She raised her hand and touched her hair. 'No, that can't be right. I dropped her off at the bus stop. She had her uniform on.'

'Is Carys here, Ffion? We'd like to ask her some questions.'

'Oh, er, no. She's out.'

'It's okay, Mum.'

Carys entered the room and settled herself on the settee. 'I didn't go to school that day because I started my, um, period. When I got to the bus stop, I realised I had nothing with me.'

'She's always bad with it,' said Ffion eagerly.

'Not so bad that she only realised after she'd got to the bus stop,' said Norman.

'So, what did you do all day?' Southall asked.

'I came back here and sorted myself out,' Carys said.

'And that took all day, did it?'

'Well, no. I watched a bit of TV.'

'You didn't go out at all?' Southall said.

'No.'

'You're quite sure about that, are you? Only someone wearing mucker boots the same size as those out there,' Southall pointed towards the front door, 'was at the murder scene, and we know it wasn't your mother.'

'Ah. Yes, well, I did go for a walk. I thought the fresh air would make me feel better.'

'And what time was that?'

'I don't know exactly.'

'Well, was it morning or afternoon?' Southall said.

'It was around lunchtime.'

'So, say, between midday and two p.m.?'

'Yes, it must have been.'

'And where did you go?' Southall asked.

'I followed the old footpath. It goes past the stables across the fields to the village.'

'Nef Anfon?'

'That's right.'

'Did you see anyone on your way?' Southall asked.

Carys appeared to make a great effort to recall. 'Oh yes, now you come to mention it, I did. I saw Jimmy Denman. He was tearing along the path on his bike, and he was carrying that stupid top hat.'

'And you never thought to tell us this before?' said Southall.

'I saw him the next day and he asked me not to say anything.'

'Because he'd stolen the top hat?' Southall asked.

'It sounded like he'd done something much worse than that, but he wouldn't tell me what it was.'

'And what do you think it was?' Southall asked.

Carys held Southall's gaze. 'I think he killed that man.'

'What man?'

'David Griffiths.'

'Did he say how he killed him?' Southall asked.

'He said something about a shovel.'

'Why would he want to kill David Griffiths?'

'I don't know.'

'You know, I've spent quite a bit of time talking to Jimmy recently,' said Norman. 'He thinks you're his girlfriend.'

Carys let out a snort of derision. 'Oh, please. Do I look that desperate?'

Norman smiled. 'I told him you'd say something like that.'

'What do you mean?'

'Oh, come on, Carys. Jimmy might have been won over by your sweet smile and touchy-feely ways, but some of us are older and less impressionable.'

'You can't be serious,' said Ffion. 'You can't possibly think my beautiful daughter would give a boy like Jimmy so much as a second glance.'

'Oh, I'm sure she would if she wanted to use him — or set him up,' said Norman.

Ffion's eyes widened. 'Are you suggesting my daughter . . . Well, that just proves you can't believe a word that boy says. He's not right in the head.'

'Just hang on a minute, Ffion, and perhaps you'll understand why we're here,' said Southall. She nodded to Norman.

'According to Jimmy, he was out on his bike,' Norman said. 'And he saw Carys near the stables. Because he's sweet on her, he headed across. As he got closer, he saw she was arguing with a man. As Jimmy watched, the man took a couple of steps towards Carys and grabbed hold of her.

'Now, Jimmy's not the sort of boy to stand back and watch his girl getting attacked, so he grabbed the nearest thing he could find to distract the man's attention — which happened to be a horseshoe — and threw it. To Jimmy's dismay, the horseshoe hit the bloke on the head and he fell to the ground.'

At Norman's words, Carys seemed to shrink into the sofa. Ffion stared at her daughter as if she had never seen her before.

Carys began to rock back and forth.

'Jimmy says Carys then gave him Griffiths's mobile phone and told him to dump it in the pond on his way home. That's right, isn't it, Carys?'

'This is all rubbish,' said Ffion. 'Tell them, Carys, tell them it isn't true.'

Ignoring Ffion, Norman carried on speaking. 'Jimmy says that when he left, David Griffiths was lying on the floor. He didn't know whether he was dead or not, but there definitely weren't any cuts on his head, and there wasn't any blood. But that's not how we found him, is it, Carys? So, would you like to tell us what happened?'

'Carys? Say something,' Ffion said. 'Why were you speaking to David Griffiths?'

Carys shook her head, her eyes wild. 'He told me he wasn't my father.'

Ffion's mouth dropped open.

'Your father?'

'He said he didn't know what I was talking about and he hardly knew you. How could he say that?'

Southall glanced at Ffion, who looked blank.

'What makes you think he was your father?' Ffion said after a while.

'I heard you arguing with Tilly about the rent. You told her it was only right for you not to pay it because she had stolen the father of your child. That's me, right? So, I thought if I reasoned with him, he'd see what he'd done and come back to you.'

'Oh, Carys, what have you done?' Ffion cried, tears coursing down her cheeks. 'David Griffiths isn't your father!'

But now Carys had begun, she couldn't seem to stop the words pouring out. 'When I told him I wanted to get our family back together, he laughed at me. He said I didn't know what I was talking about. That's when Jimmy hit him with the horseshoe.'

'And then what happened?' asked Southall.

'Jimmy went mad and started hacking at his head with the shovel. I told him to stop, but he wouldn't listen.'

'Carys, we found the shovel. It was clever of you to hide it where we'd find it, but if you were hoping it would incriminate Jimmy, you should have wiped your fingerprints off it.

Yes, Jimmy's prints are on the very top of the handle, but he couldn't have beaten anyone with it held like that. It's your prints on the shaft and it was you who battered David Griffiths to death.'

'He just lay there, while all I could hear was him laughing at me. I couldn't understand why he wouldn't admit to being my father. His laughter kept ringing in my ears and I saw red. I caught sight of a shovel leaning against the stable wall . . .'

'Oh, Carys,' Ffion whispered.

# CHAPTER 43

'If it wasn't Griffiths, who is Carys's father?' asked Winter the following morning.

'She was right about Tilly stealing her father away,' said Southall. 'She just got the wrong man. Giles Rotherby is her father, not David Griffiths. It appears Ffion was the "family friend" whose pregnancy his father was so annoyed about.'

'So, why was Ffion blackmailing Tilly?' Winter asked.

'Apparently, Ffion had long suspected that the reason Tilly and Giles were so close was because they were a bit more than brother and sister. She finally accused Tilly to her face, and threatened to make their incest public. Apparently, Ffion wasn't the only person to suspect what was going on, so she had good reason for her suspicions. When Tilly agreed to let her live in the house rent-free, she assumed it was in return for her silence.'

'You say Ffion assumed it was that. Is there another reason?'

'Giles claims the reason they let her live in the house rent-free was because Carys was his daughter.'

'So, who is telling the truth?' asked Winter.

Southall shrugged. 'They both claim they're right, so I guess we'll never know for sure.'

'And Tilly really was going to marry David Griffiths, even though she had Rocco, and he had Rhona?' Winter said.

'They thought if Tilly married Griffiths it would put a stop to the rumours,' said Southall. 'It was a business deal, if you will: a genuine marriage of convenience.'

'Did we ever find out who was the baby's father?'

'The DNA doesn't match any of our suspects, and it matches no one on the national database.'

'Does that mean it's a mystery?' asked Winter.

'Not necessarily,' said Southall. 'We now know Rocco Lombardo has never given a DNA sample, and we know we didn't get a match for the sperm sample taken from Tilly's body.'

'Oh, right,' said Winter. 'So you think—'

'If I was a gambler, that's where I'd put my money,' said Southall.

Winter shook his head. 'Wow. I bet this is one of the weirdest cases you've ever had to deal with.'

'That's true,' said Southall. 'But, in a way, it's also one of the saddest. That poor kid, Carys, spent most of her life dreaming of getting her family back together, and all the time she had the wrong man down as her father.'

'Don't forget that "poor kid" battered a man's brains out and then tried to pin the blame on someone else,' said Norman.

'But how did she know Griffiths would be down at the stables?' asked Winter.

'She sent him a text saying she knew something about the person who killed Tilly. It's still on her phone. She didn't even think to delete it.'

'Carys must have really hated Tilly,' said Winter.

'Yes, that has crossed my mind,' said Southall. 'I'll be asking her about that later. Would you like to sit in?'

'Oh, yes, please. That would be great,' said Winter.

'Sorry for butting in,' said Morgan. 'But I've just had a call from the young vet I spoke with about people who had access to the drug safe in Hywell Davies's Land Rover. He says they had a teenager doing work experience during the half-term holiday. Apparently, her mother works there and arranged it.'

'Holy shit,' said Norman. 'Is it who I think it is?'

Morgan nodded. 'Yep. Carys Howells.'

Southall let out a long sigh. 'D'you know, I'm not sure if I'm pleased or disappointed. Oh, well, come on, Frosty, let's speak to her again and get it over with.'

Ten minutes later, they were sitting in the interview room opposite Carys, who was accompanied by an appropriate adult.

'Good morning, Carys. How are you?' asked Southall.

Carys gave her a lopsided grin. 'Pretty good, thank you.'

'Do you think you could answer a few more questions?'

'I did kill him, you know. He said he wasn't my father, but why did he deny it? Why didn't he want to get back together with me and Mum?'

Southall glanced at Winter. This wasn't good.

'Carys, I need to ask you about something else now. Do you remember doing work experience at the vets where your mother works?'

'Oh yeah. That silly old vet. He's always forgetting to lock his drug safe. It was so easy to steal the pentobarbital.'

'Why did you steal it?' Southall asked.

'To inject Tilly, of course. She was the cause of all the trouble because she stole my dad from us, so I had to get rid of her first.'

'You know that drug is supposed to be given intravenously?' Southall said.

'Yeah, I know that, but I thought if I could just stab her in the leg, I might get lucky and hit a vein, or at least slow her down. I was right, too.'

'But then you strangled her and strung her up. Why?'

'Oh, that. Yeah, I wanted to make sure she was dead. D'you think it was too much? She deserved it, though. She stole my dad.' Carys nodded sagely.

Southall felt she ought to call a halt to the interview. She was concerned about Carys's mental state, and thought she needed to be properly assessed before she faced any more questions.

* * *

'Is she really crazy, or is she putting on an act?' asked Winter when they'd left the interview room.

'I don't know, Frosty. But if she keeps it up, her defence counsel will most likely suggest a plea of insanity. It might be the best way to go for a sixteen-year-old double murderer.'

# EPILOGUE

Some time later, Morgan took a call on her desk phone.

'DC Morgan speaking.'

'It's Rhona Pritchard. I'm just across the road, and I wondered if I might come in and have a word with you.'

'Just one moment, please,' said Morgan into the phone. She put her hand over the mouthpiece and turned to Norman. 'Rhona Pritchard is outside. She wants to speak to me.'

'What about?' asked Norman.

'David Griffiths, I suppose. What am I going to tell her?'

'Does she know he's dead?'

'I'm not sure, but it doesn't sound like it. I have an idea that now she's had time to think, she wants to tell us what's really been going on.'

'Well, whatever it is, you can't pretend he's alive, so you'll have to tell her the truth,' Norman said.

Morgan took her hand from the phone and returned to her call. 'Hallo, Rhona? If you come on over, I'll meet you at the door.' Looking thoughtful, Morgan slowly replaced the phone on its cradle. 'Can I ask a favour?'

'D'you want me to sit in?'

'Would you mind? Only it feels a bit of a weird one.'

Norman smiled reassuringly. 'No problem. Play it by ear and let her say what she wants to say first, then choose the right time to tell her what's happened to him. I won't step in unless I think I need to.'

Morgan thought Rhona seemed to have aged since she had last seen her. Then, it had been obvious that Rhona took a great deal of pride in her appearance. Today, everything about her looked creased and crumpled, even her face.

'Your husband reported you missing days ago,' said Morgan, ushering Rhona into an interview room. 'We've had your photograph up everywhere.' She introduced Norman. 'This is DS Norman, he's going to sit in on the interview, if that's okay?'

Rhona nodded in agreement and sat down opposite the two detectives, perching herself on the edge of her chair, her handbag clutched tightly on her knees.

'What is it you wanted to tell us?' asked Morgan.

'I suppose you guessed I've been waiting for David,' she said, staring down at the table, as if she were embarrassed to even be there.

'When your husband told us you'd gone, we figured that was the case,' said Morgan.

'I've spent days and days, cooped up in a tiny hotel room, just waiting. We were supposed to be going away together, but he never turned up. I called and called, but he seems to have switched his phone off.'

'Er, yes, I can probably explain why that is,' began Morgan, but Rhona wasn't listening. She'd come to say her piece and she wasn't going to be interrupted. She looked up, chin jutting determinedly forward.

'I finally realised what a fool I've been,' she said. 'And now I've had enough. I'm going to tell you all about David Griffiths and what a shit he is. You see, you were right when you said a man like him couldn't possibly find an old woman like me attractive.'

Morgan caught Norman's disapproving look, but her eyes remained fixed on Rhona.

'I don't think that was quite what we—'

'It was exactly what you said, and I did consider making a complaint, but now I've had time to think about it, I know you're right. All David ever wanted from me was my money. He's taken a small fortune from me, cost me my marriage, and now I suppose you're going to arrest me and charge me with being his accomplice in this scheme of his.'

'I think that's unlikely,' said Morgan.

'But what about all the investors he took money from?'

'The thing is, Rhona, as far as we can tell, you were the only one to invest in his business, and you didn't want to make a complaint.'

Rhona sat back in horror. 'But that can't be right. You told me he had cheated lots of investors.'

'That's what we thought at first,' said Morgan. 'But when we started to look into it, it turned out there was no one else involved.'

'What about the factory in Scotland?'

'I'm afraid that address turned out to be a private house.'

'But he spent two or three nights a week up there, on business.'

Morgan shook her head. 'I'm afraid it was the home of a girlfriend.'

Rhona put a hand to her forehead. 'Oh my God. This is even worse than I thought.'

'We believe David had already set up the fake business before he met you, but he hadn't been able to find anyone to, er, invest in it,' explained Morgan. 'And then he found you.'

'And I was so gullible—'

She stopped speaking for a moment, and a tear rolled slowly down her cheek. 'Damn,' she muttered, rummaging in her handbag for a tissue. She looked up at Morgan. 'I promised myself I wasn't going to cry.'

'Don't be too hard on yourself,' said Morgan. 'You were unhappy, and lonely. I'm afraid the David Griffithses of this world regard anyone in that situation as prey. They have no feelings for anybody.'

'That's easy for you to say,' said Rhona bitterly. 'It's not you that's lost everything, is it? Anyway, what about Tilly? Where does she fit into it? Was she another victim?'

'I can't say much about Tilly as her death is an ongoing investigation,' said Morgan. 'But I believe Tilly recognised David for what he was.'

'Did he kill her?'

'No, he didn't kill Tilly. That's one thing we do know for sure.'

'That's one thing going for him, I suppose,' said Rhona. 'So, where is he?'

Morgan glanced at Norman, who gave her an almost imperceptible nod. 'Rhona, I must tell you something. It will help explain why David isn't taking your calls, and it could even be the reason he didn't come to meet you.'

'Let's face it, Detective Constable Morgan, if he was going to meet me, it was only so he could finish draining my bank account. He would soon have ditched me after that.'

'I can't deny that's possible,' admitted Morgan.

'Possible?' snapped Rhona. 'It's probable, and we both know it.'

There was an awkward silence.

'Is he here?' asked Rhona. 'Have you arrested him? Serves him right if you have.'

'I'm afraid it's worse than that, Rhona.'

'What do you mean, worse?'

'I'm afraid David has been murdered.'

The look of shock on Rhona's face would remain imprinted on Morgan's mind for a long time to come, though it lasted only seconds. It was replaced by a savage grimace.

'Good,' hissed Rhona. 'I hope he rots in hell.'

### THE END

# THE JOFFE BOOKS STORY

We began in 2014 when Jasper agreed to publish his mum's much-rejected romance novel and it became a bestseller.

Since then we've grown into the largest independent publisher in the UK. We're extremely proud to publish some of the very best writers in the world, including Joy Ellis, Faith Martin, Caro Ramsay, Helen Forrester, Simon Brett and Robert Goddard. Everyone at Joffe Books loves reading and we never forget that it all begins with the magic of an author telling a story.

We are proud to publish talented first-time authors, as well as established writers whose books we love introducing to a new generation of readers.

We have been shortlisted for Independent Publisher of the Year at the British Book Awards three times, in 2020, 2021 and 2022, and for the Diversity and Inclusivity Award at the Independent Publishing Awards in 2022.

We built this company with your help, and we love to hear from you, so please email us about absolutely anything bookish at feedback@joffebooks.com

If you want to receive free books every Friday and hear about all our new releases, join our mailing list: www.joffebooks.com/contact

And when you tell your friends about us, just remember: it's pronounced Joffe as in coffee or toffee!